STALKED: THE CONTI ROSE

TH SECOND SIDE SERIES

Written by

CAY TEMPLETON ~THE FAIRY TALER~

ISBN: 978-0-9983272-0-4 (Paperback), 978-0-9983272-1-1 (Ebook)

THE
SECOND
SIDE

"The only way I could ever understand the world was to look at it sideways."

~The Fairy Taler~

My Respected Second Sider,

I will be the first to acknowledge my personal lack of interest in the telling of Jack and the Beanstalk. A dear friend once pointed out that there is no love story in this tale, so why should anyone want to read it?

You be the judge...

You now hold in your hands the true account of a very stern, yet quiet General who tries to complete his task of escorting all the available noble women to the Duke's masked ball to be his potential bride. However, he finds the heroin of this story, Lady Sarah Levine, to be a particular challenge.

Sarah is a head strong girl with her own ideas of what should become of her future, and she had not a qualm in the world expressing her displeasure to the General. That being said, he fired back with his own curt and honest responses.

No one would ever imagined, before stumbling upon this book, a passionate love story resided deep within the pages of Jack and the Beanstalk.

I do so hope you enjoy this unique recount of this fairy tale.

Ever Sincere,
~The Fairy Taler~

SPECIAL THANKS!

Mom
Sophie
Jimmy R.
Brian S.
Christine MB
Steve F.
Chuck O.

CHAPTER 1

MAGICAL BEANS

The crisp night wind cut across Sarah's cheeks as she spun around in absolute darkness. Moonlight struggled to push its way through the denseness of the forest vegetation, but just enough crept in to capture Sarah's breath as it hung in the air.

"Is anyone there?" she whispered so as to not to disturb any of the night prowlers from their evening hunt.

Off in the distance, a tree branch snapped and leaves crackled under a heavy foot. A howl broke through the intense silence.

Sarah tried not to flinch in her moment of panic, however, her feet took flight without consent. She ran as fast as her body would allow. Moving across the rough terrain, she leapt over every rock and fallen branch in her path.

Having no memory of where she had been or any knowledge of where she was going, Sarah gave way to her body's unexplainable need to move forward.

Quick steps could be heard chasing from behind, but every time she glanced over her shoulder, nothing was there.

Absolute fear that she was about to be pounced on caused her body to freeze in mid-flight. Perhaps the wolf would pass her and she could change direction? Or maybe find a tree should could easily climb?

After coming to a complete stop, Sarah turned in several directions, trying desperately to locate the sound that caused her whole body to tremble. Unfortunately, as she paused, so had the phantom footsteps. It was as if they knew her thoughts better than she did.

In that moment, the world stood uncommonly still — nothing moved. Even the chirps that often filled the night, fell silent.

An unsettled feeling carved a hole into the pit of her stomach and the only comfort she felt was the idea of creating more distance between her and the wolf she was certain was chasing her. To get away from this unknown danger. To find a safe place to hide.

Again, she took off running, as she weaved through the trees and over the uneven floor of the Allogot Forest.

Another taunting howl rang out which provoked Sarah to look back for the pursuing predator. Without warning, her body collided headlong into a dark form that obstructed her path.

"Umph," she grunted as she fell to the ground.

Disorientation consumed all her senses as she looked up at the object that she ran into.

Her eyes traced the outline of the form just before another howl sounded and caused the overwhelming want to run again.

Shaking her head, Sarah tried to wake herself from the horrific nightmare, but instead of waking, a craggy hand extended itself out to her. As her eyes adjusted, she could just make out the hunched over figure of an old woman who stood in front of her. At present, the old woman seemed so unaffected by the impact that Sarah wondered if she had hit something else.

Finally taking the hand, Sarah pulled herself up to her feet.

"Are you alright?" asked the old woman with care.

"I am so sorry," replied Sarah, a little panic-stricken. "I did not mean to-"

"Of course not! You're moving far too quickly!" scolded the old woman before she put her hand over her mouth to stop herself from talking.

After she shook her head while rolling her eyes, she then dropped her hand back down to her side.

"I do apologize. Sometimes my mouth has a mind of its own."

Sarah nodded to acknowledge the apology, but was far too distracted as she glanced around, worried the wolf would be upon her at any moment.

"However, what else could be expected if you're being hunted?" finished the old woman with a smirk.

Sarah's focus snapped back to the old woman. The unease that lingered in the girl's stomach now expressed itself on her face. Her brow crumpled and her lower lip began to quiver.

More leaves crackled and crunched that made it sound like the wolf would show itself any second now.

The old woman closed her eyes. Her chin tilted up as if to listen, and then she whispered a few words under her breath. Just then, a gust of wind weaved through the trees that left in its wake nothing but absolute calm, even to Sarah's nerves.

"We should go," she said so matter-of-factly.

"To where?" replied Sarah, unsure if she could be trusted.

The old woman put a finger up to Sarah's lips to quiet her.

Another howl sounded just down the hill from where the two stood.

"Hastiness will not save you at this time, Sarah Levine. Worry not! Old Madge will not let him harm you."

The old woman cackled loudly, which caused each and every hair on the back of Sarah's neck to stand on edge. Though it also stopped the predator from moving any closer as well.

"Come. Come now. I live just there," said Old Madge as she shuffled her way down the far side of the small hill towards a fallen tree. There was no recognition of the kind of tree it was, nor did it look like any other tree in the Allogot Forest.

As Sarah's eyes caught up with the haggard figure, they locked on a wooden door that hung in the air just above the ground.

"What is this madness?"

"Is it madness if there is some explanation behind it?" replied Old Madge as she glanced over her shoulder.

Sarah took a couple steps forward; unsure if this was the right course of action or if she would rather risk her life to the wolf that chased her.

Old Madge turned to Sarah and held out a welcoming hand.

"This door will only open if you want it to."

"What is on the other side?"

"Answers, Sarah Levine. Answers."

Sarah reluctantly placed her hand into the old knotted one, which pulled her just in front of the floating door.

She was close enough that she could see the image of a massive tree that was carved into the wood. On each branch hung a unique kind of leaf that was scattered throughout every limb.. The leaves moved ever so slightly within the wood as if a breeze blew through them.

"Knock," stated the old woman.

With great hesitation, Sarah's hand rapped on the door.

At first, there was nothing. The door continued to float just above the ground. Then she heard something snap and break. The sound was different that when a branch broke under the wolf's foot moments earlier. This sound was right in front of her and loud. Vines and ivy broke from the fallen tree and sprawled out, interweaving with each other until it reached the door. It intricately laced its way into a frame around the wooden slab.

Sarah feverishly rubbed her eyes; unsure she could trust what was unfolding. As the shrubbery locked itself into place and harden, it created a solid wall.

Slowly, the weaving continued to claw around the base of what appeared to be a small cottage. More ivy and vines made their way down from the treetops and slid into place to form the roof.

When the small home came to rest in its full form, Old Madge turned the knob and pushed open the door. From what little could be seen inside, Sarah swore a fire crackled in the fireplace and she could smell something sweet.

"Now, join me for a cup of tea to warm your bones."

The old woman chuckled to herself and gestured for Sarah to follow her in. A slight nod fell from Sarah with consent.

As she stepped onto the porch, it was hard to miss the random chunks of siding that were missing. Sarah wasn't sure if the vine had just missed its mark or if something entirely different happened to this strange place. She chose not to linger on the matter for long, but instead, thrusted herself through the front door.

* * *

Upon entering the charming little home, the first thing that captured Sarah's attention was the flames that roared in the fireplace. The stone structure was larger than what would normally accompany such a small cottage. Clearly the focal point, it was overwhelming in size as it consumed a third of the wall space. Built within its stone walls was a metal frame that had a hook for what one could only assume was to hold a pot for cooking.

The entirety of the cottage was a single room with a sitting area close to the fire, a small kitchen area and a bed in the far corner. Along the wall closest to the bed stood a simple bookshelf that looked to be wedged between the floor and the ceiling. The contents on the shelves were hard to make out in such low light, but there were certainly jars and other trinkets that resided amongst the rows of books.

The old woman slammed the front door closed, then shuffled over to the small armchair next to the fire and flung her cloak over the back. An iron pot sat on a small table just off to the side. Old Madge grabbed it and placed it onto the hook.

Finally, she moved into the kitchen area and produced two empty teacups. When she sat them downside by side on the small table, the old woman gestured for Sarah to take a seat.

"It will just be a minute for the water to warm itself."

Sarah looked at the glass questioningly before she sat down.

A howl cried out again.

"If that creature thinks he can torment you, he has another thing coming," said Old Madge. "Now, tell me, what were you doing in the middle of these woods at this hour?"

Sarah's lips parted to speak, but found that her voice was absent.

"Hm," grunted Old Madge. Her eyes thinned in thought. "I see."

Then she turned and moved back to tend to the fire.

"You have questions. I can tell by the look on your face," she said as she poked the logs with a stick.

Sarah folded her hands in her lap and looked around nervously.

"These questions, they scream from your eyes, but silence your tongue? How unusual."

Sarah couldn't help but redirect her focus back to Old Madge. The old woman's back was turned to her, still she felt like she was still being watched.

"Come now! Out with it! What consumes your mind?"

"How... how do you know my name?" asked Sarah.

Without warning, Old Madge broke into a hearty laughter. Tears streamed down her cheeks as she leaned on her knees for balance. Sarah thought she was going to fall on the floor if she didn't get it under control.

"What humors you so?"

Old Madge hobbled over to the table and rested her hands on the top of the chair next to Sarah.

"Out of all the odd things you have seen in the last several minutes, I find it quite amusing that my knowing your name should be the first question you should ask."

"It was the first question that came clearly into my mind."

"So it is. Very practical, I suppose," agreed the old woman. "Lady Levine, whether you are aware of it or not, your father is the keeper of these woods. Naturally, I am well aware his only daughter and her name."

Sarah took a moment to review the answer and found she was satisfied with the response.

"How is it I saw a door floating like a cloud in the air to only form a cottage behind it once I knocked?"

8

"There you are!" shouted Old Madge and slammed her hand on the table with such force that it caused Sarah to jump.

The old woman shuffled over to the bookshelf and kicked the bottom shelf. Like the magical door, the books slid off the shelf and started to stack themselves into a small staircase that led up to the second shelf.

Old Madge made her way up the couple of steps, then kicked the wood again. Books from the second shelf slid off and continued to add themselves to the staircase to allow Old Madge to climb to the top of the bookshelf.

Looking across the row, she grabbed one of the jars, read its contents label, and then threw it over her shoulder. Instead of it crashing to the ground as one would expect, it floated in the air, much like the front door had.

"I know they are here somewhere." Old Madge muttered to herself as she continued to search around. A stern look caused her to pinch her brow and clench her teeth.

"What did I hide them, Preitty Meermore? You were such a crafty person, so I know I hid them well!"

The old woman released her hands and took a couple steps down the stair until she got to the next row down. It appeared there were more books than bottles on this shelf. Old Madge's eyes squinted as she slid her hand across the spines.

"I know it was some time ago, but still." She had clearly lost her mind as she mumbled to herself.

"Ah ha!" chirped Old Madge victoriously as she pulled a square shaped bottle off the shelf. She came down the stairs until her feet rested firmly on the floorboards.

While the old woman made her way back to the table, Sarah could see all the books and dropped items float back to their proper places on the shelves.

Again, Sarah shook her head and realized this must be a dream, for any other explanation would simply be beyond her comprehension.

It took only a moment for Old Madge to sit comfortably in her seat across from Sarah. Once she was settled, she placed the square bottle on the table and pushed it across.

At first, Sarah wasn't sure how to respond. Taking a closer look, on the other side of the glass were six white, dried-out beans.

"Go on, take them," Old Madge encouraged.

Sarah emptied the contents into her hand, and then rolled the beans around in her palm while she studied them in great detail.

"I do not understand," Sarah finally said.

"Of course not. That's because we are only at the beginning of your story. Those right there are about to change your life forever."

CHAPTER 2

PARPOSA

"*These* beans... are going to change my life? How is that going to happen, exactly?" asked Sarah as she sat back in her chair and looked at the beans skeptically.

"All I can say is it will make... a huge impact on you," said Old Madge, followed by a little chuckle at some joke only she understood. "But for now, put them somewhere safe and show them to no one."

Old Madge put her hand down on Sarah's arm and looked deep into her eyes. For a moment, Sarah felt an unspoken weight fall on her that caused her stomach to churn.

"I can't press upon you enough that you must keep these out of everyone's sight. They're meant for you and you alone. No one else is to know of them. Understood?"

Sarah nodded her head emphatically before she dropped the beans, one by one, back into the bottle and pushed in the cork. Then she carefully tucked it away in a hidden pocket sewn into the side of her dress.

When she looked back at the old woman, she realized Old Madge was preoccupied by something else entirely. The raggedy hand reached across the table and beckoned for Sarah's.

"Are you going to read my fortune?" Sarah joked.

"Your hands!"

Without another thought, Sarah slid her hands into the open palm.

Old Madge rubbed her thumbs across Sarah's fingers, and then released them. She brought her thumbs up to her nose and inhaled.

"Parposa," she whispered.

It was difficult not to be bewildered by the oddity of the situation.

The tea kettle screamed from the fireplace that it was ready, but neither one of the women flinched. Instead, the old woman's head drifted down and smelled her fingers again.

"You've been hanging around Jack again, haven't you?"

Sarah's eyes widened at the mention of her dearest friend's name.

"He showed you where the Parposa flowers grow in the forest, didn't he?"

"Yes, but there is no harm in that, is there?" Sarah suggested as an odd sensation overtook her to want to defend her friend.

Breaking the tense silence, Old Madge hopped to her feet and quickly moved to the fireplace. The kettle was still screaming when it was pulled from the flames. Carefully, she poured the hot water into one of the cups that still sat on the side table. Then, she returned the pot to its rightful place.

"He showed them to you, but he didn't tell you to be wary of them."

Old Madge returned to the kitchen table as quickly as she had left. When she placed the cup of tea down in front of Sarah, it almost spilled over.

"I knew they are unique to these woods," Sarah replyed and looked up with a furrowed brow. "I had never seen them before. So, when Jack knew where I could find them, it was as if my deepest wish had come true."

"Did you smell them?" asked Old Madge, cutting her off.

"How could I not? Their so blue, and the winged appearance makes me think of butterflies. And they smelled like..."

Sarah's vision blurred. When it refocused, Old Madge's hair shifted slowly from a dark gray into a deep red. Years shaved off the old woman's face until she could be no mare than twenty years old and stunningly beautiful.

"Whoa," breathed Sarah and then began rubbing her eyes. "Has your hair always been red?"

Old Madge put her hands over the steam wafting from the cups and whispered a few inaudible words.

"Drink this," she demanded, as she placed the teacup into Sarah's hands.

"What is in it?" Whatever it was, it smelled so wretched that it caused her nose to crinkle.

"Enough with the questions – drink!"

Sarah pinched her nose as she guzzled down the foul stench. The taste was so atrocious that it caused her to cough uncontrollably. Her eyes teared up as Sarah struggled to catch her breath between coughs. An achy, ill feeling overtook her entire body.

"What have you done to me?" she managed to get out as she lost her ability to remain upright and collapsed onto the table.

"Parposa flowers lure people in with their beauty and sweet scent. Then the hallucinations created by their enticing aroma are so real and so scary that people have been known to go stark raving mad. This is killing that scent within your body. Not exactly the most pleasant thing to go through, I'll admit, but it will save your life."

Old Madge sat down and patted Sarah's hand while the young woman's head laid on the table with half-open eyes.

"Did Jack know this would happen?" Sarah slurred.

"I seriously doubt it. He is a boy who dabbles in things he ought not to."

"How do you know?"

"I know a great many things," said Old Madge before she glanced down to the teacup and then over at Sarah with pity.

All of a sudden, Sarah sat straight up. She shook her head and wiggled her fingers to make sure everything still moved properly.

When her eyes made their way back, they were met with a great intensity in the old woman's. Seeming to be caught in a trance, Old Madge's eyes went dark and empty as if life itself had been drawn from them. The old hand clasped Sarah's tightly.

"Your life is about to take a very dramatic turn, Sarah Levine. A hard and treacherous journey lies before you. Quick and calculated decisions will have to be made or tragedy will come to many."

"That sounds horrific," Sarah replied as she tried to pull away unsuccessfully from the tight grip.

"Fear not, for love will come from the most unlikely of places, and at the most unpredictable of times. It has the power to save you. But you must let go and not fight with it."

Old Madge's hand went limp and landed on the table. The emptiness in her eyes dissipated and her odd nature returned.

Sarah rubbed her hand as she sat in disbelief, unsure of how to react to this entire encounter.

"Oh, your cup is empty, would you like another?" was said enthusiastically before the old woman hopped from her chair as if nothing had just happened. Returning to the fireplace, she grabbed the tea kettle again.

A loud bang slammed against the front door, followed by a spine-chilling howl.

It startled Sarah to her feet.

Another slam smacked against the door. It looked as though the hinges held onto the wall for dear life.

"It must be time for you to wake, Sarah," said Old Madge.

Bang!

"Wait! I still have so many questions!" pleaded Sarah.

The old woman turned on her heel with the kettle in her hand.

"I know you do, but like everything else, it'll come in time."

Another howl broke loose from the wolf just on the other side of the door. Sarah's body slumped in dismay.

"Sarah, wake up. Wake up!"

Darkness shrouded Sarah's eyes as it felt like she was falling from a great height.

"AHHH!"

. . .

"SARI. SARI!"

Blurry vision slowly crept into focus.

"Sari," came a comforting voice.

"Jack," she whispered.

Sarah could feel her body being surrounded by Jack's loving embrace. He ran his lips lovingly across her forehead until he finished it with a kiss on her nose.

For the moment, she was more overjoyed that he was there to save her than she was angry that he never told her of the dangers regarding the rare flower. Though she knew she would give him a good tongue lashing later.

As Sarah's eyes cleared, she could see the bright blue petals of the Parposa that surrounded her. In their butterflied shapes, she was sure they could fly away at any moment.

"I need to get you out of here," said Jack as he struggled to lift Sarah from the ground. Once she was in his arms, he took a few unsteady steps until he placed her feet back down.

Exhaustion and weakness plagued Sarah's body as she leaned against Jack for balance. He pulled her forward as he tried to get away from the intoxicating scent.

"I had no idea you would come this deep into the woods alone. This is all my fault!" Jack screamed at himself.

Sarah placed her hand on Jack's chest to stop going any farther.

"I must stop."

Even through the darkness of night, Sarah could feel Jack's head nod with consent.

"There is a fire pit just there."

He pointed out into the darkness. When she didn't respond immediately, his face soured.

"I shall try to carry you again."

Jack was only a half head taller than Sarah and was built more like a twig than a tree. So, the notion of him attempting to pick her up didn't sound all that appealing of an idea.

Still, he swooped her up into his arms. Weakness plagued her body too much for protest.

Jack's intentions were good, but Sarah could feel the tremor in his weak grip. Every step he took was labored and unbalanced, and she thought he was about to drop her.

"How much farther?" Sarah asked after several uncomfortable minutes.

"Not far," grunted Jack.

Just then, Jack's legs gave way, and the two collapsed to the ground. Sarah went tumbling down a small hill. Every branch and stone could be felt as she rolled faster. Her body came to an abrupt halt when she slammed against the side of a boulder.

"Umph," she grunted.

"Sarah! Are you alright?" Jack yelled as he rushed to her aid.

Slowly, she wiggled her fingers and tilted her head side to side to make sure there was still a full range of motion. Everything was intact except for the small gash on her knee.

"Maybe we should just make a fire here and wait until daylight breaks," suggested Sarah.

"I will get the firewood. You can just rest here."

"Good idea," Sarah grumbled as she struggled to smile.

When Sarah's eyes met Jack's, it was hard not to see the affection he had for her. A moment of longing passed between the two before Sarah cleared her throat and turned away.

"I do have one question for you," Jack said with a devious smile.

"And that is?"

"Squirrel or rabbit?"

"Whatever is the quickest for you to catch."

Jack pulled out a slingshot from his back pocket.

"As my lady wishes," he said.

Taking her hands, Jack kissed them just before he popped to his feet and took off to find food.

Sarah clinched her arms tightly to her chest to try to keep the night chill away. As her hands rubbed up and down her arms in an attempt to keep warm, she felt something press awkwardly against her side.

When she slid her hand down the length of her dress, it stumbled across a little hidden pocket. In it was a small square bottle with six white, dried-out beans.

Her eyes grew large as a hint of light caught the glass.

"It was not a dream," she breathed, just as a wolf cry rang out through the trees.

CHAPTER 3

THE NONSENSICAL PLAN

The fire popped and crackled while an Acol squirrel roasted on the tip of a stick. Jack turned it over in an attempt to cook the meat evenly. Once he was satisfied, he sat down close to Sarah.

"Are you feeling any better?"

"A little, thank you," she said and rested her head against Jack's shoulder.

Sarah could feel his caring arm wrap around her. The two sat in silence and just watched the flames hop around erratically.

"You know, some say parents leave their bad children in these woods," started Jack.

"That is not true!" replied Sarah and elbowed him in the side.

"It is true. Two children were left here years ago."

"And a witch tried to eat them... You know, Jack, I never took you to be one who believes in old wives' tales."

Deeper into the woods, some leaves rustled, followed by a howl. The hair on the back of Sarah's neck rose, and she turned in the direction of the familiar sound.

"Relax. He will not come anywhere near these flames," said Jack and poked the fire with a stick that caused the flames to climb higher towards the sky.

Not sure if he was right, Sarah pulled herself closer to her friend until she was curled up on Jack's chest. A little shudder went through her body. She wasn't sure if it was fear or the chill of the night air.

"I have never liked this forest. I feel like it is watching me."

"I know. That is why I cannot believe you came this far in by yourself," replied Jack.

"I was enchanted by the Parposa flowers. I just had to see them again."

"They have that effect on people," Jack agreed.

Sarah's eyes drifted up to meet his.

"But they do not have that effect on you."

Jack didn't respond immediately. The silence made Sarah uncomfortable and worry that her statement came off accusatory. Still, she remained quiet.

"There is nothing wrong with falling in love with something so beautiful," Jack finally said and hugged Sarah tightly to him. "Just be wary of its charms or they could throw you in an oven and try to eat you."

Both Jack and Sarah laughed heartily. She could tell by his joke that he had no idea of the flower's dangers if allured in by them. From what she could remember, the first time Jack introduced her to the strange plant, the aroma surrounding them was so sweet and it made her feel light as a cloud. That initial scent lingered in her nose for days. That smell caused her torment and eventually encouraged her to wander deep into the Allogot Forest and find them again.

"I would still like to know how you were not drawn into the plant's seductiveness," spouted Sarah, as she pushed the issue once more.

"I am not easily seduced."

"Is that so?" asked Sarah in a sultry voice and looked up with inviting eyes.

"I said not easily. I do have my weaknesses."

"Oh, I know... How did you stumble across them? I had no idea you came this far into the forest either. Your father would be irate if he caught you out here."

"My father is evil no matter where I go or what I do," replied Jack coldly. He turned away from Sarah and exposed the fresh bruises around his eye and cheek.

Sarah sat up quickly and softly grazed Jack's newest wound. Tilting his head back, the firelight caught every shade of purple and black that empaled his cheek. She could only blame the darkness of night and her exhausted state to justify why she had not noticed it before.

"What has he done?" growled Sarah. Jack put his hand on top of hers and forced a smile.

"I will be alright, Sari," said Jack and pulled her hand away from his face. Sarah's expression contorted to disbelief.

"Someday I will make him pay for his crimes. If made Duchess, I will make sure he lives out his days in the stocks."

"Do remind me never to upset you in this way. I would hate to see what you might do to me," said Jack with a light chuckle.

"It is possible for you to upset me for longer than a moment. You are my closest friend. Now and, I hope, for always."

Jack's lips instantly caressed Sarah's forehead before she curled more comfortably in his arms again. They both seemed resigned to remain in that position forever.

"I do not want to leave Ditrum. I do not want to be married off to the Duke. I hate my father for making me go."

"Your father is doing what he thinks is best for you."

"Which does not include you if he had his say," reminded Sarah.

"Perhaps I might change his mind?"

"You would have to hurry. I am off at daybreak."

Just as the words left her mouth, a drop of sunlight slipped through the trees and brushed her face. The little warmth it provided caused Sarah's heart to sink and a bundle of nerves tighten in her stomach.

The tension of the day to come settled in. Sarah felt Jack's body shift underneath her.

"What are you doing?" she asked.

"We should go."

"I do not want to," pouted Sarah.

"Listen," started Jack and turned Sarah so she had to look at him. "Set off for the castle, if for no other reason than to appease your father. In a day or so, when no one is looking, I will come and get you. Then we can go anywhere you wish. Can we do that?"

"It sounds like a nonsensical plan, but I love you all the more for trying."

"You have no faith in your knight's abilities to save his damsel in distress?" suggested Jack and grabbed his shirt proudly.

"Not against the Duke's finest General. You do know he is the one who fought the battle in Longsom Pass. The Giant."

"On a battlefield, he may be a giant amongst men and win that battle," argued Jack. "But amongst the trees, with my aim and sling-shot... I will be the Giant Killer!"

Sarah pulled him into a tight embrace and kissed his cheek.

"Give me another few moments just here with you," she pleaded. Jack didn't even attempt to argue, but instead smiled.

Though as rays of sunlight made its way through the treetops, both Jack and Sarah knew the fairy tale getaway had come to an end.

* * *

THE TWO MOVED in silence for the better part of an hour. The tree-line thinned and made it apparent that they neared the edge of Sarah's land.

As they stepped out of the forest, the morning sun hadn't quite warmed the dew off the crops, but Sarah enjoyed the little warmth it did provide her on her cold travels. She grabbed Jack's hand and continued to walk towards her home which sat on the far side of the field they walked across.

The large, two-story stone house sat in such a way that it could oversee the vast farmland that surrounded it.

"Looks like your visitors are already here," said Jack in an odd tone, and then gestured his head towards the drive.

Glancing towards the front of her house, Sarah saw a brigade of twenty guards on horseback. Right in the middle of the company was an ornamented carriage with the Duke's emblem prominently painted on the door. Sarah couldn't bear to look at the wretched thing that was going to drag her away from the comforts of her home.

"Why must I go when every part of my being longs to stay here?" she huffed.

When she turned back to her friend, she noticed that Jack's demeanor had softened. He slid his hand down the length of her face and tipped her chin up so she now looked into his eyes.

"I will be there to take care of you, Sari. I promise."

Sarah's eyes began to well up so badly that she forced herself to look away from him.

"Do you hear me?" questioned Jack with great care in his voice. "I will never let anyone hurt you... ever."

Sarah struggled to nod in agreement, knowing Jack's heart was huge, but his poorly thought out plans never worked in their favor.

Jack and hugged her close.

"Are you really going to go home?" Sarah muffled into his shirt.

Jack kept his chin up and looked out into the distance. "Perhaps... perhaps not."

This time it was Sarah who nudged Jack. "I will be there for you, too. If I have any say in the matter."

"SARAH!!!" echoed across the fields from the direction of her house.

The two broke. Sarah looked into Jack's eyes once more.

"I must go..."

Maybe it was the way the light struck Jack's face in that moment, or maybe it was the perilous journey ahead, but for whatever reason, Sarah pulled Jack closer and kissed him.

Before he could respond, she broke from their romantic moment and took off as fast as she could, too embarrassed to ever look back.

CHAPTER 4

GENERAL GREGOR FURST

*U*pon entering the back door, Sarah's father's tight grip clasped around her arm and directed her into a small reading room.

"Where on earth have you been? The Duke's escort has been waiting out front for nearly an hour now!"

Sarah looked at her father sheepishly. "Father... I am... I apologize. I got lost in the woods with Jack..."

"Jack!? When will you learn to leave that riff raff in the gutter where he belongs?"

Sarah felt her lip curl back into a snarl as heat rose to her face.

"He is not riff raff. He is my dearest friend," she snapped.

"Such disobedience! You are such an impetuous little girl."

"Father, I am not a little girl anymore."

"Then act like it!" he barked back in his most terrifying tone. "You need to make new acquaintances with someone of your own stature and class."

After his last words, he looked down the full length of Sarah's attire. Sarah followed his gaze. She hadn't realized that most of her dress was covered in mud and her hem was tattered from the fall down the hill. On her hand was dried blood from when she tended her wounded knee.

Finally, her eyes drifted up to catch his disappointed ones.

"Well, if I am to be married off to the highest bidder, then I am sure I will meet higher society when I join their circle of friends at the castle," Sarah replied defensively.

"Go make yourself more presentable before you travel – Now."

Sarah dropped her head and started to make her way to the door when something in her gut forced her to turn back.

"You do know that the Duke has many suitors attending this ball, right?" she pointed out. "The only way he would ever look at country nobility like me is if I had some magical power to turn our crops of hay into gold and make him even more rich than he already is."

Sarah's father stroked his gray beard at the thought. "If only you could."

She came back to him and kissed him on the cheek.

"I know how much you wish this match to work in our favor," she whispered.

Her father dropped his defenses and smiled back at her brilliantly.

"Oh, my girl," he said as he pulled her into a hug. "There is not a man in this world who would not fall in love with you. You are too endearing."

Sarah remained blank faced as she knew Jack would come save her after a half day's time. She was certain of it.

"Now, go change. The General is waiting for you in the front sitting room."

Sarah bowed her head and hurried out the door to change.

* * *

Once Sarah entered her room, she noticed that many of her things were missing. The only assumption she could conclude was that her father had already sent someone up to pack for her. Everything was most likely already attached to the back of the carriage outside.

The bottle with the six beans was transferred to an identical hidden pocket sewn into the clean dress she put on.

Taking a moment to collect her thoughts, she sat down at her

STALKED: THE CONTI ROSE

vanity mirror and thoroughly brushed the knots out of her long, mahogany-colored hair. Each stroke took longer and longer, knowing she wished to delay leaving as long as she could.

Thoughts rushed erratically through her mind. A several days trip was before her and the truth was that her noble bloodline was far weaker than many of the nobility that already resided in the Duke's Court. That fact alone made her less likely to be favored as the Duke's new bride.

There was no more stalling to be done. She placed her brush down on the table and made her way down the stairs into the large sitting room.

* * *

Upon entering, Sarah was taken aback by the giant figure as he stood in the far corner with his back to her. His head just barely missed the ceiling, and his frame was larger than a workhorse.

At present, he was looking very closely at a small painting that hung amongst many on the wall. This gave Sarah a moment to observe him before their long-awaited introduction.

Clearly, he was the Duke's General based on the number of decorated bans sewn into the sleeves of his uniform. From what Sarah could tell, he seemed well groomed with his short, dark hair and the little she saw of his thick beard. At his side hung an enormous war hammer that had a worn handle from use. Clearly, a warrior stood before her.

"My humblest apologies for my tardiness. It took longer than expected to get ready."

The man didn't turn to acknowledge her but instead leaned closer to the painting.

Sarah cleared her throat loudly and try to force the General to look at her, but his attention was still focused on the picture.

"Is there something wrong?" asked Sarah impatiently.

"Yes. Your inability to be punctual makes me realize that staying a few minutes longer will not influence your otherwise timeless day," he said in a deep yet calm tone.

A moment of annoyance and anger at this stranger's curtness flashed across her face. Her teeth clenched involuntarily as the man chose to continue studying the painting instead of addressing her properly.

He probably had no care for the painting at all. Instead, he just came up with a reason to make her stand there a little longer.

"I must confess, I cannot make out the purpose of this painting," he finally said.

"It is a Brenton," she blurted out. "I am an admirer of his work. After all, he is highly regarded around the world."

The giant of a man took a step back from the picture as he still looked it over.

"I am well aware of his work. I am just fascinated that you would have an Aenglton painting in your home when we are nowhere near there."

Sarah moved next to the large figure and studied the painting more closely herself. A cottage rested comfortably in the woods as the sun was almost out of sight. One flickering candle rested in the window and it was trimmed outside with purple flowers.

Old Madge's cottage dashed through Sarah's mind, which caused her to look away.

"I was intrigued with this cottage abandoned to the woods. When I saw the painting, I asked my father if I might have it."

It was hard to make out the expression under the giant's thick beard, but he seemed unmoved by Sarah's explanation.

"You do not approve?" she observed.

"I have no taste for Aenglton or its people," replied the General starkly.

"I guess that is the beautiful thing about art. Beauty can come from anywhere."

"You give your opinions very freely. I think the Duke will be quite taken with you."

"Because he likes good art?" Sarah growled.

"No. Because he likes impertinence," shot back the General.

Sarah could feel the insult strike her like a smack across her face.

"And you do not, I take it?"

"I like silence," snapped the General and finally turned to look her straight in the eyes for the first time since she entered the room. The glare only tarried for a moment before he redirected it back to the painting.

Sarah took a step towards the massive figure with her head cocked to one side, not sure what to think of this strange creature.

"I guess I will not look to you for conversation during this trip then?"

"Ah!" hummed Sarah's father. "I see you have met my daughter, Lady Sarah Levine. Sarah this is- "

"General Gregor Furst," the giant said curtly with a rigid bow of his head.

"General," Sarah repeated, and felt her knees involuntarily bend underneath her into a curtsy.

"What kind of trouble you must be in?" she said.

"Trouble?" replied the General, puzzled.

"To escort one of what I can only imagine is many suitors to the castle. It does not exactly seem like a task for the Duke's top General."

"Sarah!" scolded her father.

"Perhaps you misunderstand the care the Duke gives to each and every woman that is being invited into his home. The road can be a dangerous place, especially in lands this far south. It is very... restless here. I offered my services to him."

Sarah struggled to remove her eyes from the giant's strong face, but finally forced her gaze out the window to the guards who had waited for her.

"Well, I would hate to detain us from such an exciting journey. Perhaps we should be off?" Sarah said with the most sarcasm she could without sounding overbearing.

Sarah's father pulled the front door open and hugged her close.

"My dear, if you can make a good impression on the Duke, he could build you a life of which you have always dreamed."

"You mean the life that you have always dreamed for me?" Sarah snipped back.

Her father looked at her with discontent, and then over to the General, "I do apologize, my daughter is still young and... spirited."

The General held his look of ill humor that Sarah started to believe was his usual expression.

"Spirited is a kind word," the General said, and moved past the two on his way outside.

Sarah kissed her father on the cheek and reluctantly made her way out to the company, who were all mounted on their horses.

The General stood rigidly by the open carriage door and held out his left hand as Sarah approached.

Upon taking it, she could feel the rough texture of what was no doubt his sword hand. For a moment, his firm grip clinched around her tiny hand and provoked her to scowl as she crawled into the back seat.

"Ouch!" she hissed, but her complaint could not be made before the carriage door slammed in her face.

"Heartless," Sarah scoffed as she crossed her arms and threw her back against the seat cushion with annoyance.

As the company started to move towards the woods, Sarah kept her eyes on her father, who waved from the front step. She could not bring herself to wave back, for she would rather have spent her afternoon with a good book or walk down by the brook with Jack.

"Jack," she whispered.

As her friend entered into her mind, her eyes began to well up and a single tear glistened down her cheek. With all the adventures she had been on with him since she was just a little girl, she knew that she might never have another quiet moment alone with him again.

Thinking on the previous night's events, it wasn't the oddities that came to her mind first but instead, the comfort she found while she lay in Jack's arms. Though she could not get the word "love" to pass through her lips, she felt a great affection towards Jack. An affection that was stronger than friendship.

All of a sudden, a little clink hit the window. Not loudly, but just enough for Sarah to look out.

A little distance off the road, just inside the first row of trees, Jack stood with a devious smirk. In his one hand was a pebble that he flicked up into the air while the other held his slingshot.

Sarah couldn't help but smile back at him.

"This is going to be some journey," she muttered to herself.

As soon as the words were spoken, Jack took off as fast as he could, and disappeared into the density of the Allogot Forest. Sarah's faith was now placed into Jack's unsteady but loving hands that he would come save her. That he would protect her.

She allowed her back to fall once more against the seat. The tears that filled her eyes only moments earlier were now replaced with comfort and hearty laughter.

CHAPTER 5

FALLEN TREE

*T*he humid spring air clung to every inch of Sarah's body as the carriage traveled half a day closer to the Duke's castle. In the Southlands, it was remarkable how the extreme of heat during the day could turn to such bitter cold at night.

In a vain attempt to keep cool, Sarah fanned her face with her hand, but with no success

A rap on the window caused Sarah to almost jump out of her skin. When she looked out, the General rode alongside the carriage on the back of his massive horse, which held a militaristic stature.

"Yes?" she asked gruffly.

The General held out a fan that was dwarfed in size as it rested in the palm of his large hand. Sarah's face softened.

Without saying a word, she took it and immediately began to fan herself. The new gust of air felt refreshing against her sweaty skin and gave her instant relief.

"Thank you," she said and turned back to the General, but he had already pushed forward towards the front of the company. She could just see his horse's tail flick back and forth before he was out of her sight.

"Do not take the General's bluntness to heart," said another voice.

Sarah turned to look towards the back of the carriage. A handsome man, with a full beard and reddish-brown hair pulled his horse up next to her. His uniform was not quite as grand as the General's, but he was still a man of rank. He tipped his hat to her as a kind hello.

"When the General has orders, he is a very focused man."

"Is that how you would describe him? Focused?" Sarah hissed.

The man smiled brilliantly with a hint of charm in his expression. "That is what he is."

"You do not seem as cold as he. What is your name, might I ask?"

"Captain Anton Lowe, at your service, my lady," he said with a bow of his head.

Sarah poked her head a little further out of the window to see if the General was near, but all her eyes could catch was the dense trees along the path.

"I would guess that the General is not from this part of the world by the looks of him," Sarah suggested.

"Well, you are right about that, my lady. He comes from an island up north called Gaente."

"Gaente? I thought only beasts lived up there."

The Captain raised his brow at the statement. "Bedtime stories mothers tell their children."

"I have no mother. So, you will have to come up with a better explanation than that."

"Gaente is a rough terrain that many men are not built to travel. The harshness of the weather and the land builds people larger and tougher to survive," said the Captain.

"Does tougher also entail being curt to your guests?"

"I am afraid the clans there are tightly woven and do not take kindly to strangers."

"Clearly," Sarah blurted out.

"Before you judge the General too harshly, Lady Levine, please understand that he has come a long way from his homeland and has been through more than you or I will in our lifetimes."

Sarah's eyes drifted while the Captain's observation ruminated in her mind. It sounded as though the General had been in the position that she now found herself in. Being forced from his land against his will. Though, he was now the top General in the Duke's army.

When the last thought passed, her eyes refocused on the object in her hand. She held up the fan and looked at it more closely. The scene painted on it was a little girl in a pink dress knelt by a waterfall, singing. At least that's what Sarah thought the little girl was doing.

"He is a good and honorable man. Best I have seen in my life," said the Captain.

"Despite all you say, I find him to be... difficult," Sarah replied shortly.

"You have only just met him. Give him time. You will warm up to him."

"Doubtful."

"You never know, maybe he already has."

A light chuckle slipped through the Captain's lips. He quickly turned away from Sarah as he tried to hide his amusement.

"You are all so infuriating!"

"We come by it naturally," replied the Captain with a smirk.

"That is true enough," agreed Sarah.

A bright flash lit up the Captain's face, followed by a loud bang. A large tree creaked as it started to fall and crashed down onto the path just in front of the company.

The guard splintered, as their horses became hysterical from the severity of the noise. Some horses reared up while others took off into the woods.

"Staida! Staida!" screamed the General as he tried to gain control of his own horse.

A thick cloud of black smoke engulfed the carriage that suffocated Sarah. Her chest started to burn and her eyes watered. She kicked open the door, slid out of the back seat, and held up her arm to cover her face.

She ran to the front of the carriage as she gasped for fresh air. As she heaved in and out, Sarah slowly regained her breath and she turned to see smoke billow from the base of the tree that had just fallen.

The General had dismounted his horse and examined the unusual situation.

Sarah kept her hand over her mouth as she walked closer to him.

"What is it? What happened?" she shouted out.

The General ran his finger along the jagged edge of where the tree split, and smelled it. He hastily pulled his war hammer off of his belt and spun around to look at the forest behind him.

The Captain pulled his horse to an abrupt halt next to the General, unleashed his sword, and pointed it towards the woods.

"Sir, I caught a glimpse of something just there, but it was moving too quickly for me to see what it was," said one of the guards.

The General pointed his hammer directly at Sarah with a crumpled brow, "Get her back in the carriage and put four guards on both sides. Now!"

The General continued to look around the forest as if something was about to attack him.

One of the guards helped Sarah into the carriage and closed the door behind her. Just as the General ordered, four guards on horseback remained at attention as they filed along both sides of the carriage.

"What is going on?" Sarah shouted out the window.

"Grah!" roared from outside. Sarah looked around nervously still not being able to see what the General was doing.

"Grah!" sounded again.

"General? Captain?" she screamed with a tremor in her voice.

For a brief moment, Sarah thought the company was under attack but the four guards on either side didn't flinch from their post.

"Grah!" sounded again and again. "Grah!"

Finally, a loud CRACK sounded, followed by cheering.

"What has happened?" Sarah pleaded for an answer.

The guards off to the left side of the carriage separated as the Captain appeared.

"This is unsafe territory. We must get to Lankenshire before nightfall."

"Will you tell me what has happened?" Sarah asked with concern.

The Captain held out his hand which had a black grainy substance on it.

"The General found this at the base of the fallen tree," he said bluntly.

"Black powder?"

"This was no accident. Someone meant for this tree to come down on us," he said and looked out at the forest cautiously.

"Who would possibly?" Sarah started, but found her words trail off when she looked at the Captain's hard expression.

"I know you are not the biggest admirer of the General, but he is right about the dangers of these roads. There has been unrest in Ditrum for some time now. What could make a bigger statement to the Duke than an attack on his military while traveling these roads?"

Sarah could tell by the concern in the Captain's voice that the situation was quite serious.

"We are going to push on at a quicker pace," said the Captain. "I am going to move ahead of the group to make sure that there are no other surprises waiting for us."

With that, he kicked his horse's sides and took off up the road. While the rest of the company continued forward.

As the carriage passed through the fallen tree, Sarah couldn't help but stare at it in wonderment.

How could the tree have been cut in half and pushed enough off the road so the carriage could pass through? she thought to herself.

"You looked surprised," remarked the General while his horse now trotted alongside the carriage.

"How could men move a tree this fast? I have lived amongst the greatest of woodsmen and it would have taken an hour at least to move this."

"Maybe for a woodsman you are correct, but not for a giant beast from Gaente."

Sarah almost thought she could make out a smile under the General's dark beard.

Before another word was spoken, the General pushed his horse forward and moved to the head of the company as they galloped up the road towards the little town of Lankenshire.

CHAPTER 6

THE LITTLE INN OF LANKENSHIRE

*D*usk settled into the sky when the company came to a halt in the center of a quaint village square. Next to the carriage was a small fountain where two women dipped their buckets to collect water, and then scurried off down the street. Most of the storefronts were dark and the surrounding streets seemed fairly empty. That is – except for one place.

The entire company's focus was drawn to the music and merriment that came from the tavern on the northeast end of the square. Boots could be heard stomping on the wooden floorboards in time as two or three fiddles bowed a cheerful tune. Several people could be seen entering the lively place.

"Hooray! Hooray!" the villagers cheered as the song came to an end.

The applauses prompted Sarah to shift her gaze from the bright lights that streamed from the tavern down a couple of buildings to the more dimly lit inn. Nothing at all about the structure invited her to enter. The thatched roof looked like it was thinning at the top. The walls, from what she could only presume were clay, seemed to lean a bit, which made the inn look like it could fall over at any moment.

With a hard shove, Sarah pushed the carriage door open. She

hadn't even gotten a foot onto solid ground before she heard the General's gruff voice.

"Stay here," he ordered.

"I am coming in with you."

The General paused for a moment and let his scowl of disapproval be seen as clearly as possible to her. Sarah simply brushed past the menacing figure that blocked her path and stepped into the inn.

Upon entering the peculiar little abode, it appeared to be vacant. The only light to be found was a single candle melted down to the last bit of wax and wick. Behind the counter, the old innkeeper leaned awkwardly against the wall while he slept. The loud snoring was the only indication that he was alive. His spectacles sat askew on his nose and a small book lay overturned in his lap.

The General and the Captain entered quietly through the front door and walked up to the dilapidated looking counter.

The Captain waved his hand in front of the innkeeper's face, but the old man didn't move.

"Should I?" asked the General and placed his hand on the handle of his war hammer.

"Why not? He looks like he could use a new counter anyway," said the Captain, and looked over his shoulder with a light chuckle. "Besides, a small town like this could use a good story to tell."

"What are you going to do?" asked Sarah, unsure of the General's intentions.

The General unhitched the hammer from his belt while he ran his hand across the top of the uneven counter surface. His eyes flickered down to meet Sarah's apprehensive glare.

"This!"

Smash!

With one stroke, the General pulled the war hammer off his hip, rolled it up into the air, and let it fall down hard onto the counter. Splinters of wood went flying in every direction while the main structure collapsed to the ground.

The innkeeper jumped so high from his chair, he could have easily touched the ceiling. He fell back into his seat and he quickly adjusted his glasses on his nose. His eyes grew to the size of saucers when they refocused to the General's large figure, then looked down at the pile of wood on the floor.

Sarah turned, surprisingly amused by the whole event. Still, she tried to remain somewhat serious as she spoke to the General.

"Was that really necessary?"

The General hung the hammer back into its holster.

"Define necessary. He is awake, is he not?"

"Only because he did not die from fright," Sarah snapped back.

"My goodness! What has happened here?" said the innkeeper, a little out of sorts.

"We have a company of twenty men," stated the General.

Sarah cleared her throat loudly to try to remind the General that she was also in the room.

"And Lady Levine," the General grumbled. "We need housing for the night."

The innkeeper adjusted his glasses again while he forced his eyes to look from the collapsed counter up to the General.

"Twenty, you say? I am afraid we only have fifteen rooms here. And all but one of them are taken because of the festival in the neighboring town."

"We shall take the one," said the General and threw a small bag of coins into the innkeeper's hands.

"Oh, my goodness," chirped the old man, a little surprised by the immediate payment.

The innkeeper's eyes grew in size as he inspected one of the gold coins. Once he was finally satisfied, he took a closer look at the massive man who stood just past the wreckage.

"A large barn is just out back there. If you would like, your company is welcome to sleep there for the night," he proposed.

"We will be out before dawn," said the General with a slight nod of agreement.

"Alright," said the innkeeper. "But if you choose to stay a little longer, there is a wonderful festival like you have never seen."

The General waved him off with an uncaring hand and moved towards the door.

"After having been to the best festival this world has to offer, all pale in comparison."

"Are you suggesting you have been to the Gluhen Festival?" said the old man in amazement.

The General looked over his shoulder and nodded once in affirmation.

"How did you ever find it? I know so many who have tried but its city is hidden in the sky," questioned the man with curiosity.

"It is not hard if you are from that town," said the Captain.

Sarah noticed the harsh glare the General shot at his second in command as soon as he finished speaking. The Captain seemed to not even notice the unkind glower and held his jovial demeanor.

"Oh, I have been to so many wonderful festivals across this great land. But I fear I will never get to see that one."

"Why not?" asked Sarah.

"It simply is not possible at my age," replied the old innkeeper.

"It might not be probable, but it is still quite possible," countered Sarah. "Please never lose hope you will see it someday."

She could feel a heaviness in the room when she turned smack into the General's disapproving scowl. But the heaviness lifted when the old man nodded with agreement and a smile on his face.

"Come," growled the General and shoved the front door open.

"Do not worry, he is in a mood," the Captain whispered in Sarah's ear.

"Is he ever in a good mood?"

"Well, spend enough time around him, he is bound to crack a smile once in a while," said the Captain with a grin.

"I seriously doubt it," replied Sarah as she stepped out to the street.

The first thing she noticed were the two men who took a piece of her luggage off the carriage and walked past her into the inn.

"Where are they taking my things?"

"I believe the General intends for you to stay in the inn," replied the Captain.

"No! I am staying out in the barn with the company. I am a country girl after all."

"You are a noble woman," reminded the Captain.

"Yes, who grew up amongst animals and grain fields. I have spent a night or two on a stack of hay as a bed."

The Captain pursed his lips for a moment.

"Honestly, My Lady, I have no cares to where you sleep. However, it is not me you must convince," said the Captain, and then gestured to the General.

Sarah sighed, and knew that no matter how much she wanted to fight with this decision, she would lose. That didn't stop her as she made her way to the General in protest.

"I wish to stay wherever the company is sleeping tonight."

The General brushed past her while he carried another small bag of hers.

"Does my opinion count for nothing?" she growled.

"Not at this time."

"What if someone sneaks into my room and attacks me in my sleep? You will surely regret your decision then!"

"I am willing to take that risk," said the General before he let the door to the inn slam behind him.

"Insufferable! Horrible! Ogre!" Sarah screamed after him.

"Believe me when I say he has been called much worse by more threatening people than yourself, My Lady," said the Captain, and then offered his arm to escort her inside.

Sarah looked down at his elbow, uncaring.

"I never asked for any of this," Sarah snapped, and then turned her back to the Captain as she walked back into the inn alone.

CHAPTER 7

THE CONTI ROSE

Sarah sat on the edge of the bed and hugged a pillow tightly to her chest. She was thankful to be away from the General for the first time all day. The only downfall was the loneliness that set in from being the farthest she had ever been from her home.

"Why do I have to marry the Duke? He knows nothing about me or Ditrum. And that horrible General Furst, hand-picked to escort me to my grave."

A rumbling started in the depths of her belly and escalated until it erupted from her lips. Sarah screamed, as loud as she could, into the feathery fluff held between her fingers. Then she took the pillow and hit the bed with it multiple times. Feathers flew from the seams as she swung and hit whatever she could.

All that remained in the room after she released her fury were sheets of white plumage and silence. One last huff shot from her nose when a sound rose to her consciousness.

Music.

Fiddles still strummed happy tunes that conflicted with her present attitude. Slowly, Sarah found herself rise from the bed and drift over to the window. Just as she looked out, she caught a glimpse of some of the guards as they ducked into the front door of the tavern.

"If I am to be sold off like property, the least I can do is have a little fun before we get to the castle," Sarah said to herself with a half smile.

Quickly pulling the pins from her intricately wrapped hair, Sarah let her mahogany locks fall into perfect curls down her back. She pinched her cheeks to bring the color back to her pale complexion and dabbed some red onto her pouted lips.

Looking into the mirror once she was finished, Sarah was content with her simple attire. Though she would much prefer to go chase frogs at the pond instead of going to a tavern.

She exhaled a deep sigh.

"Here I go."

* * *

When Sarah entered the tavern, she was not surprised to see most of the guard had already partaken in the festivities. All the humble villagers had smiles on their faces and dance shoes on their feet. The one figure she was pleased she didn't come across was that of the oafish General.

Taking a closer look at the room, the ceiling was higher than she envisioned when she saw the tavern from outside. Other than some low hanging beams to frame the walls, the ceiling extended to a second level and gave an open feel to the place.

Three fourths of the room was filled with wooden tables that were surrounded by groups of people with glasses of ale in their hands. Beyond the tables was a large dance floor filled with villagers and guard members alike. Then, at the far end, rested the bar that ran the width of the room.

Out of the corner of Sarah's eye, she noticed some of the guard waved her over to their table.

Sarah had to admit; it was nice to see the company at ease for once. They were freed from their militaristic formations and their strict General. They now rested comfortably in their seats while they each held a cheerful demeanor.

One of the men rose to his feet and offered his seat as she came closer.

"Please, I could not possibly," she said and held up her hand up in protest.

"It is not needed," replied the guard as he winked in the direction of two girls who giggled uncontrollably at the next table over.

"I believe I will be dancing in this next one," he said just as the two girls approached him and laced their arms into his. Sarah watched with pleasure as the three moved towards the dance floor.

A glass slid across the table to where she stood. When Sarah looked up, she saw the Captain pick at his teeth with a thin wooden stick as he looked her over with a mischievous smile.

She sat down and placed her hands around the handle of the stein of ale.

"I am surprised the General is not here leading his troops into the world of merriment," she said with no effort to remove the sarcasm from her voice.

"It might seem hard to believe from his loveliness, but the General does not usually go out to places like this," replied the Captain.

"Is this not what most warriors do at the end of a long day? Drink and be merry?"

"Atou! Atou!" cheered all the soldiers around the table as several of them held up their steins before they took a swig.

"Not all soldiers," stated the Captain. "The road to the Vasfale castle is a treacherous one. The General is probably looking over maps to see where he can anticipate trouble."

"What kind of trouble? I would think everyone would quake in the presence of the Duke's royal guard."

Looking around the table at the strong builds and worn eyes, these were men who had seen the harshness of war.

"Some of you have fought in legendary battles, have you not?"

"None more so than the General," the Captain pointed out, "But he did not win those because he was ill-prepared. Besides, just because we are well liked by most, does not mean we are liked by all."

"Who would not love and admire you?" nudged Sarah for an

answer, but could tell by the Captain's hardening expression that he really didn't want to respond.

"Tell her about Baer," one of the men said while he looked down at his glass. "She is not a feeble woman, despite her nobility."

"I would never doubt that, but Baer is not good table conversation," retorted the Captain sharply.

Just as he abruptly ended the conversation, the fiddles began to bow another tune. Many of the guard were approached by fawning admirers and asked to dance. Though Sarah had a couple offers to join in, she turned everyone down with a gracious smile and remained with the Captain.

"As much as I am sure this Baer fellow might be a threat to us, I am sure one drink would do no harm. Even for the General. After all, does drinking not create some kind of bond amongst soldiers?"

The Captain leaned back in his seat with a half smirk and half quizzical brow before it suddenly relaxed and he broke into hearty laughter.

"What?" asked Sarah genuinely confused.

"I thought you did not care for the General," pointed out the Captain.

"I find him difficult, yes."

"And yet here you are, wondering where he is."

"I was trying to be hospitable. I really do not care if he is here or not."

The Captain plopped his chin onto his hands and looked at Sarah with a bemused smirk. "Lady Levine, I will not profess to know you well, but it does sound as if you have taken a liking to the General."

Sarah could feel her face instantly burn like it was on fire as his words panged her ears and rattled around in her thoughts. The shouting started before she even knew what she was saying. The Captain just held his satisfied countenance while she screamed at the top of her lungs.

"How could you possibly think that I would take any interest in such a horrible, despicable creature like the General?! Every part of me is absolutely repulsed by his very nature! You are absolutely, without a doubt, completely and utterly out of your senses!"

In the moment her last words left her mouth, she quickly noticed that the music had stopped and everyone around her seemed frozen in time, just staring.

When she glanced around the room, all the villagers stood like statues. The guard, too, had stopped in their tracks.

For a moment, Sarah thought her yelling might have gotten a little out of control, but then she noticed that no one was looking at her.

No! They looked past her.

When she turned and followed everyone's gaze, her eyes landed on the large figure that consumed the entire doorway.

"You wonder why he never comes out?" said the Captain, and rose to his feet. "You just got your answer."

Sarah, in turn, sat back down and allowed the Captain to take the attention of the room off the General.

Holding up his glass in a celebratory gestured, the Captain said, "I know most of you are stunned, flabbergasted, brought to absolute awe to see such an amazing hero in your presence. But I assure each and every one of you that he can drink with the best of us. Am I right boys?"

All the guard joined in as they held their glasses up.

"Atou! Atou!" they cheered.

A wave of ease settled into the crowd and the music started to play again.

Sarah watched the General move slowly across the room. He careful not to hit his head on the beams or run into any of the cowering villagers that didn't realize they were in his way. Finally, he arrived at the table and sat down across from the Captain and right next to Sarah.

"Another drink!" yelled the Captain.

A portly, bubbly girl hustled over and dropped three more large steins in front of them.

Sarah kept her focus on the glass. Her stomach twisted into knots and she found her breathing become labored the longer the General sat in silence.

"To what do we owe this unexpected pleasure, General?" asked the Captain casually.

"I was tasked with protecting *her*... Best if I keep an eye on her at this time," the General replied.

"Really?" Sarah shot back hotly. "That is comforting considering that I am the only one staying in the inn. I did not see you keeping an eye on me there."

The General turned his glare towards her as she crossed her arms tight to her chest. The heavy weight that sat behind his dark eyes shook her to the core, but she tried hard not to show it. Instead, she slid her hands under her legs and sat on them to stop them from trembling. By the looks of him, the General clearly wasn't used to being talked to with such an aggressive tone.

"I do not need to be in your room to know you are there," he said sternly. "But with more people around you comes more... complications."

"Complications?"

"You could easily sneak out of here with all these diversions," continued the General and motioned to the glass in his hand.

"I think you are giving me too much praise," said Sarah with a whimsical laugh that instantly eased the tension in her body.

"One thing I am known for, Lady Levine, is assessing the battle-field before me and having a plan of attack."

"This is not a battle, General."

"Oh, but it is," hummed the General. "And you are my worthy opponent."

Sarah forced a smile, if for no other reason than to try to get under his skin.

"Despite your quick temper and your insistence to always be right, I find you do understand what you are doing," said the General.

"And yet, I cannot comprehend the situation I currently find myself in," Sarah argued back.

"You comprehend it, you just do not care for it."

"Yes, because I have no choice in the matter," she scoffed.

"There is always a choice, even if you do not like the possible outcomes."

"What are you? A fortune teller?"

"I am a man who has seen enough to know."

"Is that so?" said Sarah as she expected a snide retort. Instead, the General relaxed on his stool and spun his glass in circles between his fingers.

"You are a passionate soldier. I will give you that," admitted Sarah.

The General's gaze lifted up to meet Sarah's. This time his eyes were softer, so much so that she felt a tranquility wash over her. The rejuvenation put Sarah back in control.

She grabbed the beer that rested in the General's hands, and guzzled it down. Her face soured at the taste before she wiped the froth from her lips.

"You think you know how to handle things, do you?"

The General nodded his head confidently. Sarah leaned on the table and asked, "Then how will you get out of dancing with me?"

The General's eyes looked calmly over at the Captain.

"I will allow my second in command to handle such an assignment."

Sarah shot a look at the Captain who smiled at the amusing situation unfolding between the General and her.

"As much as I would love to dance with this fine young lady, General, I do believe she has asked you. I would hate to deprive you of such an honor," said the Captain as he raised his hands up in surrender to Sarah.

Before another word was spoken she wrapped her arm through the General's and pulled with all her might for him to follow her to the dance floor. She couldn't even make him shift on his stool; he was so big. The Captain almost fell on the floor with laughter.

"Come on, General!" implored Sarah.

"Yes, General! You fear nothing! Not even the dance floor!" urged the Captain.

The General looked over at him with a hint of irritation.

The Captain nodded his head with encouragement. Finally, the General's shoulders dropped with consent.

Sarah smiled as the General slowly rose and she dragged him towards the dance floor. She didn't even notice that the rest of the guards throughout the room went silent, completely stunned.

"Where is she taking the General?" Sarah overheard one of the men ask the Captain.

"To the dance floor," came the chuckled response.

"She knows she is going to die out there, right?" another one of the men said. "He surely will make it known that he does not *dance*."

Sarah just turned her nose up at all the cynicism. As she and the General stepped onto the dance floor, everyone who had previously occupied it scattered like rats, leaving just the two alone in the middle. She looked at the fiddlers, who waited to hear her song request.

"I think the Conti Rose will suffice," she said, contentedly.

The General leaned into her with a scowl.

Sarah took her first position with her hands clasped together by her ear while her head was tilted towards the floor. Her eyes shot up to meet the General's large brown ones. He began to breathe more heavily.

"Is that fear I see in your eyes, General?" she goaded him on. "All you have to do is stand there," she explained.

Sarah was impressed that he didn't retreat, but instead remained ever so still as she nodded to the fiddlers and the lively tune began. Her hands started to clap together and she circled the entire floor as she coaxed the villagers to clap along.

She then fixed her eyes on the General. Lifting her skirt to her knees, her feet tapped a complicated rhythm on the floorboards. Around the General, she spun and spun. The crowd cheered her on, while the soldiers laughed with excitement until the music came to a crescendo. Sarah slid her arms around the General's neck and collapsed in a heap of giggles into his arms.

The entire crowd cheered loudly at the spectacle. All, that is, except the General.

Breathless, Sarah looked back into his eyes. His hardened expression had not changed over to amusement as she had hoped. Though, just for the second, when their eyes were locked, she felt his body shift and he leaned closer to her. Her heart fluttered unexpectedly and she could feel the warmth of his breath graze her skin.

"Worthy opponent," he said.

Then the General raised her carefully to a standing position.

"I believe you will be safe here without me," he concluded.

Without looking at her again, the General pushed his way through the group of his soldiers who patted him on the back, and he made his way out of the tavern.

As Sarah returned to her place at the table, all the guard congratulated her on surviving the General's ill-humor.

"I would never have thought in a thousand years I would see the General dance," one guard spouted out.

"Technically, he just stood still while I moved around him."

"Still! Best thing I can recall seeing in years," followed another guard.

"Listen, men. Because of the oddity of the situation tonight, I think it is best if you just put all these events from your minds come morning," suggested the Captain.

The entire guard fell silent as they looked around the table at each other, concerned about the backlash. The moment broke into roaring laughter by everyone there, which included the Captain.

Sarah couldn't help but join them for she thought the night would be spoiled by the General's presence, and yet, she thoroughly enjoyed her dance of mockery with him.

But her satisfaction only lasted a few moments longer before the Captain leaned over and whispered into her ear, "It was just an observation, what I said earlier. But, I do believe I am correct about you and the General."

CHAPTER 8

THE ESCAPE

Sarah was hardly surprised to find the innkeeper passed out again in his seat when she enter the inn at the end of the evening. Despite the fact that the General had smashed the front counter into pieces, the guards must have gotten rid of it before they went out. All that remained was a little night table that sat next to the old man.

The staircase creaked as Sarah made her way up to her room. The weight of the evening's events and the festivities made her body feel heavy from exhaustion as she collapsed onto her bed. There were no cares that she was still fully dressed including the shoes on her feet. With great effort, she pulled herself up to her pillow and allowed her eyes to close.

Her hands moved clumsily across her body until they landed next to her head.

"That giant oaf," she mumbled into her pillowcase.

Sarah sat up abruptly and shouted, "I do not like him! You hear me, Captain? I do not like anyone!"

Then her whole body fell back down onto the bed. Her hand slid under her pillow when something crackled under her fingertips. One eye popped open then the other. As she tried to identify the foreign object, she slid it out. When her eyes refocused, they stared at a small envelope that rested in her hand.

"What could this be?" she started and sat up in the bed.

Sarah lit the candle on her night table and held the folded parchment up to look over the nondescript wax seal.

Across the top read "SARI" – She hugged the letter close to her chest. "Jack!" she exhaled, excited.

She feverishly ripped the envelope open and began to read.

> Sari,
>
> I slipped some sleeping powder into the innkeeper's drink earlier this evening. He should be asleep for some time. When you get back to your room, grab what you need and meet me behind the blacksmith's barn. I will be waiting there with two horses, ready to ride. Be quick and safe.
>
> Love,
>
> J.S.

SARAH HELD the letter in her hand for a long moment. When the plan of their escape settled into her mind, she looked out the window.

"The blacksmith's barn?" Sarah repeated and studied the storefronts in the square. Finally, in the far corner, she could just make out the word 'smith' and a large barn roof could be seen off to the side of the building.

"That must be it!"

Before Sarah knew it, she had thrown together a satchel full of clothes. She made sure to tuck the small bottle of beans away in the hidden pocket of her dress. Blowing out the candle on her nightstand, she quietly made her way down the staircase. A light chuckle escaped when she saw the innkeeper still asleep. She now knew that it was Jack's doing.

The door opened easily enough as she poked her head out to get a good view of the square. It was empty of most everyone and she was in the clear to make her escape.

As soon as her feet hit the dirt, Sarah made her way along the edge of this town as she crept quietly by the empty stores. As she passed the last shop, her feet picked up the pace. The thought of the General catching her and what he might do to such an 'impertinent' girl made her nervous.

CHAPTER 9

QUMA

*T*he morning light had barely broken when Sarah's eyes fluttered open to the gentle tap of the Captain's fingers on her arm.

"Good morning, My Lady. Decide to join us, did you?" he said in a humored tone.

Sarah tried to sit up but her neck was stiff and her body was uncooperative after a night on uneven bedding. Every inch of her ached and a throbbing slammed against her temples repeatedly. Part of her wondered why she fought so hard to sleep out in the barn.

"What time is it?" she asked groggily.

"Early. But we must be on our way if we hope to make it to Ambrea by nightfall."

"What or who is Ambrea?"

"It is a wall. Well, it is a gate in a wall."

"Unusual name."

"The man who designed the gate named it after his daughter who he lost at a young age. He built a gate that is so big it could almost touch the heavens so he could be closer to her."

"That is a sad tale for this early in the morning," Sarah muttered as she closed her eyes and draped her hand over her forehead.

"I think it quite beautiful, actually."

A the Captain's words, Sarah's eyes half opened and looked at him. The Captain's cockeyed smirk made Sarah realize that she had lived a sheltered life in Ditrum. There was so much to the vast world she had never even heard of before, let alone seen.

After the story, Sarah found her interest peaked and she all of a sudden looked forward to seeing a gate that could touch the sky.

"Your things have already been packed onto the carriage," said the Captain as he regained her attention. "After seeing your room with my own eyes, I must ask, did you get in a fight with a large bird or are all those feathers from something else?"

Sarah dropped her head a little embarrassed from her outburst the previous night that she took out on her pillow.

"Take a minute to collect yourself and when you are all set, the company will be out front ready to depart."

With that, the Captain rose and stepped out of the stall.

"Wait!" said Sarah through her exhaustion.

The Captain paused to look at her.

"How is the General this morning?"

The devious smile held on his face and his eyes clenched shut as if he suppressed a laugh. He shook his head and then walked out of the barn without any reply.

"Wait! No! This does not mean I like him! GRRR!" growled Sarah.

Sarah slammed her hands down next to her, truly frustrated with the Captain's nonsense. She could only guess that the General laid into his men for their behavior last evening and because he felt they lost sight of the task at hand.

Time was of the essence. Sarah dipped her hand into the water bucket that hung by the stall door, splashed her face a couple of times, and then made her way out to the company.

At the front of the inn, the guards had already mounted their horses except for the one guard who waited next to the carriage door to help Sarah in. Dark creases rested under most of their eyes, and a handful of them struggled to sit up straight in their saddles.

The General was the only one who looked alert as he sat sternly on his colossal horse. Sarah glanced over at him to gauge his attitude towards her this morning, but he didn't return her look. Instead, he steered his horse towards the path that they were ready to travel.

Sarah took the extended hand of the guard and climbed into her seat. After she was settled, she turned her gaze to look out the window. The carriage began to move. Just as they were about to exit the town, she noticed the imprint in the dirt of where Jack had been knocked off his horse. But the General's massive steps and the place where she had collapsed on the ground looked like they had been brushed away.

"Interesting," she muttered just before the carriage moved back onto the country road.

* * *

THE MORNING TRAVEL was quite dull and humid. Sarah cooled herself with the fan the General had given her a day earlier. The events of the previous night played over and over again in her mind which provoked questions. Why had the General showed compassion towards her after all the hate and rage she spouted at him? The attempted escape alone could be seen as a treasonous act, punishable by a good lashing, but instead he granted her wish to let her stay in the barn with the guards.

The Captain pulled up alongside the carriage with his usual smile.

"Are you feeling any better? You looked ill when I woke you earlier."

"I have had better mornings."

"Not uncommon when you had an exciting night," suggested the Captain.

"Indeed," Sarah replied sharply, unsure if the Captain knew the full meaning of his statement.

"In all the years I have known the General, I have never seen him dragged to the dance floor before."

"Is he not light on his feet?"

"I would say most women are too intimidated by him to ask him to dance."

"Well, the General is highly esteemed in the Duke's army. That can be intimidating."

"That did not stop you."

"Not much does," retorted Sarah.

"I gathered that," stated the Captain with his amused smile. "For what it is worth, you have given the men a memory that they will not soon forget."

Sarah couldn't suppress the goofy grin that crept onto her face. No matter what had come from the previous night, she will always have that dance. When she looked back at the Captain, the knowing look he returned made her blood boil.

"I know what you are thinking!" Sarah snapped. "It is absolutely absurd!"

"I am not thinking anything!" defended the Captain.

"That is good because you would be wrong!"

"Wrong about what?" poked the Captain as he goaded her on.

"You know what! I think the General is a beast! He is in absolute refusal to believe anything else could be correct outside of his own opinion!"

"Is that right?" said the Captain.

Sarah instantly noticed a change in his tone and his eyes shifted to look past her.

Sarah turned to look out the other side of the carriage to see the General ride just outside of the window. His eyes were cold and looked forward while his face remained hard.

"We are coming to Somar. It is mostly farm country but it has it's dangers. I would advise you to stay silent for this stretch of land," said the General, and then pushed his horse past the carriage.

Sarah's head fell into her hand as absolute mortification rushed over her. Nothing could be said to undo the damage caused by her careless mouth. Though she was quite conflicted about her feelings towards the General, she had no intent on being so direct in her opinion of him. Especially not out loud and certainly not for him to hear.

When she looked back to the Captain for him to console her, he had already gone. Sarah fell back into her seat and kept her gaze out the window.

The carriage broke from the last line of trees into acres upon acres of what looked like some sort of puffy, soft grain. It ran from the forest all the way up to the base of the mountains.

Sarah had never been this far north before. The thick mud and hard work of her land in Ditrum was all she had known. Her breath was swept away with the sea of golden grain bent back and forth in the light breeze. After many years of breaking her back on her own land's crops, never could she imagine a field of such richness and beauty.

As the carriage entered the field, she extended her hand out the window and allowed her fingertips to clip the tops of the soft grain. Even the texture was fuller than what she was familiar with at home.

"Amazing," she breathed with an effervescent glow about her. "What is this called?" she shouted out the window.

"Quma. It is used mostly for drink. Strong but good stuff," replied one of the guards.

Sarah nodded her head, satisfied.

"AHH!"

A cry of pain broke out. Sarah was ripped from her moment of splendor to hear a loud crack followed by another scream.

"What was that?" yelled Sarah.

The guard rode up next to the door.

"Nothing that concerns us, My Lady."

"Really?" replied Sarah with annoyance.

Looking down a row of Quma, her eyes caught a glimpse of a man on a horse with a whip raised over his head, and then came down hard onto the back of one of the workers who was on the ground.

Acting on instinct alone, Sarah kicked open the carriage door and was about to jump out when the door quickly slammed shut. On the other side was the General's foot. He leaned closer to the window.

"You will only make things worse for them," he hissed.

"So you let people be beaten? To think moments ago I felt horrible in calling you a beast when, in fact, I was just telling the truth!"

"That is not my concern," said the General and pointed in the direction of the screams.

"What is your concern exactly?" Sarah barked back.

"You!"

Sarah felt flutters break loose in her stomach again at his response.

"Me?" she said breathlessly.

"Yes. Getting you safely to Vasfale is my only concern right now."

"Are you going to tell her stories to put her to sleep, Gregor?" jeered a deep voice.

The company came to a halt as a group of eight armed men on horses appeared from the fields. The man who spoke was large and burly, but still wasn't quite as big as the General. He had not one hair on his head, his teeth looked black and worn, and a scar cut across his right eye that pinned it closed.

The General turned his horse towards the group of armed men, as the rest of the guard filed to either side of him.

"Bernard," said the General simply.

"That is Lord Baer to you," shot one of the armed men in the field.

"Lord?" scoffed the Captain as he took his place next to the General. "When did you give yourself that title?"

"It was always mine," growled Baer.

When the Captain looked away, it was the first time Sarah noticed the Captain look annoyed.

Her attention was pulled back to the men in the field when she could feel Baer look over every inch of what he could see of her. It made her feel uncomfortable and almost dirty.

"To think you were once the great General Gregor Furst, and now here you are – a lady's handmaid. My, how you have softened in your years," goaded Baer.

The eight men chuckled at the mockery of the General.

"I guess that is a far better than beating innocent people for amusement," replied the Captain.

"Anything to pass the time," cameBaer's retort.

Sarah snickered at the insensitive answer.

"What, you do not like it rough?" said Baer and coaxed his horse a couple steps towards the carriage. "Come spend a night with me and you might see things differently."

The General side stepped his own horse a few steps that forced Baer's horse back.

"I see. Maybe this woman is not for the Duke of Baldwin at all, but for your own personal pleasure?"

Even through the General's thick beard, Sarah could see his jawline tense and his eyes fierce. Was there an ounce of truth to that statement? Any second now, she knew he would pull out his hammer and crush this tyrant. But the General remained oddly still.

"If I pull my sword, will you protect her?" continued Baer.

At this comment, Sarah could hear the General's breath grow heavier, as if this comment had a deeper meaning. The General put his hand on the hilt of his sword.

"Come, come now, Gregor, no need to become defensive. I was just seeing if you cared. Now that I know you do, I can think of much more creative things to do with her innocent face."

"You would have to get through me first, and you know how well that worked for you in the past," said the General, and then swiped his hand across his eye that matched Baer's missing one.

"You cannot always protect everyone, or perhaps you have forgotten Eleanor," taunted Baer.

At that, the General ripped his sword from his side. All his guards followed suit.

Baer, too, pulled two long, fighting knives from his side. All the men grew restless with the exchange. In only a matter of seconds, a brawl would break out, and at the end of it, some would stand while others would not.

"Tell me, *Lord* Baer," Sarah blurted out to try to break through the tension. "What do the people do for amusement out in this part of the country?"

Sarah drew all the attention upon herself as she rested her arm on the frame of the window and threw on the brightest smile she could against the pressure in the air.

Clearly by Baer's perplexed expression, she had caught him off guard.

"Lord Baer, I feel my question might have been too complicated for you, please allow me to simplify, if I may. I am new to these parts, and I just wondered what you do at the end of a long day of... 'work'? You know, to take the edge off?"

Baer looked to his men for an answer but they seemed as confused by her question as he did. Sarah thought she caught a smirk on the General's lips for a brief moment but she kept her focus on Baer.

"Nothing? Well that is a shame. Perhaps if I see you again, you will have taken up some hobby that could be put to better use than your goading tongue or beating helpless people," she said assertively. Not allowing Baer time to respond, she continued. "In the meantime, General, I do believe we have somewhere to be and I know how you hate to be late."

The General turned his horse to face the mountains off in the distance.

"I do believe you are right," confirmed the General.

The guards returned to their place in front and behind the carriage.

"I will cut that insolent tongue out of that pretty little head of yours," growled Baer, and threw one of his knives right at Sarah.

The General's sword cut through the air, lighting fast, and deflected the knife to the ground.

The General pointed his sword at Baer, who scowled back at him.

"Do it again, Bernard, and your other eye will be mine," stated the General with unflinching eyes.

A long moment frozen in time passed before Baer slid his other knife back into his belt.

"We will be out of Somar by nightfall, and you can continue with your horrible existence."

The General kept his sword pointed at Baer while the carriage started to move.

Sarah left her eyes on the General as she looked through the back window. The General held his sword out until the carriage was at a safe distance from the armed men. Sarah was relieved when the General's arm finally dropped and he took off up the path and found his place right outside of the carriage.

CHAPTER 10

AMBREA'S GATE

A bump in the country road jostled Sarah awake. Red and orange hues painted the clouds as the sun tucked just behind the mountain. As she looked out of the window, Sarah could see a long stone wall run the length of her view.

Ingenuity was put into the design of this particular wall. It sat over forty feet high and she noticed little slits towards the top every ten paces or so where a guard could just barely be seen.

The company came to rest just before a large metal gate that looked like it could clip the top of the mountains that rested both behind and on either side. Sarah had to lean out of the window to see the gate in its entirety.

"Ambrea's Gate," she whispered to herself in awe.

The carriage had remained still for a long time and the only audible sound was that of muffled voices. The longer time passed without movement, the more Sara's curiosity grew. It grew to the point she slid out of the door.

"My Lady, you should remain in the carriage," instructed one of the guards but she simply waved him off and continued to move in the direction of Ambrea's gate.

The first thing she noticed as she moved lightly forward was that the General and the Captain had both dismounted their horses. As her eyes flickered to the wall, they quickly landed on the General as he spoke with a guard who stood off to one side of the gate. She moved alongside the horses until she was close enough to hear the conversation more clearly.

"I understand, General Furst, but Lord Baer was very specific about who could travel through Füller Pass," said the guard.

"We are traveling with a guest of the Duke of Baldwin. Our lives would be made much easier if we could just pass through this gate," replied the Captain.

"We have our orders, Captain Lowe. I do apologize for this inconvenience."

The guard's voice quivered a little at his own words. Sarah could instantly recognize the fear that the guard must have experienced.

The Captain took a threatening step towards the guard, but the General grabbed his arm and pulled him back.

"Anton."

The General bowed his head to the guard. "We shall find another route to Vasfale."

"We should be allowed to pass!" said the Captain in protest.

The General pulled the Captain close to him and said, "That guard is not our enemy, Anton."

The General gestured with his head for the Captain to look up at something. When Sarah followed the General's gaze, her eyes widened in horror and she covered her mouth from the ill feeling that took hold.

Dandling over the top of the wall was a cage that had a small skeleton.

"How much more will Baer have to do before you kill him, General?" spouted the Captain. "He grows stronger every passing minute and yet you stay your hand."

"I could not say what will tip the scales," replied the General.

The General turned away making it hard to see his reaction.

"Bernard Baer is the only man I have ever seen torment you. You have cut less venomous tongues out, yet you show him mercy. Why?"

The General kept his stern face but deliberately kept himself turned away from the Captain.

"I have my reasons."

Finally, the Captain grabbed the General's muscular arm and spun him around to face him.

"General, I am more than just a Captain in your army, I am your friend. We have been in many tough scrapes together, along with celebrations. You were there when my son was born. I am asking you as your friend, what does Baer hold over you?"

The General rested his hand on the Captain's shoulder with brotherly affection.

"I wish I could. Someday. I promise."

"I just hope it is not while you are on your deathbed."

"It will not be," replied the General.

An intense moment of looks exchanged back and forth between the men before the Captain finally nodded his head.

"So, what should we do? Whichever way we go is going to add a day to our travel."

"I think we will travel east into the Banting Woods."

"Do you think Raff would welcome us at this hour?" asked the Captain.

The General stroked his bearded chin in thought.

"I think we should see what the old dodder is up to."

"Do you think he will let a lady into Branch?"

The General shrugged his shoulders.

"I suppose it depends on his mood. Either way, night is falling and we have no time to lose."

Sarah wasn't ready when the General turned towards his horse. She had leaned too far forward while she had listened to the conversation. The General looked right at her. Guilt hit her hard that perhaps she had lingered too long in the private conversation.

While the Captain jumped on the back of his horse, the General continued past his towards Sarah. She wanted to run back to the carriage as fast as she could but, instead, she remained still.

As he approached, Sarah could feel her legs tremble like leaves on a windy day. Much to her surprise, he didn't appear to be angry or even disappointed.

"You should get back into the carriage. We have a little farther to travel tonight," said the General softly.

"The Captain is right. They should let us pass if that is the fastest way."

"You are not from this land, so I do not expect you to know the horror Baer has done here."

"Then tell me."

"This is neither the time nor the place for such a discussion."

Sarah gave the General a hard look over until she finally landed on the torment that dwelled in his eyes. They were tumultuous and hard to understand.

"What does Baer hold over you?" Sarah asked and had not realized she had put a caring hand on his arm.

The General pulled his arm away. It took only a second for Sarah to realize she stepped too far.

"No more than what I hold over him," said the General.

Sarah's head cocked to one side with curiosity as she tried to figure out what riddled her about his answer.

The General, too, studied Sarah. She could feel his dark eyes burrow deep into her own until she was uncomfortable and was forced to look away.

A rustle brushed through the fields of Quma behind the company.

"We must go," the General said with more urgency. "Baer is coming, and I would like to be gone before he arrives."

The General grabbed Sarah by the arm and pulled her towards the carriage door.

"You sound scared of him."

"I am scared of what I might do to him if provoked."

Sarah put her free hand on the General's arm and urged him to stop his quick pace. Freeing herself, she turned and looked up at him.

"How much farther can we travel tonight? It is already nightfall and I am sure the horses are tired," Sarah pointed out.

"I know another way besides this gate. But it is a little way down that abandoned road," said the General.

Sarah looked over her shoulder and saw an overrun path that ran along the wall. It was almost completely hidden by brush and weeds.

"It sounds dangerous. Especially if bandits are out tonight."

"We will be alright. Many men of this wood are honorable despite their way of living. They will not bother us."

"If you think so..."

"Get in the carriage," ordered the General a little more assertively.

Sarah glared at him disapprovingly, and then climbed into her seat. Before he could close the door she said, "You have pointed out, not so quietly, that I am not from this part of the world."

"And?"

"Do not chastise me, General, for trying to make sense of all this," finished Sarah.

She took the door from his hand, closed it behind her, and left the General to stand alone.

He spun on his heel so that he looked out to the fields. Sarah noticed his eyes close and his head jut forward while he listened to something intently.

The Captain pulled up on his horse, waiting patiently for the General.

"What is it?" asked the Captain.

The General held his finger up to his lips for silence.

A light breeze blew as the silence lasted a moment more. Then, the General's eyes slid open. "Baer is not far away now."

"We must hurry if we want to escape his eye sight," stated the Captain and held out the reins of the General's horse.

Without hesitation, the General mounted and pushed the company onto the abandoned path that lead deep into the Banting Woods.

CHAPTER 11

BRANCH

*T*he terrain that ran along the stone wall was more overrun than Sarah originally thought. Past the out of control brush that sprawled everywhere, there was also large tree roots that pushed up through the rugged path which caused the ride to be much bumpier than before.

Sarah clenched onto the leather straps that were designed to hold back the curtains. At that moment, they were used to brace her from being thrown around the back seat compartment.

An unease of Sarah's mind accompanied her physical state. She wrestled with the relationship between Baer and the General.

The General seemed fearless in every situation but this one. Also the General was larger and more intimidating in size and stature. So, for anything to hold him back for resolving the issue with a tyrant like Baer had to be significant.

As she glanced off to her left, she just realized that the dominating wall fell away and was now replaced with trees.

The carriage pulled off the rugged path and came to a stop in a little clearing that was just big enough to fit the carriage and the company.

Bright torchlight flooded the compartment when the Captain

opened the door and held out his hand to help Sarah out of the backseat.

Taking a few steps forward, her legs felt tight from bracing herself for the past hour. How fortunate they were to find this clearing to make camp.

When Sarah actually looked around at the wooded area, she noticed the General and he held something in his hand. Taking a closer look, she was able to make out a tiny rope that was attached to a shrubbery covered net.

When the General pulled on the rope; the brush curtain lifted up and blocked the view of the hidden clearing from the rest of the world. The surrounding leaves were too dense to see just how high the net went up, but it was more than enough to create a wall of privacy.

"Where are we?" asked Sarah, a little nervous.

The Captain looked more relaxed than when he was at Ambrea's Gate. He gave a smirk which Sarah had grown accustomed to.

"It is a secret," he replied.

With that statement he pulled a blindfold out of his back pocket and held it out to her.

Sarah instantly crossed her arms, and turned her nose up at the notion of being blindfolded. The company in her immediate eyesight tied off their horses to nearby trees, and then moved down a small, unlit path on the far side of the clearing.

"Is this absolutely necessary?" asked Sarah.

"I do not make the rules," replied the Captain honestly.

"Why is no one else being blindfolded?" she asked, impatiently.

The General moved past the Captain, took the blindfold out of his hand, and shoved it into Sarah's.

"This is *not* a discussion," said the General bluntly.

Begrudgingly, Sarah placed the blindfold over her eyes. The sensation of the night air as it blew over her sweaty skin heightened the evening coolness while in this dark, mysterious place. She reached out her hand and waited at length for someone to take it.

"Well? Are we going somewhere or am I to continue standing here all night?"

A hand finally grabbed hers. In just two days' time, she was already familiar with the callused hand that now rubbed against her smooth skin. She placed her other hand on top of the General's and then slid around his forearm until she was comfortably latched onto him.

The uneven ground made her first couple of steps uneven and unbalanced. Every rock and twig made her foot slide a short distance but the General's strong arm held her steady enough to walk.

"Are we close?"

As soon as the words came, she could feel the General's muscles tense up and she was pulled to a stop. In her mind, she could imagine his facial reaction of annoyance to her question.

Just then, the cloth was lifted from her eyes. Her image of him was not too far off from the General's actual expression. He took a step back to reveal the biggest tree Sarah had ever seen. A house could easily be built in its circumference. The breed of the tree looked much like that at -

"Old Madge," she breathed.

The General's head snapped over to look at her with his hard expression but then returned to what he was doing.

Just past the tree, Sarah noticed another one, and then another.

She wasn't quite sure why the group stood in front of this particular tree. Outside of its enormity, there was nothing else unusual about it.

When her eyes focused back on the General, Sarah realized he and all his men, for that matter, looked up.

She, too, looked straight up. In the tree tops there appeared to be a flickering light next to a guard post. It seemed well protected by a wall of sharpened stakes, from what Sarah could make out. Though, the distance was too far to see anything past that clearly and the dark of night did not help.

"What have you brought us tonight, General?" shouted down a haggard voice.

A small gate opened and an older man with long, scraggily, gray hair stepped to the edge.

"We are taking Lady Levine to Vasfale," said the General.

"A Lady, huh? We seldom get the likes of any 'Ladies' out in these parts."

The General chuckled for the first time since Sarah had met him. It looked unnatural and perhaps a bit uncomfortable to him.

"I was hoping you could make an exception for me this once. She is expected to be at the celebration in the Duke of Baldwin's home by week's end."

The old man stroked his rugged chin in thought.

"Who's askin'? Is it the Duke or you?"

Sarah glanced over at the General. He was contemplative as if he was about to make the toughest decision in his life.

After a long pause, the General said, "I guess I am."

"You don't sound so sure of that," jeered the old man.

The General then looked over at Sarah.

"Honestly, Raff, I have already been through too much with this one to just leave her down here for the wolves... figuratively speaking."

The old man looked away at a small group of guards that stood next to him.

"You know the laws of Branch, General," the old man shouted down. "It doesn't set a good precedent if I start going lenient for you. Pandemonium just might break out."

The General looked over at the Captain for some kind of answer. The Captain just shrugged his shoulders in response.

"We could stay down here for the night?" suggested the Captain.

"Are you coming up or not, General?" shouted the old man.

The General waved him off while he continued to think in silence.

"I don't have time for this," said the old man. "The Gluhen is about to start."

"He is a tough old bird if he will not break the rules even for you?" observed the Captain.

"He is an honorable man that is duty bound. I will never fault him for that," replied the General somberly.

The old man had a piercing glare, much like the General's. Even from that distance, Sarah could see the unspoken weight that rested on the General's decision.

"Well, the guard will be standing-by should you make up your mind anytime soon. Have a good evening!" shouted the old man and closed the gate behind him.

"Thirty eight!" blurted out the General loudly.

Everyone froze, even the old man. Looks of shock hung on many of the guards' faces. Even the Captain looked lost for words as he stared at the General in awe.

"What was that?" shouted the old man for clarification.

The General looked back over at Sarah. He didn't just look at her; his eyes buried so deep into her that she was uncomfortable. He exhaled a deep sigh.

"I invoke law thirty eight," shouted back the General.

"General," the Captain started, but was cut off by the General's leer.

"I will never need to invoke it for my own personal use, so what does it matter if I use it on her?" asked the General.

A slight head shake was all that came from the Captain.

"You just said she was on the way to the Duke of Baldwin's. If you are escorting her that suggests she is for him, does it not?" shouted down the old man.

The General stared at Sarah while he spoke. "You never know with the Duke of Baldwin, he may just pay me back for all my good deeds," finished the General.

A moment of silence gave Sarah a chance to look around at all the guards who still appeared uncomfortable about the conversation. Tension felt high and it grew increasingly frustrating to her that she didn't understand what was going on.

The old man broke the tension with a cheerful cackle. "Well I suppose we better let her in with the rest of yer horrible lot."

The General bowed his head with thanks while two guards lowered down a long rope ladder.

"What is thirty eight?" asked Sarah.

The General swung around to face her and the Captain who stood next to her.

"The laws of Branch are not permitted to be spoken aloud."

"I did not say a thing," said the Captain with his hands up in surrender.

The General then spun around to look at his men.

"I need you to understand this was a last resort. We must get Lady Levine safely to the Duke."

The guards didn't seem to be overly judgmental of what had just transpired. They actually looked relaxed for the first time since the conversation with the old man had begun. Most of the company nodded their heads with understanding, though Sarah felt like she was going to remain permanently in the dark on what exactly thirty eight was.

What was she getting herself into going up into this peculiar city in the treetops? How was she to behave if she wasn't even allowed to know the laws? Most unusual.

"Can I at least ask how a man got the name of Raff?"

"Try not to feel too bad for him," said the Captain in a hushed voice. "After all, he did pick it himself."

"Too much riff raff over the years, you might acquire the name too, Captain!" shouted the old man.

Sarah looked back up to the platform. Raff leaned against the opening as he picked his teeth with a small twig.

"He has good hearing as well, so watch what you say around him," finished the Captain.

Sarah grabbed the first rung and looked apprehensively up the length of the climb. The thick wooden rungs looked sturdy enough, but it was at least forty rungs to the top.

"One. Two. Three," she whispered under her breath as she began her ascension.

"Fourteen, fifteen, sixteen," she continued as she made it half way up. Her body's weight took hold and she made the mistake of looking down. Her heart raced at an alarmingly fast rate and her vision blurred.

"Are you alright up there?" called out the Captain.

Sarah looked down at the ground where he stood with the rest of the men and while he watched her. She hugged the rung tightly to her chest.

"I am not the best with heights," she finally admitted.

"Before you started to climb up, that would have been a better time to have mention such a fear," pointed out the Captain in his sarcastic yet serious tone.

All the men started to laugh despite the fact that Sarah felt like it was no laughing matter.

"Lady Levine," came a deep voice that cut through all the jeering.

Sarah looked up to see the General. He laid flat on the platform above with an outstretched hand held out to her.

"Keep your eyes on me," he instructed.

She had no idea how the General had already made it to the top. She clenched to the rung more tightly.

"Everything is spinning," she squealed.

"I am coming up," countered the Captain.

"Stay where you are, Captain Lowe. She can do this on her own," ordered the General.

Sarah couldn't understand why the General denied her the Captain's help. She grew dizzier by the second from anxiety. Her knuckles were white from clinching the rungs between her fingers. A loud roar rushed over her and she was pretty sure she was moments away from falling to her death.

"Sarah, look at me," said the General in a gentle tone.

"I cannot," she hissed with her eyes shut while she hugged the rung of the ladder.

"You can. I am pretty hard to miss."

Unexpectedly, a chuckle slipped through Sarah's lips and her body started to relax after the General's light-hearted joke.

"There you go. Now reach your hand up to the next rung."

Sarah hesitated to let go of what she held to so steadfast, but finally she followed the General's instructions. Once her hand was securely around the next rung, she hoisted herself up higher.

"Good. Now, look up at me."

Again, followed his request and looked up. The torchlight caught pieces of the General's face. Something seemed off, as if she had never seen his face before that moment. It seemed softer and the air that surrounded him was calm. The windblown black hair. The pale skin that lay safely behind his full, black beard. She became so entranced by her observation that she hadn't even realized that she had climbed six more rungs.

"Just a few more," said the General, encouragingly.

Sarah nodded her head ever so slightly in agreement. Her hand extended out to grab the General's hand when her foot slipped out from underneath her.

"Ah!" she screamed and slammed her eyes shut.

Sarah's body went weightless as it was suspended in air.

When her eyes popped open, she saw that the General caught her by the arm and pulled her up the safety of the platform.

As her feet hit the wooden planks, Sarah hugged herself tightly to the General in an unexpected embrace.

Raff chortled loudly at the whole scene.

"Are you sure you want her to stay here?" Raff asked.

Sarah wanted to wallop the old man, but she found that her body trembled too much to move.

The General patted Sarah on the shoulder and then took a step away from her. His usual hard look resumed in his face.

"For now she may stay," he replied.

Raff clapped the disheveled Sarah on the back, "Welcome to Branch, my dear. I do believe you're going to love it here."

The man smelled as if he hadn't bathed in weeks. The stench was so foul, that Sarah covered her nose with a handkerchief, and pretended to sneeze.

"Now, let me get a better look atcha with these old eyes."

Raff wrapped his boney fingers around Sarah's hand and pulled her closer to him. He leaned forward so that his nose almost touched her skin as he examined her closely. Then, he took a step back until he could observe her in full. When he finished, he looked over to the General.

"Are you hungry?"

"Might be," admitted the General.

"Couldn't have picked a better night with the Gluhen upon us."

The General nodded his head with approval. Raff led the General across the first rope bridge to the next platform.

"Is that it?" Sarah asked.

"Raff is not known for his warm welcoming abilities," said the Captain as he joined Sarah on the platform.

"Crazy old man is what he is," replied Sarah, aloud.

"Maybe so, but he is also one of the smartest tacticians the Duke's army has ever known. Ever heard of the battle of Felsen?"

"Of course."

"Who do you think took out a thousand man army with only a hundred archers?"

Sarah's head whipped around to look at the Captain.

"No..." she said in awe and quickly looked back at Raff cross another bridge with the General.

"Ah. He is also responsible for the General."

"What do you mean?"

"The General was fifteen or so when Raff plucked him from Gaente and put him in his military. Being one of the Duke's most skilled swordsmen and the General being the size he is, Raff took interest in him. I would guess the General sees him as a father of sorts."

As Sarah listened to the Captain, she noticed Raff's hands gesture towards her. The General's eyes followed until they locked with Sarah's for a brief moment. Sarah dropped her head as she did not want to draw too much attention to the conversation between the General and Raff.

The Captain leaned in close to Sarah. "I know he is the foulest smelling creature, but I would not mention it."

When she looked over, the General was back into his conversation and shook his head 'no'. Sarah wasn't sure what they were talked about, but it didn't look pleasant.

The Captain took a step past her and started down the first bridge behind his company of guards.

"Come on," he shouted over his shoulder. "It is time for the Gluhen."

"What is it? I remember the innkeeper mentioning it last night," said Sarah with great curiosity.

"Come and find out."

The troublesome questions that grew in Sarah's mind were going to have to wait for another time. She looked once more over the several rope bridges all the way to where the General and Raff stood.

"Wait, Captain, how did you get up to the platform so quickly," she shouted as she chased after him.

"Well, that is for me to know and you to find out!"

CHAPTER 12

THE GLUHEN FESTIVAL

No time was wasted before Sarah and the Captain joined the company on the rope bridge that sat at the edge of what looked like the center of this town. Sarah couldn't help but find her way over to the General's side.

As she stood on one end of this vast town square, she looked out at two rows of eight trees that ran parallel to each other down this main stretch. Wooden platforms ran along the outside of the trees, and then connected the two rows at each end which created a large rectangle of empty space in between. Huts also resided on the platforms and multiple torches were lit along both the bridges and the platforms. But unlike a normal flame, the fire glowed blue and green.

All the town's people were also dressed in blue and green colored clothing. They stood and looked out at the emptiness where torch-light dangled at different lengths in intricately crafted iron balls that were suspended in air by invisible strings.

Sarah's lips parted at the magnificent sight.

"Wow," she breathed.

"Indeed," agreed the General with a little smile. "Just wait."

"What is this place?"

"They call this 'the Hollow'. It is the place where people convene every day."

"Like a town square?"

"Exactly."

"I am without words," Sarah admitted.

The General leaned on the hard rope handrail and clasped his hands together with amusement. "Why do I feel that is a first for you?"

Sarah elbowed him in the arm, and found herself surprisingly amused by his words.

"What is down there?" Sarah asked as she pointed to the darkness that rested below the Hollow.

"Just wait."

"You cannot tell me?"

The General turn towards Sarah as she crossed.

"In many cultures, patience is a virtue," he said.

"So is hospitality," she shot back.

The General's eyes narrowed with her sharp remark and he turned his attention back out to the Hollow. Sarah weaved her fingers through a loose lock of hair while she struggled to not lose the light-heartedness of the last few minutes.

"Perhaps it is because I do not want to ruin the spectacle for you. I promise you will see what lies below soon enough," confessed the General.

"The Captain mentioned that it was time for the Gluhen?" replied Sarah.

The General pointed out to the Hollow.

Just as she turned, a loud whoosh rushed through the trees that extinguished all the torches. Sarah could feel her hands grip the rope of the bridge tightly.

From the dark silence came the sound of a pan flute. A low hum shot up to a high twitter. Bup bup bup, it whistled.

A pinprick of light twinkled in front of Sarah's nose. Her eyes widened, unsure of what she saw. Then another pinprick of light glowed, and then another.

One little light landed on her hand. When she held it closer to her face, she could see a beetle with ambient wings march its way up to her wrist. She placed her hand down on the General's arm and watched the bug crawl off of her arm onto his.

Sarah chuckled heartily while the bug climbed up to his shoulder and flutter to the top of his ear lobe. The General's pleasant demeanor ended abruptly. She wasn't sure why but all of a sudden his face flushed red as he clasped his hand around his ear, and pinned the beetle.

For a second, Sarah was sure the bug was crushed under the General's large hand but it squeezed through the sprawled fingers. Sarah scooped the beetle back up into her palm.

"It is just a harmless bug, General. It has done you no harm."

"Keep it away from me," he snapped.

Bup twuu whup bup bup bup, sang the flute's magical notes.

The Hollow was filled with an ambient glow that flew all around the people and consumed them in the bugs' luminescence. Thousands of the glowing beetles hung in the air while others landed on peoples' hands and arms.

Sarah noticed that one landed on the lady next to her. Much like the beetle that walked onto the General, it marched up to the woman's ear and fluttered.

A high-pitched twitter sang out from the flute that called the beetles back.

The bugs made their way through the crowd of people. Most of them flew up to the forest ceiling which highlighted the green canopy of leaves. A smaller group chased after the pan flute, and attached themselves to the musician that played it.

Sarah rubbed her eyes with disbelief. For the first time since the music started, she could see the girl who played the instrument. The bugs started by landing on her, but then they weaved themselves into her fiery, red hair which created the illusion of flames spitting from the girl's head.

To watch the red flame-like hair move so fluidly through the air as the musician ran freely over the emptiness of the Hollow was like magic.

The flute whistled one last low note that slowly faded with the dimming of the light.

The crowd roared with applause at the display. Sarah, too, clapped her hands as hard as she could with enthusiasm. The General's heavy hand laid down on her forearm and pulled her closer to him.

"If you thought that was impressive, you will like this even more," stated the General.

Sarah found it hard to believe anything could be more impressive, but she hoped his words were true.

The pan flute hummed again, but this time it was accompanied by a single fiddle. At first the bow created a low, dissonant noise that the flute raged against with its deepest tones. Then the two instruments seemed to speak back and forth between each other, neither of them sounded happy nor pleasant. The two combated against one another in pure darkness until it crescendoed into one loud final note.

Silence.

The flute sang softly again and it sounded worn from the fight. The fiddle joined in too, but this time it sounded more harmonious. The two instruments worked together to provide a harmonious song.

Sarah was so lost by the emotional clash with the previous song that she hadn't even realized that she didn't stand in absolute darkness anymore.

Far below the Hollow, two blue glowing lights swam in unpredictable patterns back and forth. In no time at all, more green glowing lights joined them. Dots of blue and green swam in soothing motions, up and down, back and forth, the full length of the Hollow.

The fiddle slid down to a low note and remained there while the lights below moved into one blue-green ring perfectly centered in the middle of the Hollow. Then, the pan flute whistled again. At this the dots jumped out of the water and high into the air.

With each pop of sound created by the pan flute, the fish jumped higher and higher, so much so, that Sarah thought if she reached out far enough, she could have caught one while they were in full flight.

"What are they?" she asked as she leaned on the rope bridge.

"The town's people call them Gluhen Fish because they glow at the sound of music."

"So, *they* are 'the Gluhen'?"

"Exactly."

Sarah allowed her head to rest comfortably on the General's arm and became lost in the glowing fishes' dance. The peace that the music created in the atmosphere unexpectedly calmed her, and a deep sigh exhaled from her lips.

The music concluded and the entire crowd cheered loudly through the darkness.

The torchlight ignited again, and lit the paths for people to turn in for the night.

"Come with me," said the General, and took Sarah by the hand.

The two moved against the flow of people to make their way to a small platform that stood a few feet out over the Hollow.

Sarah could see the long, fiery-red hair of the young woman who ran along a vine across the emptiness. If Sarah hadn't seen the vine's connection with the opposite bridge, Sarah might have thought the young woman walked on air.

"Maddi," said the General.

The young woman smiled as she jumped down onto the platform and instantly hugged the General. He seemed to have dropped his guard and smiled brilliantly as he lifted the young woman off of her feet and into his arms.

"It has been too long," she said.

"It has," agreed the General as he put Maddi back down.

Sarah was taken in by the young woman's natural beauty. Though she did not wear any makeup, the young woman's green eyes shone brightly against her pale skin. She was a couple years younger than Sarah.

"Maddi, I want you to meet Lady Sarah Levine. She seemed very taken with your performance tonight."

While the two shook hands, Sarah saw what looked like confusion on the young woman's face.

"I have never seen anything like it," admitted Sarah, while she tried to deflect an unspoken growing tension with the young woman.

"I am glad you enjoyed it. I find I am always a little more inspired when I hear Gregor has joined us."

Hearing the General's first name sounded strange when it came from another's mouth. Though she heard it come from Lord Baer, this time it seemed a little more personal.

"Well, I was certainly impressed. All the lights and the creatures that were involved in this event were absolutely marvelous," said Sarah.

"You are too kind," said Maddi graciously.

"If Branch is known for anything, it is putting on a spectacle," the General interjected.

Maddi elbowed him but it was accompanied with laughter. Just then, the Captain broke in between them, picked up Maddi, and swung her around.

"There is my girl!" said the Captain and kissed her on the cheek.

Sarah took a step back and allowed the Captain, the General, and Maddi to continue their conversation together.

"I cannot believe you brought this lot with you, Gregor. I thought you were cleaning up your image," said Maddi, and then gestured to the Captain.

"Never," spat the Captain. "He will never change his deceitful ways."

"Really?" replied Maddi. "Still not going out with the guys for a night of drinking, huh?"

"Weeeelllll, aaaactuallllllyyy, he might have changed his tune a little bit," admitted the Captain as he held his fingers up to show the short distance between his thumb and forefinger.

"Really? Do tell," said Maddi as she tried to egg him on.

The Captain came over to Sarah, looped his arm inside of hers, and pulled her closer to the group.

"Do you see this charming young lady here?"

"I do," replied Maddi.

"She dragged this poor, defenseless man to the dance floor, making him dance with her."

"Impossible," said Maddi in disbelief.

"She did," reiterated the Captain with a head shake.

Sarah glanced over at the General to see if she could decipher his expression. Other than he looked like he was going to hit the Captain for making him the brunt of the joke, she was impressed that he remained quiet.

"In all fairness, she did most of the dancing," recalled the Captain while he tapped his finger on his lips in thought.

"She did do *all* the dancing," corrected the General.

Maddi nodded and seemed mildly impressed with Sarah's great accomplishment. Still there was an element of disapproval to her expression that Sarah couldn't quite figure out.

"You sound like a special girl. I have been trying to get Gregor to dance with me for years."

"I have danced with you."

"For years," Maddi emphasized again.

Sarah could feel the heat rise in her cheeks as a bashful smile clipped her mouth. A part of her wanted to go hide in a corner the more she realized her decision to dance with the General was quite a noted accomplishment.

Seeing the General, Sarah slid her arm into his and desperately hoped his body would shield her from the world of embarrassment. Just as soon as she had, she could feel everyone look at her. Even the Captain expressed apprehension.

"He was a good dance partner," said Sarah jokingly with an attempt to lighten the mood. "He remained where I left him the entire dance."

A scowl flashed across Maddi's face but it disappeared so quickly behind a smile that Sarah thought for sure she was just seeing things. All was drowned out by the Captain's laughter as he recounted the previous night's folly.

"Maddi, I had another reason for coming over here," said the General, and he rolled his eyes at the Captain.

The Captain held up his drink to the General with a smile.

"You always come with an agenda," said Maddi. "Alright, what can I do for you this fine evening?"

"I was hoping you could show Sarah to the guest housing, and make her feel a little more comfortable."

Maddi's body shifted a little and her expression hardened ever so slightly. Then, she smiled brightly.

"Anything for you, Gregor," she said as she leaned in and kissed the General on the cheek.

When Maddi leaned over to hug the Captain, the General released Sarah's arm.

"She is the best person to show you this town. She knows it better than almost anyone else here."

Maddi moved to the rope bridge that led out of the Hollow.

"There should be some hot food in your quarters when you get there. I will come check on you before I turn in for the night," said the General.

"Thank you, but I am sure Maddi here will take good care of me."

The General nodded his head in agreement.

"Come this way," said Maddi.

Sarah bowed her head to the Captain and the General before she followed her guide through the Hollow.

CHAPTER 13

ALWAYS

Sarah allowed her hand to gently slide along the handle of the rope bridge as she looked down into the darkness below the Hollow.

"Might I ask, what moved down there while you were playing your flute?"

Maddi's brow crumpled and her lips pinched tightly to one side of her mouth at the question. Sarah probed her expression before she realized that Maddi didn't look at her but, instead, past her. She looked over her shoulder to see the General while he carried on with the Captain and Raff.

Sarah looked back at Maddi, sternly.

"Is it a secret?"

"Is what a secret?" replied Maddi, and shook her head as she came out of her trance.

"The glowing things that are under the Hollow. What are they?"

"Gluhen Fish," said Maddi with slight annoyance, and then continued to move down the first bridge that led out of the main part of Branch.

"Thank you for clearing that up for me," Sarah muttered as she glanced back to the Hollow.

"Psst."

Sarah looked up and saw Maddi wave frantically for Sarah to follow her.

"Come on," Maddi ordered.

Sarah turned with a wave goodnight to the General and the Captain, but they had already gone. Her eyes surveyed the crowd, and looked for the distinct figure, but was disappointed when she couldn't find him.

"The General has already gone to Maggie's Mead with his men."

"Hm," grunted Sarah.

"What?"

"I just did not think he spent a lot of time with his men at the end of the day."

Maddi laughed mockingly, and accompanied it with a light clap of her hands.

"Perhaps Gregor is more comfortable in Branch than he is elsewhere. After all, this is his home."

"I thought he came from Gaente?" said Sarah as she tried to understand the General's story more clearly.

Maddi's smirk washed away.

"*Branch* is his home."

Sarah held her hands not wanting to argue.

"I apologize. I must have misunderstood."

"I would say so," agreed Maddi, strongly.

The fiery, young woman turned on her heel and charged down the next bridge. Sarah watched the wavy, red hair dance back and forth as she moved.

Once Maddi came to the next platform, she turned right and moved down the another bridge. The farther Sarah walked through this web of bridges and platforms; she began to see the enormity of this unique city.

On some of the platforms there were actual huts, while others were just surrounding one of the massive tree trunks. But oddly enough, a door could usually be found built into the tree.

"So, you are to be married to Emrick?" inquired Maddi.

"Are you acquainted with the Duke of Baldwin?" asked Sarah, a little surprised Maddi called him by his first name.

"He comes to Branch from time to time. Outside of his own home, this is his favorite city in his land," said Maddi with pride.

"This city is magnificent. I hope to return here someday soon," agreed Sarah, with an attempt to look past the growing aggression from Maddi.

Maddi chuckled unexpectedly and stopped from moving any farther.

"What?" blurted Sarah with agitation.

Maddi glared at Sarah. "If you had not noticed, you are not welcomed here."

"Have I done something wrong?" asked Sarah.

"There are very strict laws in Branch," growled Maddi, snidely.

"And you are not allowed to speak of them. I am quite aware," Sarah shot back.

"Raff only allowed you into Branch as a favor to Gregor," replied Maddi before she huffed off to the platform at the end of the bridge. She opened the door that entered into the large tree.

"I hope this is up to your noble standards, *My Lady*," said Maddi with a contemptuous bow.

Sarah could feel her blood boil as she got closer to the hostility that awaited her on at the end of the bridge.

"It was no favor," Sarah mentioned as she past Maddi. "It was thirty eight."

"Excuse me?" Maddi hissed.

Sarah had no idea what she was talking about but she could clearly see that it was the perfect fuel to the fire.

"The General invoked law thirty eight for me to get into Branch," Sarah explained.

"Impossible!"

Maddi's eyes bore deep into Sarah's as her hand shot out, grabbed Sarah's arm, and pulled her closer.

"You are lying to me! The General would never waste thirty eight on you! "

Sarah could feel Maddi's nails dig deeper into her skin as the tone of the conversation grew dark.

"And yet he said it loud enough for the whole company and Raff to hear. If you do not believe me, go ask him yourself."

"Stay away from him!" Maddi snarled as she leaned closer to Sarah's face. "And you need to remember that your entire safety to Vasfale is part of his orders. He does not care about you! *You* are just a name on a piece of paper that he will cross off as soon as you are delivered to Emrick."

Sarah yanked her arm free from Maddi's grip. "At least I got to dance with him which is more than I can say for you."

A cold moment of silence passed between the girls.

Then a sharp pain smacked Sarah's cheek as Maddi slapped her hard. Sarah held her face for a second in disbelief before she thrusted her full weight onto Maddi. The two girls toppled over onto the bridge and rolled a couple paces.

"Rah!" yelled Maddi, while she lifted Sarah's body onto her feet and launched her backwards.

Once Sarah got her bearings, she ran full speed at Maddi, wrapped her hand around Maddi's head and grabbed a fistful of her red hair. Maddi's head pulled back as far as it would go.

Sarah could hear cheering surround her. When she glanced around, several of the villagers had come from their homes to watch the altercation.

Maddi wrapped her arm around Sarah's shoulder but Sarah refused to release her grip. The two girls tussled back and forth, each with an attempt to gain the upper hand. The two broke apart.

Then Sarah lunged with what little energy she had at Maddi, and knocked the young woman over. As Sarah landed on top, she pinned Maddi's arms down under her knees. Maddi's legs reeled up and locked around Sarah's neck. They squeezed tightly together and made it difficult for Sarah to breathe. She clinched Maddi's legs, and tried to get free. Though, it was quite obvious the air slowly left her body.

. . .

"THAT IS ENOUGH!" boomed a commanding voice.

Maddi released her legs instantly. Sarah collapsed onto her side as she gasped for air. Maddi rose up and brushed off her clothes, in a failed endeavor to compose herself.

"Everyone return to your homes, now!" ordered the General.

The first thing Sarah felt was a gloved hand on her arm. When she glanced over, the Captain knelt next to her with concern.

"What is going on here?" demanded the General.

Maddi held her hand up to the black and blue mark that started to form around her eye.

"Maddi?" the General pushed.

"Why did you bring her here? No one is allowed into Branch without the proper invitation. You, of all people, should know that."

"Maddi."

"Thirty eight?"

"We were in trouble."

"Did you invoke it?"

"Maddi."

"Did you really invoke it!?" she screamed.

"Yes," the General finally relinquished.

"Why would you waste such a gift on her?"

"That was my choice!" he growled.

Maddi's face turned so red, it matched her hair.

"Tell me what happened," the General asked with more sensitivity.

"Are you not supposed to be drinking with the Captain right now?" Maddi asked through on coming tears.

"I wanted to make sure Lady Levine made it safely to her sleeping quarters."

Maddi clenched her teeth. A snarl curved her lips and crinkled up her nose.

Gregor tried to put a caring hand on her face, but she instantly slapped it away.

"I do not owe you an explanation. After tonight, I do not owe you anything at all," Maddi barked at him and turned away with her arms crossed in front of her chest.

"This is the task I was given - to deliver Lady Levine safely to the Duke of Baldwin. No matter the cost."

Sarah could feel her stomach wrench as the General talked about her like she was a piece of cargo or a name on a list he was ready to cross off.

"You are always duty bound," confirmed Maddi, hotly.

The General straightened up to attention.

"Always," he said simply.

Maddi shook her head with agitation before she turned back to him. "Where was the duty to protect our city? To protect me?"

"I do wish to protect you," said the General.

"The only duty you have is to yourself! No one else really matters!"

"That is absolutely not true!" said the General.

"It is true! Let me tell you where your duty will lead you, Gregor. Alone. You are going to be old and dying in a bed someday, with no one to tend to you because you shut us all out!"

Maddi's eyes bubbled over with tears.

"These are my orders, Maddi."

"Then go, do your duty!" she said with a wave of her hand.

"Duty is all I have in this world. It has held me steadfast for all these years. Do not dare try to take that away from me."

Before another word could be spoken, Maddi ran and jumped onto a vine that hung just off to the side of the platform.

Everyone watched as she swung from vine to vine and out of sight.

The General was immobile for a long time.

Sarah leaned into the Captain and whispered, "What is wrong with her?"

"She is a very passionate girl," replied the Captain, as he helped Sarah up to her feet and then gestured to the General.

"I am glad to see you have not lost your touch with the ladies, Sir."

The General turned his stern look to Sarah.

"Captain, you are dismissed."

The Captain bowed his head and moved past the General. He patted him on the shoulder as he went by the large figure.

"Take it easy on her. She does not know Branch as you do," defended the Captain, and then continued on his way.

Sarah thumbed the cut on her lip while she held the General's glare with her own look of disapproval.

"What happened?" demanded the General.

"A disagreement."

"I have had about enough of your insolence!"

Sarah noticed his stern tone switched to a yell.

"What do you want me from me?" she asked.

"Silence! That is all I have ever wanted from you, but you continually fail at doing so."

"That girl hated me from the moment her eyes landed on me."

"I brought you into a city that is very close to me. I introduced you to my friend..." the General's words trailed off.

"Who is in *love* with you."

"She is confused."

"She is in love with you!" said Sarah more emphatically.

"You know nothing about Maddi... or me," seethed the General.

"It is so obvious," shouted Sarah.

She gave a moment for the General to take in her words before she continued.

"Why did Maddi get upset when I said you invoked thirty eight for me tonight? What is thirty eight?"

The General drew closer to Sarah. He clasped both of her shoulders firmly in his grip. Sarah could feel her heart race so fast, not fully understanding what was going on. He leaned into her in a threatening manner.

"You know nothing about the world or about me. So, stop acting like you do."

"What is thirty eight?" replied Sarah simply.

The General's lip curled back into a snarl.

"A mistake. One that I will have to live with forever."

"Let her go, General," said the calm voice of Raff.

There was a long pause where no one moved.

"Gregor."

The General released Sarah with a little shove that caused her to take a couple steps backwards.

"I am sorry I brought you here. I should have never taken this assignment. I do not need this... or you," Gregor huffed.

"You called me your worthy opponent. How could I have bested you so fast, General?" said Sarah with her sharp retort.

The General raised his hand, ready to strike her.

"General! Go to the Hollow, now!" barked Raff more assertively.

The General didn't flinch.

"That is an order!" yelled Raff.

The General turned his back to Sarah and walked away. It left Raff on the next platform while he puffed on some kind of pipe.

"You sure have a way with him, Lady Levine."

Sarah's eyes followed the General until he disappeared from sight. Running her hands over her dress, she straightened up her attire and started to walk to her guest housing.

"I have my suspicions about you, Lady Levine," Raff continued with a disconcerting smile.

Sarah found herself spin on her heel to look at the old man. He seemed relaxed despite all that had just happened and he carried a grin as if he knew something she did not.

"I have been on the road for a couple days now and I am tired of everyone else telling me who I am and what I think!"

"Perhaps we all see something you do not?" he suggested.

"There is only one person besides myself who holds the luxury of being able to tell me what can be "seen". And I promise it is neither you or the General."

"Ah," grunted Raff.

"What? What is it you think you see?" hissed Sarah.

"The same thing that the Captain sees and what Maddi sees. I see what the General probably already knows based on how much he tries to hide it."

"And what is that, exactly?"

"You and the General," he said.

"Me and the General? What does that even mean?" hissed Sarah.

The old man continued to puff his pipe and studied Sarah as she screamed as loud as she possibly could manage.

"Don't worry yourself about anything else tonight," Raff finally said calmly. "These are Sacka trees and they don't take on flames."

Before Sarah could retort, Raff turned with a little puff of his pipe and headed towards the Hollow.

CHAPTER 14

A LATE NIGHT CONVERSATION

*C*losing the door behind her, Sarah was surprised to find that there was a torch already lit within the dwelling. As she surveyed the cylindrical room, she noticed there was a two-person bed off to one side and on the other was a four-person table that was covered with a small feast for one.

A smell of spices that seemed somewhat familiar loomed in the air. As Sarah walked over to the table, she could see some kind of roasted bird on a platter. Surrounding the main course was a bowl of different kinds of root vegetables basted in oil, a small bowl of sliced fruits, and a loaf of bread.

Sarah quickly took her seat at the table and filled her plate with the delicious feast. She had no idea how hungry she was until she slid the first forkful of food into her mouth. The taste was overwhelmingly delectable.

By the time Sarah was finished eating, all that was left was the empty plate on the table and a contented smile on her face.

While allowing her food to settle in her stomach, she looked up through the top of the tree and out at the night sky. She stared up at the cluster of stars in the small view she had and considered it her little piece of heaven.

Slowly, Sarah made her way over to the bed and returned her focus up to the sky. Thoughts started to plague her mind. As much as she wanted to dismiss her fight with Maddi and the General, it was too present. Many times she forced her eyes to close but they would pop back open again. The General's words repeated over and over through her mind.

"I do not need this... or you!" she reitterated out loud.

In her mind, Sarah was done with the General too. She was so tired of him criticizing her and how he made her feel like she could do nothing right.

As Sarah rested her hands at her side she felt the uneven object that still remained in her hidden pocket.

Pulling out the bottle from the hidden pocket in her dress, Sarah studied the dried out beans as she rotated the bottle back and forth between her fingers. What was she supposed to do with them? Actually, there was a part of her that felt ridiculous for still carrying them around. Did they really have any significance to her life?

Yet, she found some comfort in having them with her. A sense of importance came from these seemingly useless objects. Sarah shook the bottle and watched the beans dance around before she tucked it back in her pocket.

Again, she looked up at the night sky.

"I wonder what happens in these houses when it rains?" she muttered to herself.

Time passed by slowly as she tossed and turned over and over in her bed.

"Uh," came a little huff.

As the incidences continually marinated in the foreground of her thoughts, the walls felt like they closed in on her. Sarah's chest felt heavy and made it difficult to breathe. She sat up abruptly, wrapped the sheet from the bed around herself and stepped outside.

As Sarah looked out, it was difficult to see but the maze of bridges and platforms were evident. A single torch lit on the next platform was the only source of light. Only the animals of the night could be heard hoo-ing through the trees.

Sarah found her feet moved in the direction of the light. Out of the corner of her eye, she noticed a second unlit torch sat in a mirrored location on the other side on the platform. She quickly grabbed and lit it.

Now able to see, she continued down the next bridge and around the corner which she knew could lead back to the Hollow.

The wooden planks creaked under her feet more than she remembered them doing so earlier in the evening. The sound concerned her enough that she almost went in the wrong direction a time or two because she was too wrapped up in the noise they made.

Some relief came when Sarah made it out to the empty Hollow. Time by herself was a luxury she had lost after she tried to escape in Lankenshire. But her time in solitary was not her sole interest in coming back to the Hollow, but instead, her interest lied in the Gluhen Fish.

The town square was dimly lit. Only embers glowed in the iron balls that were still suspended in the air. Sarah saw an empty holder that she rested the handle of the torch down into, and extinguished it so all that was left was a faint glow of moonlight.

Then she turned her focus to the empty abyss that was at the heart of the Hollow. She walked slowly, and slid her feet along the wooden boards to make sure she didn't step too far. Her outstretched hands finally came in contact with the thick rope railing. She clenched it, and then closed her eyes.

Taking in a deep breath, the cool air felt refreshing. A rush came over her until she found a tune that started in the back of her throat.

"Dum dee dum dum dum dum. Dum dee dum dummmmmmm," she hummed out loud. "Dum ba dum dum de dum dum. Ba dum de dum dum dum dum."

The slow notes of the Conti Rose sung out of her mouth. The song was just as sultry as it had been the night before, and just as clear as if the fiddlers were right next to her. A smile crept up on her as she continued to hum.

Then a strong rush of wind whooshed over her, much like it had at the beginning of the Gluhen festival. The gust blew her hair around carelessly while she continued to hum.

"Ba da de dumm dumm a dumm de dum dum. Ba da de dumm dum dummmm."

Another gust of air swirled around her that revived her spirits. The weight she had been caring with her had lifted and made her feel lightheaded and giddy.

"Wishes," whispered the wind.

When Sarah's eyes slid open. On her hand, she was surprised to find one of the glowing beetles from the festival. It seemed to look right at her as it fluttered its radiant wings. The little bug cocked its head to one side as if it waited for an answer, but when nothing was said, it took flight.

Sarah's eyes followed it until she saw the Gluhen Fish that had illuminated down below. She hadn't even noticed it until now.

A slow clap echoed through the trees.

When Sarah turned, Raff had already started to move towards her.

"You have a nice voice," he said.

"You are being kind," said Sarah modestly.

"They are a tough crowd, Lady Levine," said Raff and gestured to the glowing light below them. "They would be the first to tell you if you were good or not."

Sarah couldn't tear her eyes away from the beautiful blue and green dance that swam in unique patterns in the water.

"Would you like to get a closer look?" Raff offered.

Sarah's head popped up with excitement.

"Really? You would let me do that?"

A crooked smile edged Raff's lips and he gestured with his head for Sarah to follow him.

The two walked out to the small platform where Maddi had played her flute during the performance. Raff knelt down on the platform and slid his hand over the board until his finger caught on something.

"Ah hah," he hummed.

He lifted a hook and a trapdoor opened. When Sarah looked

through the hole, she noticed below was a large wicker basket just big enough for two people.

Raff slid down into it first, and then held his hand out to Sarah.

"I am not sure about this. You saw how difficult it was for me on the ladder climbing into Branch."

"And yet you made it," Raff pointed out.

Sarah could feel her forehead start to moisten as she took a tentative step forward. She sat down on the platform and slid her legs through the hole until her entire body fell down into the basket.

Her heart raced at full speed and she clung tightly to the siding.

"I promise this will be worth it," Raff said as he grabbed the rope and lowered them down.

"Besides, I was hoping to have a moment alone with you, Lady Levine."

A look of concern pierced Sarah's face.

"It seems as if you have stirred up a lot of trouble on this journey thus far. Fighting with Maddi, talking back to Baer … dancing with the General in front of his men?" hummed delightfully out of his mouth.

Sarah couldn't help but roll her eyes.

"Yes," she replied. "Is a lecture coming next?"

"Not at all," said Raff in a calm tone.

"Really?" said Sarah with a mix of surprise and skepticism. "You mean you are not about to scold me?"

"Nah. The three people in question are all headstrong and think they are in control of everything. Someone such as yourself is a fresh reminder to them that they aren't."

"They sure think they are."

"Gregor thinks he is but I explained a thing or two to him tonight."

Sarah's face softened with thanks, and her whole body relaxed into the side of the basket as it drew closer to the water. It was nice to have someone on her side for a change.

In that moment, she missed Jack. Someone who usually listened to her council though lately, he seemed to also be growing head-strong. The one thing that still remained true though, Jack was the only person in her life that had stuck up for her no matter the consequences.

"Believe me when I say you have the General quite perplexed. He has never met a woman that had enough gumption to approach him on her own, let alone dance with him."

"Maddi did. At least she said she did."

"Maddi is a dear friend that Gregor has known since she was just a babe. He will never look at her as more than a sister."

When Sarah looked over at Raff for further explanation, the old man's head leaned towards his shoulder with a knowing look. Sarah looked away.

"What's worse is Maddi knows it. That is why she was so upset tonight."

"That might explain why she was upset, but what about the General? Why was he yelling at me?"

Raff shrugged his shoulders while he leaned back on the edge of the basket.

"Despite his overly strong figure, he is still human. You have stirred things within him that he has never experienced before. Give him a little time to sort it out."

"He said he never wanted to speak to me again," Sarah said in dismay.

"Of course he did," chuckled Raff lightheartedly.

Sarah looked at Raff confused, as if that statement was expected.

"Listen, he needs you as much as you do him."

"Is that right?" replied Sarah.

"Let me tell you a little secret. Tomorrow, when you are walking past him to your carriage, just say 'good morning' as pleasantly as you can, and then keep on moving. Don't say another word to him and see how much he doesn't talk to you."

"That is all I have to do? Just say 'good morning' and then move on?"

"As pleasantly as possible. The longer you stay in silence while in a happy mood, the more you will drive him mad."

"How could you be sure?" she asked.

"Let me just say this, that trick has never failed me with regards to him."

Sarah half smiled at the old man just before she looked over the side to the water. They had touched down in it and now bobbed up and down on the current.

The light of the Gluhen Fish had dimmed since they had started their descent.

"Sing to them again, they will light right up for you," proposed Raff.

Sarah closed her eyes and began to hum.

"La de dah dum dum dum dum. Ba da da de da."

When her eyes slid open, not only were the fish glowing brighter, they came to the right side of the basket where she stood.

"Put your hand into the water," Raff instructed.

Sarah followed his order while she continued to hum. A smooth, slick texture grazed her fingertips.

"Wow," Sarah exhaled with enchantment.

"You think that's amazing, look at your fingers," suggested Raff.

Sarah pulled her hand from the water. A warm, tingling feeling pricked at her fingertips while they glowed as brightly as the Gluhen.

"Incredible," she whispered.

"This town certainly has its charms."

Sarah nodded her head in agreement.

"You can't tell anyone you came down here. As you have already found out, Branch is quite particular about the people it lets in and what they are allowed to do when they are here."

"Am I going to be in more trouble?"

"Not while you are with me, but for my sake and feeble heart, let's just keep this between us."

"Of course," affirmed Sarah.

* * *

IN NO TIME AT ALL, the two made their way back up to the platform and started back towards Sarah's housing for the night.

Just before she went through the door, Sarah wrapped her hands around Raff's side and hugged him close. She could tell by the clumsiness of the hug, the old man wasn't used to this kind of gratitude.

"What was that for?" he asked.

"So much has changed in the couple days I have been away from my home. Sometimes I think I have quite forgotten who I am."

"That can happen."

"Thank you for giving me something to hold onto again."

When she pulled away from him, Raff smiled at her through a puff of his pipe.

"Will I see you in the morning before we go?" Sarah asked.

"I wouldn't have it any other way," replied Raff, and then waved his hand for her to go inside.

CHAPTER 15

THIRTY EIGHT

A white wall of clouds engulfed Sarah as she walked forward slowly. The surroundings were unfamiliar and an unexplainable knot sat in the pit of her stomach.

"Hello?" she said.

Her voice echoed as if she were in a cavern. Hello bounced back and forth as it moved farther away from her. She spun around. The smoke attached to her clothing and it spun in circles with her as she turned.

The denseness of white cloud overwhelmed her, yet it was luminous much like the Whisper Beetles. Despite the ever-growing fear that something was wrong, Sarah was enthralled with the anomaly that surrounded her. Trying to touch it, she extended her hand but it floated through the mist.

The white denseness washed over her like a wave washes over sand, except it caught her bare skin and would not release her.

"Help! Help me!" she screamed into the emptiness and the only answer she got was the echoed cry.

Sarah felt the denseness collapse around her which made every breath more labored than the previous one. She clenched her eyes tightly shut and with her last breath, she screamed as loud as she could. All the hate, anger, and bitterness exited her body as she released it all in that moment.

When her eyes opened, Sarah found that the white cloud had gone, but she was now wrapped in what looked like an elegant wedding dress.

When she turned towards the echoing abyss, she found she stood in front of a mirror. She looked picturesque, as only a Duchess could. She lifted her hand up to the divinely styled hairdo upon her head. She looked ravishing.

Thud!

Sarah quickly spun around on her heel to find that the General laid on the ground, lifeless. She tried to walk towards him but after several steps, she was no closer than before. Frustrated, she broke into a run, but his body drifted farther and farther from her like he was caught on a current.

"General! General!" Sarah screamed as loud as she could, but the body just drifted away until it looked like it fell over a waterfall.

SARAH SAT STRAIGHT UP in her bed and gasped for air. Her clothes were drenched in sweat. She brushed her forehead with her sleeve.

Beams of sunlight snuck over the top and down the inside of the Sacka tree. Sarah thought for certain that the General would want to leave before sun up. An image of him lying dead flashed through her mind.

"General!" she muttered to herself.

She was still dressed from the clothes she wore the day before; partly because it would have been difficult to get her trunk into Branch. She slid her shoes halfway on her feet when she opened the door and took flight across the first bridge.

As she moved, she realized no one seemed to be around. The town felt eerily quiet. By the sixth platform on the path, she stopped, short of breath, and looked around puzzled.

"You look out of sorts this morning, Lady Levine," said a haggard voice.

Sarah turned to see Raff as he sat relaxed in a chair, and smoked his pipe.

"I was looking for… You see, I was just…" Sarah stammered, lost for words. The image of the General lying dead sat heavy in the pit of her stomach and urged her forward.

Sarah turned and was about to run down the next bridge.

"Ah," hummed the old man just as he brought his pipe up to his lips for a puff. The calming words had her pause.

"What is it?" asked Sarah as she tried to find solace from her nightmare.

"Take a walk with me," Raff said as he rose and gestured with his head for her to come join him. Sarah wasted no time as she made her way to his side and they leisurely strolled from one bridge to the next.

"Something about our conversation last night didn't sit right with me. Once I figured out what it was, I realized that I had to make a decision."

Just the tone in Raff's voice made Sarah nervous, like she was going to get that lecture after all.

Raff let his eyes wander freely around the surrounding area as if he looked for something or perhaps someone who wasn't there. When nothing stirred or made any sound, he returned his gaze to Sarah.

"The laws of Branch are very stringent and meant to keep outsiders out, even when they are here."

"That makes sense, I suppose," agreed Sarah.

"Having said that, last night I wrestled a lot with the laws of this city and I have come to realize that I must break my own rule. You wish to know something, don't you?"

Sarah nodded her head and involuntarily said, "Thirty eight."

"Yes. Thirty eight. You wish to know what it means?"

"Very much."

Raff pulled the pipe from his mouth and exhaled one last puff before he spoke.

"I have known Gregor a long time. Military and tactics, these are areas in which he excels. I thought for sure he would live a good, long life but he would do so alone."

"I could see why," Sarah interjected honestly.

"But when he asked me to let you into Branch last night-"

"Thirty eight," Sarah repeated.

"I realized that something was different about him. It did not take me much longer to recognize that the difference was you."

"Me? Now I know you are being ridiculous."

"You think so?"

"Maddi was not wrong, I am just a name on a piece of paper that he is waiting to cross off," Sarah argued.

Raff chewed on his end of his pipe as he looked around. His head bobbed up and down ever so slightly.

"As much as you believe the General is disinterested in you, you could not be more wrong, Lady Levine. He knows when he hands you over to the Duke that you will no longer be a possibility for him."

"A possibility for him to do what?"

Raff's head fell to one side as it had the night before. He seemed filled with curiosity and yet answers all at the same time.

"To be with you."

Sarah's lips parted and she took a staggered step backwards and landed on the bench next to her.

"Be with me? He cannot even stand to be around me!" said Sarah and took no care in how loud she spoke.

"Are you sure about that?"

"Absolutely!" said Sarah as she tried to stamp her disapproval.

Raff dropped his head in submission and sat down next to Sarah.

"Law thirty eight allows someone who has traveled abroad to bring a companion into the city."

"So?"

"That is one companion during his or her entire life."

"How did the Captain get in?"

"Well there are other laws that allow for military men in the Duke's army."

"You are telling me that the General has never had a companion come with him to Branch?"

Sarah watched the plume of smoke zigzag from the pipe as Raff shook his head 'no'. Her heart sunk in her chest as if the weight of the world fell on it again.

"What if I do not want this?"

"Well that is up to you," said Raff, resigned.

"I do not want him to waste his thirty eight on me," whimpered Sarah.

Raff chuckled.

"What?" responded Sarah.

"I don't think he has wasted it at all. You might think so. He might think so. However, if you could have seen how you both looked when you were attached to his arms last night... there is no mistaking it."

"He hates me. You saw how angry he was last night," Sarah grumbled.

Raff's brow raised and he nodded with understanding.

"Then how can you say that?" Sarah finished.

"Gregor is a composed man, never really showing emotion. Last night I saw a bigger range of emotion than I have ever seen out of him before. Even with Maggie..."

Raff trailed off. When Sarah looked up at him, Raff seemed lost in his own thoughts. Sarah remained silent out of respect for the old man. Finally, he shook his head and looked over at her.

"Remember, you need him as much as he needs you."

"You said that last night and I do believe you are wrong," she replied defensively.

"Mmm," hummed Raff. "Listen, we all have our roles to play in this world and despite your current protest, you know what you must do. Even your body betrays your true feelings right now."

Sarah looked down at her arms clenched tightly together and pinned against her body.

"I thought so too," said Raff with confirmation, and then he pointed across several bridges. "The company is just there for break-fast. I think it time for you to join them."

Sarah's eyes followed until they landed on a large hut that was tucked between three entangled trees. From where she stood, it looked as though two branches pierced through the side of the building.

"I am quite fond of this city," said the old man.

Sarah turned back to find Raff as he now leaned on the wooden railing of the platform and looked out at the magnificent village mounted across the forest ceiling.

"You should get a good breakfast before you go on your way," he finished.

Sarah nodded in agreement. As she started to move, she heard Raff yell out behind her, "Sacka trees get their water from the tips of their branches, not their roots. Rain would never make it to the heart of the tree before the tree would catch it. Though, it's pretty astonishing to watch a rain storm from inside one of them."

Sarah spun to look at him, amazed.

"How did you…" Sarah started, completely dumbfounded.

"It's an amazing place, Branch. One of a kind."

"I would say so," said Sarah with a nod. "I hope to come back someday."

"I believe you will," said Raff as he returned his pipe to its rightful place between his lips. He turned and slowly moved down another bridge. Sarah watched the odd fellow a little longer, and then hunger took hold.

Without another word, she moved down the bridge towards the large hut.

CHAPTER 16

A SIMPLE REQUEST

Sarah wasn't sure if it was her thoughts or her stomach that moved her forward to the large hut, but she made her way there in no time at all.

When she pushed the door open, the smell of meat, cheese, and freshly baked bread wafted in the air.

Most of the company sat at the large branch that was carved into a table and cut across the middle of the room. The villagers occupied the rest of the smaller tables around the perimeter.

Sarah made her way to the Captain and sat down next to him.

"I thought we were leaving early this morning?"

The Captain removed a fork of food from his mouth and chewed happily.

"We were, but then the General felt it more hospitable if we stayed for breakfast," said the Captain as he pushed another pile of food into his mouth. "You know, fill our bellies."

He leaned back so Sarah could watch him rub his belly. She just rolled her eyes and took her first bite of food.

"Mm," she hummed and put her hand on her lips as she burped.

"The people of Branch do make exceptional food. It is one of the things I look forward to when I know we are going to stop here."

Before Sarah could question anymore, hunger got the better of her. She shoveled scoop after scoop of food into her mouth until her stomach no longer cried in pain.

"Hungry?" asked the Captain.

Sarah looked over at him, a little embarrassed by her unladylike behavior. She swallowed her mouthful of food and wiped her lips clean with a cloth.

"Famished," she smiled coyly.

She slowly looked around the room and carefully paid attention to who she recognized and who she didn't.

"He is not here."

"Who is not here?" asked Sarah as she tried to pretend she had no idea who the Captain spoke of.

"The General is preparing the horses for travel," stated the Captain bluntly.

Sarah just nodded her head and tried to look like she didn't care.

* * *

STANDING by the ladder from her heroing ascension the night before, Sarah looked down at the distance to the forest floor and felt queasy.

"How am I supposed to get down?" she asked the guard who stood next to her.

"Well, we can throw you off and let the men catch you," joked the Captain.

Sarah snickered at him as if he would ever do such a thing.

"Or we can lower you down in the basket?" suggested Raff and opened an escape door in the middle of the wood floor.

Sarah spun on her heel to look at the Captain, who seemed to suppress a laugh at the moment.

"You knew about this?" she hissed.

"I did," the Captain admitted.

"And you did not tell me?" Sarah said with more agitation in her tone.

"Lady Levine, I had no idea you had a fear of heights. By the time we realized it, you were already halfway up the ladder."

"This is how Gregor got up here so quickly." said Raff with a little puff from his pipe.

Sarah's teeth started to grind together as she pointed directly at the Captain.

"You are a horrible individual."

"Why thank you," said the Captain with a tone that suggested that he was more proud than embarrassed.

Sarah's eyes narrowed before she slid across the floor and climbed into the basket.

"Can we please go now?" she demanded.

She clinched her eyes tightly shut as the basket descended to the forest floor. Beads of sweat lined her brow and she felt a little woozy until the barrel landed on solid ground. In no time at all the blindfold was placed over her eyes again and one of the guards led her back to the clearing.

When the blindfold lifted, Sarah was pleased to see the General as he stood next to his horse. The moment was ready for the taking.

Raff's instructions ran through her mind before she started her walk to the carriage.

The General carried the same hard expression from the night before and clearly ignored her presence. Sarah mustered up the most radiant smile she could manage and as she passed him said, "Good morning, General."

He scowled with condemnation but never turned to acknowledge her.

Sarah never allowed her smile to fade while she knew she was in eyesight. Once she got to the carriage, she hopped into her seat and closed the door behind her.

Great satisfaction filled her and she knew that Raff would have been proud that his tactic was a success.

A hard knock on the door startled her. The Captain stood just outside.

"You spoke to Raff recently, correct?" said the Captain.

Sarah nodded her head. The acknowledgement caused the Captain's lips to purse and his nose to scrunch.

"What?" asked Sarah with concern.

"I know that you think you are making a point to the General, but we have at least a two-day ride in front of us. It would be best if you just leave him be."

Sarah was a little taken aback by the Captain's straightforwardness. It might be the first time he talked to her where a smile wasn't present. Enough seriousness had replaced his usual happy demeanor so much so that guilt inevitably followed his stern words.

Sarah crossed her arms and rested her head on the seat as she looked up at the ceiling.

"Look, I know you think the General is hard on you."

Sarah's eyes slid over to look at the Captain for a brief second then went back up to the ceiling.

"And I must admit, there have been times he has been."

"You want me to leave him alone?" Sarah reiterated the Captain's previous words.

"Please," replied the Captain sincerely.

"Is that an order?" said Sarah snidely.

"No, just a simple request. I have seen the General angry before... I just do not want to see him take it out on any of us. Yourself included."

"What does he do when he is angry?" she questioned.

"He wins wars," replied the Captain emphatically.

Sarah looked away with a mix of annoyance and fear.

"I will be quiet."

"Thank you. We are about to go. Try to make yourself comfortable."

The Captain tapped the side of the carriage door with his fist, and then headed towards his horse.

Tears overwhelmed Sarah's eyes as feelings of being outnumbered and unwanted consumed her.

The carriage jolted forward down the road.

Sarah looked out the window at the curtain of leaves pulled back to allow the company to return to the dirt path.

Just as the curtain returned back into place and the illusion was complete, a head of flaming red hair raced out and Maddi stood there, watching.

Two tear-filled, green eyes looked on as the company pulled farther away from Branch. Just as the carriage was about to turn the bend, a loud shriek cut sharply through the air.

Sarah could feel Maddi's pain resonate throughout her own body. Before she knew it, she brushed away the tears that streaked down her own cheek. But the tears flowed freely and the entire world blurred behind them.

CHAPTER 17

AMBUSHED

*T*he morning passed as the Captain had requested… quietly. For a change, the road was smooth and Sarah took this time to enjoy the beautiful scenery. She learned that Sacka trees were only in a small part of the Banting Woods. So, if that was the fallen tree next to the hovering door by Old Madge's house, it certainly would be out of place. Though, Sarah guess it could be argued most everything in her life seemed to be out of place at the moment.

However; the different kinds of plant life found along the path was enough to keep Sarah entertained and silent.

A clink clipped the back window as a few drops of rain grazed the glass. She stretched her arms out in front of her, and tried to alleviate the kink that grew in her shoulder. Then another light clink hit the window.

This time, Sarah spun around and looked behind her with more scrutiny. The woods seemed quiet except for the occasional smack of rain against the leaves. From what she could see, even the soldiers appeared oblivious to anything out of the ordinary as they traveled.

Sarah leaned past the doorframe and yelled, "Stop the carriage!"

In a moment's time, the company came to a complete halt as she commanded. The Captain was the first to ride back to see what was going on.

Sarah hopped out and looked around at the woods suspiciously.

"What is it?" insisted the Captain.

Sarah closed her eyes and strained her ears to hear every sound that she could.

"Lady Levine, we do not have time for this," stated the Captain.

Sarah ignored his complaint and took a few steps off the path.

"The General is already upset that we have stopped."

"Hush," Sarah hissed at him. "Did you hear that?"

A single branch cracked, followed by leaves that crunched under foot. Her eyes popped open with panic.

"Be on guard! Someone is out there!" Sarah said with urgency.

"What are you talking about?" replied the Captain, unconvinced. "I hear nothing."

"We must hurry!"

The Captain and the two guards next to him sat in silence while they looked around skeptically. One of the guards pulled his horse around and took a few steps past where Sarah stood.

"I do not see anything, Sir," admitted the guard.

Just then, an arrow whizzed through the air and hit him in the shoulder.

"We are under attack!" screamed the Captain.

All the guards readied themselves with swords and bows. A shower of arrows flew from unseen archers that were hidden in the forest foliage.

The General rode back in a fury to where Sarah stood.

"Back in the carriage, now!" he commanded.

Sarah didn't even hesitate to follow his orders.

A rush of leaves rustled, arrows flew, swords clanked together, and tree branches broke. All the sounds consumed the air.

Without knowing who was in control, the carriage took off in a fury, and left the escort of guards behind to fight off the surprise attack of Lord Baer and his men.

The carriage flew down the path. Every rock, every fallen branch, every bump in the road could be felt tenfold when the carriage wheels hit it. Sarah's body was thrown around recklessly. It took all of her strength to pull herself to the door and throw it open. It instantly hit a tree and slammed shut again.

There were far too many trees along the path to keep the door open long enough for her to escape, so she did the only thing she could think to do. Clenching tightly to the top of the wooden frame, Sarah hoisted herself out the window.

Her body clung to the outside of the door; her skin grazed a tree trunk or two. While the ground moved at a rapid pace, she clenched her eyes shut and exhaled a deep breath.

Without warning, Sarah thrusted her body forward. The next thing she felt was her full weight slam hard onto the ground and roll over and over until she came to a halt.

"Uh," was knocked out of her body.

Stunned from the fall, it took a moment to regain her senses. When Sarah's eyes opened, she stared up at the forest canopy. Then a gruesome-looking man with burn marks scrawled across his face leaned over her.

"My, my. What do we have here?" asked the man in his gristly voice.

His two big hands grabbed Sarah and dragged her several steps before he released her next to the base of a tree. She looked around desperately for signs of help, but the guards were left far behind in the fight. For all she knew, Lord Baer's men killed them all.

The large man put his sausage-sized fingers into his mouth and whistled loudly. Another whistle farther off into the woods responded back. The man smiled.

"Ah, Lord Baer will be happy to see you again. He has a plan for that pretty little tongue of yours."

"You think you scare me," snapped Sarah, in a sad attempt to sound less threatened than she actually was.

"Ha. Feisty, I like that. Do not worry yourself, Lord Baer will enjoy taking his time as he cuts it out."

A shiver went down Sarah's spine. She knew Baer loved to torture and she was sure that he had little cares for what nobility she possessed which might protect her.

The man grabbed Sarah by her hair and yanked her head back while he drew close to her face. His stench was so repugnant she thought she would gag. When his lips pulled back from his rotted teeth into a smile, it made Sarah's lip curl back into a sneer.

"Those lips are begging for a kiss," said the man with gross excitement.

Sarah slammed her eyes shut and braced herself for his assault.

Just as the man's warm breath brushed her face, her body was released to the ground.

"Sari!" screamed Jack. "Are you alright?"

No words could be spoken. Instead, Sarah threw her arms around Jack and squeezed him tightly. She thought she would never let him go. How much more could she endure on this trip without her friend?

"We will have time for this later. Right now we must hurry," Jack said before he pulled away.

He helped her up to her feet, grabbed her hand, and pulled her forward.

"Come on," he said.

Sarah looked down at the disgusting man dead on the ground with a small bleeding gash in his forehead.

"I think you have become quite skilled with your slingshot," Sarah noted.

"When I need it most, my aim is pinpoint."

"Thank goodness for that," agreed Sarah.

Jack took Sarah's hand and kissed it, but the sentiment didn't last long before he pulled her a couple more steps forward.

"We must go," said Jack as he looked around cautiously. When his eyes came back to her, she exhaled a deep breath.

Jack cupped his hand on her cheek.

"I know you have been through a lot. But I will get us through this," he emphasized.

Sarah's skepticism was worn on her sleeve. Even with how impressed she was that Jack killed Baer's guard, she still wasn't sure if he knew what he was doing. Jack was notoriously careless and constantly got the two of them into trouble.

"I will!" he said more firmly. "I have a secret weapon on my side."

The two of them inched forward and looked for any signs of danger. When they seemed to be in the clear, they moved as fast as they could across the uneven ground.

"We must find the river. It will guide us to safety," said Jack and he pulled Sarah at a faster pace.

The gasps for air were the only thing Sarah could hear as she pushed herself to the brink of collapse. Her body ached and was uncooperative. When she tried to leap over a fallen branch, her toe caught the wood and she went face first into the ground.

A whistle echoed through the trees.

Trying to shake off the fall, Sarah looked up at Jack. He spun around to listen.

"What is that?" asked Sarah.

"Trouble," said Jack shortly.

Jack helped Sarah to her feet and yanked her back into a run. Hooves hit the ground at a quick pace not far behind them.

A loud whinny trumpeted. Before Sarah knew what was happening, a rope lassoed around Jack's neck and he was ripped from his feet backwards. The horseman took off through the forest and dragged Jack behind him.

"Jack!" squealed Sarah, and was about to take off after him. "Jack! No!!"

A loud clap sounded from behind her which stopped Sarah dead in her tracks. She spun on her heel to face Lord Baer.

"I was so hoping to get a private audience with you, Lady Levine. It seems like today is my lucky day."

CHAPTER 18

A LIFELONG DISAGREEMENT

"What have you done with the General and his men?" demanded Sarah.

"No need to worry about them. Or should I say him?" Baer chuckled to himself and started to move towards her one calculated step at a time. "You could say they are all indisposed at the moment."

Horror flashed through Sarah's mind as she imagined the entire company's dead bodies strewn across the dirt path. The General... lying lifeless with his cold, brown eyes glazed over like in her dream. She quickly shook the thought from her mind.

"Impossible!" she hissed.

Lord Baer took one final step so he now towered over her. Much like the General, Baer dwarfed her in size.

"Is that so?" asked Baer, menacingly.

Sarah's teeth clenched tightly together and she was filled with so much rage that her face burned like fire.

"Rah!" screamed Sarah and slapped Baer as hard as she could across the face without a care that no good would come of it.

Baer's face took the hit and he was slow to turn back to her.

"I could see earlier that you had a lot of fight in you," said Baer with more pleasure in his voice than Sarah cared to hear.

Without a second thought, Baer clasped his hand around Sarah's throat and lifted her off the ground.

"I could kill you right now if I wished and not even think twice about it."

The grip Baer had on Sarah tightened. Her vision blurred and her ears began to ring.

The air was strangled out of her. No matter how hard she flailed or kicked at Baer, his grip only grew stronger.

What little Sarah could see became hidden by dark spots as her body started to shut down. She was sure the last ounce of breath she had was about to be squeezed out of her, and only her lifeless body would be left behind.

"GRAAH!"

The sound of Baer's ribs as they crunched at the end of the General's war hammer became the most joyous sound Sarah had ever heard. Baer dropped her as he doubled over in pain.

Rolling around on the ground, Sarah coughed and gasped, and did whatever she could to regain the air that she had lost.

"If you want to kill me, Bernard, you will have to try harder," the General growled.

"I will see to it," grunted Baer, and then he unsheathed his two knives.

The General dropped his hammer to the ground and he, too, unleashed his sword and pointed it directly at his target.

From what little Sarah could see, the General and Baer kept their eyes on each other as the two danced around in a slow circle across from one another.

"Are you alright?" shouted the General.

Sarah felt too weak to respond. She tried to lift herself up, but she collapsed back to the ground.

"My, how you have softened, brother," quipped Baer.

Sarah's brow struggled to contort her brow at the odd sentence, not fully sure if she heard Baer correctly.

"When I beat you within an inch of your life, you will not think so... brother," barked back the General.

"I would love to see you try!"

With that, the General lunged at Baer, and clashed sword upon knives. One strike followed by another. Baer lunged back, which struck hard and fast.

Sarah's head pounded as she hoisted herself up onto a boulder with concern to try and see the altercation more clearly.

As the weapons were locked together, the General punched Baer hard in the face, and sent him back a couple of steps. Hastily, the General followed with another strike of his sword, but Baer pulled his sword from his hip fast enough that he stopped it.

The two blades remained connected with the full weight behind each man as they pushed against one another. The General quickly released his hand and flung both swords off to the side.

Baer slid another knife from his sleeve and swung it at the General. The General deflected the blow with his arm and then elbowed Baer in the face.

The giant man fell backwards before he spat out a mouthful of blood.

"RAH!" screamed Baer, and ran full speed at the General. He locked his arms around the General's waist. Both fell to the ground. The General got one or two solid punches into Baer's side, while Baer countered with a hit into the General's jaw.

Just then, a loud whistle blasted through the trees as one of Lord Baer's men barreled on horseback towards the fight.

"Lord Baer!" screamed the man.

Baer twisted out of the General's grip and jumped up just in time to catch the man's outstretched arm that pulled Baer onto the horse's back.

Baer looked over his shoulder at Sarah, who was still propped up on the boulder, just before he disappeared into the forest.

Sarah struggled to get to her feet while she gently grazed her tender neck. After she acknowledged she was going to be alright, she quickly staggered towards the General, who was on his knees.

"General?" she said, gingerly.

His eyes shot up as they bitterly met with hers.

Sarah took another step forward. Without warning, the General wrapped his arms around her waist and pulled her close to him. He relaxed his head against her stomach.

There was no struggle or contemplation. Sarah placed her arms around the General's shoulders and embraced him the best she could.

She fought against the shock that trembled through her arms. Just when she was going to give in to her body's yearning to quake, the General's strong hold calmed her nerves.

"I was afraid Baer had killed you," slipped out of Sarah's mouth.

The General looked up at her.

"Never," he replied simply.

As their eyes remained locked on one another, Sarah ran her fingers through the General's thick, black hair in a comforting manner.

They remained in silence for a time before the strength of the General's hands released Sarah and he pulled away. He rose to his feet, collected his weapons, and then stood before Sarah once more with a look of concern.

"What is wrong?" she asked.

The General carefully ran his thumb across the cut on Sarah's forehead. A fiery sting burned which caused her to hiss.

"We need to get you some care," he said softly.

"I could say the same thing to you as well," Sarah said as she placed her hand onto his which stopped him from tending to her wound.

"I need you to keep this encounter to yourself. I will explain in time, but right now we must get back to my men."

Sarah nodded her head and fought off the urge to ask anymore questions. They all drifted away when the General took her hand and guided her through the woods.

Just a short distance away, she could make out the large frame of the General's horse.

"Are your men alright?" Sarah asked and quickly counted the number of soldiers she could see.

"Yes."

"But Lord Baer said that he..."

"Bernard has always been better at talking than he is about following through with action."

As the General finished his last words, the Captain and the company trotted up the path. They all looked a little worse for wear.

"General, I do say, if we are to make it the Vasfale on time, we need to stop these silly antics and be on our way," advised the Captain in his humored tone.

"I could not agree more, Captain Lowe!" shouted the General, and then turned his focus to Sarah. "Do you know how to ride?"

"Yes," said Sarah, a little uncertain if she could ride a horse as large as the General's.

"Good," said the General as he picked her up and placed her onto the back of his horse.

"Move up a little," he directed her.

Next thing Sarah knew, the General lifted himself up and sat behind her. With one hand on the reins and the other around Sarah's waist to secure her to him, the General pulled his horse around to the path.

Sarah could feel every eye of the company on her as she sat in front of the General.

"General, we can provide another horse for Lady Levine if that would make you both more comfortable," proposed the Captain.

"I have my orders, Captain. I believe this is the safest way to travel with Lady Levine to Vasfale."

The Captain quickly bowed his head at the General's observation.

"Let us be on our way!" ordered the General, and moved his horse forward.

Ever so slowly, Sarah allowed herself to relax back into the General's muscular body. His grip shifted around her waist, and secured her more closely to him. She even thought maybe his hand caressed her side when she was convinced that it slid ever so slightly up and down. In that moment, she felt safe from all the harms of the world.

CHAPTER 19

CAMPFIRE STORIES

The campfire spit and popped in front of Sarah as she sat on top of a fallen tree with a damp cloth pressed against the cut on her forehead.

"Let me see that," said the General as he sat down next to her.

Sarah's eyes flickered up to him with hesitation before she let down the cloth. The General placed his hand on her chin and tilted her face towards the light as he tried to get a better look. Sarah unconsciously pulled away from him before his fingers could reach the cut.

"I am sorry," she said softly. "I think I am still a little shaken."

"Battles of any kind can shake the strongest of men," agreed the General.

"But I am not a man."

"Indeed. Now let me take a look. You do not want to risk infection."

The General carefully brushed Sarah's hair off of her forehead before he ran his thumb over the gash which caused her to instantly hiss. He held up the small, wooden bowl with a clear, creamy paste in it. Sarah's nose crinkled at its smell.

"What is that?"

"An old herbal remedy Raff taught me. It has gotten me through many scrapes over the years."

"He seems to be a very learned man despite his rough exterior."

A hint of humor grazed the General's lips as he dipped his thumb into the paste.

"This will sting a little, but it will help it heal faster."

His eyes looked submissively into Sarah's before he slid his thumb across the gash.

"Ssss!" she hissed and tried to lift her hand to the point of the pain, but the General caught it.

"I know it hurts," said the General in a soothing tone. "But you must not touch it."

A huff shot through Sarah's nose while she tried to weather the sharp sting above her eyebrow.

"How do you suggest I deal with this pain?"

"You simply need to divert your attention with something else," replied the General.

"Would now be a good time to ask you about Lord Baer?"

The General's eyes immediately dropped to the bowl in his hand.

"If it makes you uncomfortable, I understand," she quickly followed.

The General chuckled a little to himself.

"Did I say something amusing?" Sarah asked.

The General looked back at Sarah, "You have never taken my opinion into consideration before. It is amusing that you should do so now."

Sarah's lips parted at the harshness behind his remark but found herself remaining silent. The General rose from his seat, walked to a little bag on the far side of the campfire, and returned the bowl to its rightful place. When he turned back to her, she could feel the weight of his judgmental eyes look over her tiny figure.

"Bernard and I are brothers, yes," said the General. "That is what you wanted to know?"

Sarah's head fell in confirmation. The General wiped his hand off on a clean cloth before he made his way back over to where Sarah still sat.

"As children we were the best of friends, but time changed things," he said and sat down, once again, beside her.

"He mentioned a girl's name the other day... Eleanor? Who is she?" asked Sarah.

She could see the General's jaw tighten at the question as he picked up a nearby stick and poked the fire with it.

"Eleanor was my sister," the General finally said.

"Was?" Sarah repeated. "What happened to her?" persisted Sarah.

"For someone I have just met, you are getting quite personal with your questions," admitted the General as he started to lose his patience.

"I have been traveling a few rough days with you, and I know nothing except the fragments of your life I have seen through other people's interactions with you. Am I wrong to be curious about you?"

"Curiosity can kill a man dead if he stretches himself too thin with it."

Sarah felt a sting to her ego as her whole posture readjusted to the General's warning. Her lips pursed in thought, and she turned her focus to the flames that bobbed up and down in front of her.

"You deflect your answers regularly. Why are you afraid?" sighed Sarah.

"I am not afraid. I just do not see a point in telling you. Not even Captain Lowe knows anything about Baer and my relations," said the General.

"Maybe that is why I am your worthy opponent and the Captain is not."

The General seemed impressed by her retort as his brow lifted and he nodded his head in agreement.

Sarah was relieved that the burning sensation on her forehead had subsided. The air was more chilled than it had been the previous night in Branch. Interesting how different the landscape was from day to day, and town to town.

Grabbing a small blanket next to her, Sarah wrapped it around her for warmth.

"I was only a boy when I saw the evils of this world," started the General as he broke the silence. "A group of rebel warriors were pillaging villages along the eastern coast of my homeland. I was fifteen, maybe, at the time that group of men decided to sneak into the forest that sat right at the edge of our village and try to catch our people off guard. We had no real weapons; just wooden spears, rocks, and some old, rusted swords. Looking back, we were fools to think we could stop them.

"When the group of rebel warriors rode up, they were far more men than we could have possibly imagined. Worse than their number was their skill set. These men were warriors, and they knew it. The group I fought with dwindled quickly. I knew little of fighting back then.

"Before I knew it, Bernard and I were the last two to be standing. We took out fifteen of the fifty men on our own. But when a couple of horsemen started moving onto the village, Bernard told me to go and protect our people.

"I ran after them as fast as I could. Something heavy smashed into the back of my head, knocking me unconscious.

"When I woke, most of my village was burned to the ground. Many bodies laid brutally beaten to death or had been burned alive. Many of the women... suffered worse. Those warriors were heathens.

"I found Eleanor's body among the wreckage of my house. Stripped of all clothing and marks that no girl of eight should have ever suffer. Bernard and I could not leave this unanswered.

"After we buried her and our parents, we grabbed our father's hunting knives and went after them. Two young men hunting down thirty-five warriors seems ridiculous. But we did find them... while they slept.

"This encounter would end very differently than the last one. Rage and malice consumed Bernard and my hearts. Silently, we slit each and every one of their throats until they all choked to death on their own blood."

The General poked the fire with his stick while Sarah felt ill from the images evoked from his story.

"To this day, Bernard believes I should have been able to save Eleanor. After the massacre he told me that we were no longer brothers, that he would become the thorn in my side that I could never remove. A rumple - we call it.

"We had the worst of fights and parted ways. Raff found me and brought me to Branch."

"Are you responsible for the scar across Baer's eye?"

"I guess you could say I am a rumple to him too."

"You stayed your sword with him in the fields."

"I mark his taunting me down to bitterness in his own heart. He has become the heathen he once killed those many years ago. When he took you, the image of Eleanor came back to me. I could not let him..."

Sarah rested a caring hand onto the General's forearm.

"You got to me in time. I am still here. Nothing happened to me that time cannot heal."

"But..."

"No, General. You saved me. You did your duty well."

The General took his time as he slid his free hand over and put it on top of Sarah's.

"Hopefully, that is enough of my life story to satisfy your curiosity for now."

The General rose from his seat unexpectedly and started to move past Sarah when her hand reached out and grabbed his. He stopped and looked down at her. She popped to her feet and when she realized she was only tall enough to barely reach his chest, she climbed up onto the fallen tree she just sat on so she could look him in the eyes.

Placing her hands on both of his shoulders, partly for emphasis, partly for balance, she said, "I never meant to pry so deeply into your horrible past. Seldom do I meet a man that intrigues me as much as you have. Ever since I saw you criticizing the painting in my drawing room.

"And once I am intrigued by something, I have a tendency to find

139

out all I can without considering the hurt it might bring with my questions. This is a great fault of mine, that I am sure will one day get the better of me."

"Is that your way of apologizing?"

The General raised his brow with curiosity. Sarah rolled her eyes and tried to not let her apology be mocked.

"I suppose."

Sarah could feel her heart race as her eyes returned to his.

"Are you going to hold on to me all night?" asked the General.

"Perhaps," came Sarah's unexpectedly honest answer.

The General scooped Sarah's hands into his and secured them on his chest.

"Though Raff saved me in Gaente all those years ago, it was the Duke who put me in his army. He and I have been, dare I say, friends for more than twenty years. I respect and honor him. So, when he gives me an order, I always follow it."

"Always," Sarah repeated as she remembered Maddi's words.

She slid her hands out from under the General's and stepped down to the ground. Turning towards her tent, this time it was the General who reached out and grabbed her hand.

"That is..."

She instantly spun back to him with bright eyes.

"That is, until I met you," admitted the General. "You are so brash and unforgivably straightforward to the point of being offensive. Still, your naivety to the world, and the poise you show in the most tense moments, makes you quite endearing."

"Endearing? I guess I can accept that."

"You smile at the world despite the fact that it is not smiling back at you."

The General whisked Sarah up and put her back on the tree so she was roughly the same height as him once more. The two stared into one another's eyes with conviction and passion.

Sarah's hand slid onto the General's cheek and she drew her lips closer until they collided with his.

140

A jolt of energy rushed through her veins and she hoped that this moment would never end.

"General?"

The General and Sarah broke from their embrace and moved to opposite sides of the campfire.

"What is it, Captain?" asked the General in a stern voice.

Sarah looked over at the Captain who stood by a tree just past where she and the General had been. Captain Lowe's eyes glanced between the General and Sarah with a look of incomprehension.

"I am sorry to interrupt, but I believe someone is following us. The men heard some commotion on the far side of camp."

"Baer?"

The Captain shook his head 'no', and then looked over at Sarah.

"I think there is only one person," he finally said.

Understanding set in with whom the Captain suggested was near to them.

"Would you like us to set a lookout?"

"No. I know what he wants and I am on guard," said the General.

"Of course," replied the Captain and bowed his head before he retreated back to the camp.

Sarah placed her hand over her mouth as she felt her stomach churn to the point she thought she was going to be sick.

"Do you think the Captain will say anything to the Duke?" asked Sarah.

The General shook his head 'no'. Sarah moved closer to him and tried to take his hand for comfort but he pulled away.

"This is a dangerous game, Lady Levine. With your curiosity and my being wooed by it. I cannot do this."

"But you just said…"

"I made a mistake. It was a moment of weakness that I cannot repeat. I must remember what I was sent here to do, and that is to get you safely to the Duke."

"Always concerned about your orders. What about you? What about what you want?"

"To fulfill my duty *is* what I want! It is the only thing I can trust in this world," snapped the General. "The Duke is a good man. Charming – and any woman would be lucky to have him."

"Many available women will be attending the extravaganza. There is no telling who he will pick." Sarah moved closer to the General and turned him to look at her. "And if he chooses another girl…"

"You will be chosen," acknowledged the General so matter-of-factly.

"You cannot know that for certain."

"I know the Duke. And I know most of the other women that are at the castle already… he will see you as exotic and unlike the girls he is accustomed to."

"You make me feel like a trophy that will be put on the Duke's wall."

"Do not misunderstand me…"

"Stop!" yelled Sarah and waved him off with her hand. "Just stop this."

The General resigned and took a few steps towards the camp before he finally turned towards her.

"You should get some sleep. We will be arriving at the castle tomorrow and you will want to look rested for the Duke," said the General.

Before he could completely withdraw, Sarah grabbed his hand but he quickly shook it free again. And with that, he marched away.

Sarah watched him until he tucked himself away in his tent.

"Damn!" she screamed and threw a rock into the fire that kicked the flames up higher.

She sighed deeply and knew that her potential happiness had ridden alongside her for the last couple of days and it was about to slip away from her forever.

She pulled her blanket around her again and curled up next to the fire.

The crackle of the wood started to calm her nerves. As the time passed, her eyes began to grow heavy until they finally fluttered closed. She was just moments away from a dreamy state when a cold hand clamped down around her mouth.

Her eyes shot open to see Jack's eyes looking back at her.

CHAPTER 20

I CANNOT GO

"Jack!" whispered Sarah loudly, and threw her hands around his neck. "You are alive! I thought Baer's men killed you when you were dragged off."

"Quite the other way around, actually."

"How did you possibly?"

Sarah pulled away from him and looked at the smooth skin where the rope had been lassoed.

"You do not have marks on your neck. Not even a burn..." Sarah trailed off as she ran her fingers over his neck with astonishment.

"I have my ways," said Jack with a dark laughter that put a chill in Sara's bones.

She was unsure if this was the same carefree man that she had always known or if this was a complete stranger. There was a firmness to his grip that she hadn't noticed before when they had just embraced.

"I told you. I will keep you safe," Jack said sincerely.

As Jack pulled back and his eyes surveyed Sarah, they landed on the cut across her forehead.

"Did that ogre do this to you?" growled Jack before he leaned in to kiss the wound.

"If by the ogre you are referring to Baer, then yes."

"I knew Baer could not be trusted," Jack growled.

Sarah's eyes widened with horror.

"Did you help him attack us?" asked Sarah repulsed.

"I sent them to be a distraction so I could rescue you."

"Rescue me?" she said as she became more upset. "Is that what you call it? As far as I can tell, you almost got both of us killed, and put the rest of this company in danger."

"Things got out of hand, I will admit. But you are safe now," Jack said with a vain attempt to defend himself.

"That is how things always are with you, Jack! I was fortunate that the General got to Baer before I was... before he could..."

"What would you like me to say, Sari? I do apologize."

Jack took Sarah's hands and tried to draw her closer to him, but she pulled away.

"I will kill the man who hurt you," vowed Jack, upset.

He rose to his feet and looked at the sleepy camp around them.

"Listen to me, my horse is just up the road, there. Come with me."

"And go where?" exclaimed Sarah, not buying into his proposal.

"Wherever we want. We can just start riding."

Sarah chewed on her lower lip as the thought developed in her mind. Jack quickly got down on his knees and scooped her hands into his.

"I want to spend the rest of my days with you. Can you not see how much I love you, Sari," he pleaded with her.

Jack hesitated for a moment to gauge Sarah's response, but then leaned in to kiss her. Disgust quickly filled her before his lips reached her that caused her chin to turn so that all Jack kissed was her cheek.

Sarah was lost for words. She stared at her hands that still rested comfortably in his. They looked more at home there than in the General's overly large ones. But still...

There was no suppression of the image that she and her oldest friend could escape if she wanted. Rapid images of their wedding surely follow, and a small cottage with children that would run out in the front yard. Sarah knew that she would never be able to show her face again to her father nor step foot in her homeland... she would be marked as a disgrace.

An unexpected smile crept up on her face that invited Jack closer. He slid his hands around her waist and pulled her close. He rested his forehead on hers. The intensity in his eyes was overwhelming.

"I..." she started.

As soon as the first words of acceptance were spoken, the tree falling and almost hitting the carriage replaced it all. Reality versus the dream.

"Come with me, Sari. It is what we have always dreamed of. Exploring the world. No one telling us how to live our lives. We can be free."

Sarah rose to her feet and turned her back to him. She paced back and forth as confusion set in, followed by anger.

"What do you want from me, Jack? To run away with you and live happily ever after?" asked Sarah.

"I want to marry you, Sari."

This had Sarah stop dead in her tracks. She knew the thought was always present but now the words were spoken.

"I..." Sarah started again, and then exhaled a deep breath. "I cannot, Jack."

The exuberance that was on the young man's face melted into a pale sadness.

"Why? I thought you never wanted to marry the Duke," stated Jack in an insinuating tone.

"You are right, I do not," agreed Sarah.

"Then why will you not marry me?"

"I have my reasons."

"What reason could you possibly have?" asked Jack, his voice broke as he held back his frustrated tears. "Why will you not come with me, Sari? Why?"

"Because I do not love you, Jack." Sarah screamed back. "I am sorry. You are my dearest friend but no matter how I try, I will never love you over..."

"*him*," Jack finished her sentence, snidely.

147

"Yes."

"You are being a ridiculous girl," Jack said and grabbed her by the wrist. Trying to drag Sarah towards his horse, she did not budge.

"I think the lady was quite clear in telling you to leave her be," said a deep voice.

Both Jack and Sarah turned to see the General only a couple feet away from them. He leaned against a tree and smoked a pipe. Sarah couldn't get over his resemblance to Raff.

Jack tucked Sarah behind him as he tried to protect her.

"This does not concern you, you giant oaf," snarled Jack.

"Oh, but it does," said the General in a low threatening tone.

"I just said it doesn't!" yelled Jack.

A puff of smoke crept from the General's lips as he exhaled.

"I will ask you just once to let her go."

A fierce scowl crossed Jack's face.

"This girl means nothing to you. All she is is bag of gold in your pocket. I can pay you double to let her come with me," offered Jack.

"No."

"You can take my horse."

"No."

"What would you like in exchange?"

"Nothing can replace her."

"I could not agree more," said Jack.

Sarah felt butterflies take off in her stomach at the General's kind words.

"So, the only way you can have her is if you get through me," argued Jack.

As fast as it took for Sarah to think 'What a foolish threat from Jack,' was the brief time it took for the General to leap across the campfire. Before Jack could speak another word, the General had his hand around the entire circumference of Jack's neck and lifted him into the air, much like he had in Lakenshire.

"Listen to me carefully. This girl means more to me than any money or property you could possibly put before me. I suggest that you be on your way before I break you into two."

Jack's face was beet red as the General clenched his hand tighter, but that didn't deter Jack.

"You have no idea what I am capable of," grunted Jack, attempting to sound menacing.

The General pulled Jack close enough to see the whites of his eyes. "Nor do I care."

At that, the General tossed Jack onto the ground like a rag doll. Jack burst into a coughing fit while he rubbed his neck.

"Now get out of here," ordered the General.

Jack rolled over to his feet as he struggled to stand. He glanced at Sarah. "I will always love you, Sari."

Sarah just crossed her arms.

Jack shook his head with disappointment.

"Never forget that," he said as he punctuated his previous statement.

Sarah looked back at Jack, who seemed so certain in his thinking. But before she could retort, Jack backed away until he was shrouded by the darkness of night.

Sarah stared blankly at the emptiness where Jack had just stood. "Would you have stopped me had I wanted to go?"

"You chose to stay."

"But if I had?"

"I guess you will never know."

Sarah shook her head at the General's tenacity.

"Jack was right about one thing. I do not want to live the life of a Duchess."

"You have never been a Duchess before. How could you know if you want to be one or not? Wait until you meet the Duke. You might change your mind."

"I suppose anything is possible," she said as she forced a smile. "Will you stay out here until I fall asleep?"

The General didn't hesitate to pick up his pipe where he dropped it and sat down on a nearby boulder.

Sarah resumed her place on the blanket by the fire while she kept her eyes on the General. She could see the glowing embers in his pipe with every puff he took. How different would tomorrow be after they arrive at the castle? How would she be able to let go of this man she once hated but now had great affection for?

As the questions mounted, exhaustion took hold. The glowing red cinders from the pipe blurred until they faded into a peaceful sleep.

CHAPTER 21

THE LAST LEG

Air seeped out of Sarah's lungs one gasp at a time as the rough hand squeezed her neck tightly. The image of Jack's saddened face blurred as the last breath of air escaped her body. Everything went dark.

Sarah sat up abruptly, startled awake from her newest nightmare.

"Shh. You are going to be alright. Take a breath," said the Captain as he knelt beside her.

The morning light made it easy to see that the camp had already been packed and the company was ready to leave.

"Why did you not wake me earlier?" she asked groggily.

She didn't need to look into a mirror to know how out of sorts she appeared and the gash on her head throbbed again.

"The General wanted to let you sleep as long as possible. The last couple of days have been-"

"Horrible?"

"To put it kindly," agreed the Captain.

"Are you telling me your travels with other ladies have not all been as exciting as this one?" asked Sarah with a forced smile.

The Captain chuckled a little while his thumb stroked the stubble that now emerged on his chin.

"I would have to say that you have certainly created a new experience for us all on this trip."

Sarah thought about the full meaning of his words before her eyes diverted.

"Please do not say anything to the Duke about what happened… It was my fault…"

Sarah could instantly feel the warmth of the Captain's hands around her cold ones.

"My Lady, I would never do anything to break the confidence of the General or you. Please never let that fear enter your mind again."

A contented smile pressed into her cheeks.

"Now that we have that all sorted out, we have a horse ready for you to ride, if you are up for it?" asked the Captain.

Sarah nodded with enthusiasm before she hopped to her feet.

It took no time at all to splash some cool water on her face and make her way over to the where the company waited for her on their horses.

The Captain held the reins to a handsome, chestnut-colored horse with a long flowing mane that trickled down his neck and back.

"Beautiful," breathed Sarah.

"A gift for you, to get you safely to the castle," said the Captain.

"What is his name?"

"Duke calls him Chops."

"Chops? What sort of name is that?" asked Sarah as she rolled her eyes at the strangeness of the name.

"Lady Levine, I find it best not to question the Duke of Baldwin on anything, let alone names."

Sarah gave a slight nod, then made her way to the horse's muzzle and stroked his nose. She whispered something softly. The horse bounced his head up and down and smacked the ground with his front hoof.

Sarah broke out into laughter and patted the horse's strong jaw.

"Are you ready?"

"If he is ready, then so am I," confirmed Sarah.

Mounting the horse with ease, Sarah took hold of the reins and pushed the eager horse forward a couple steps.

"Where is the General?" she asked when she noticed the absence of the large figure.

"He went on ahead to make sure this last leg of the trip would be... less eventful."

"Thank goodness for that," agreed Sarah.

"If we are all ready, let us be on our way."

In unison, the company pushed their horses forward at a quick pace which left only a cloud of dust kicked in the air as a reminder that they had been there.

* * *

THE WARM AFTERNOON sun beat down on the travelers as they cleared the trees close to the base of the mountain range. Not too far in the distance, at the edge of the mountainside stood an overly indulgent castle, complete with towers at each corner and a drawbridge across the precipice that rested just in front of it.

"I suppose the ladies love the grandeur of this place," stated Sarah.

The Captain nodded with agreement.

Out of the corner of her eye, Sarah noticed the General move at a rapid pace towards them.

When he drew closer, the General went around the company and into the first line of trees of the forest. The Captain pushed his horse after him. Sarah turned in their direction and watched as the two men talked to one another just inside the shadows of the Banting wood.

She could tell by the Captain's alarmed expression that something had gone amiss. Both the General and the Captain turned their gazes towards her. An uncomfortable feeling settled in.

The two men steered their horses back to the company.

"Is everything alright?" Sarah asked even though she already knew the answer.

The General kept his focus on Vasfale while the Captain pulled his horse next to Sarah's. He wore a distressed look.

"We must hurry."

"Baer?"

The Captain head bounced up and down. "He is trying to catch us before we get to Vasfale."

"I was more afraid you were going to say Jack was still following us," admitted Sarah.

The Captain looked away from her for a moment before he returned his gaze.

"Is Jack still following us too?" asked Sarah.

Both the General and the Captain tried to avoid eye contact with her.

Sarah's lips parted and she knew that the longer they lingered, the more her life and the lives of the company were in danger. The images of Lord Baer and Jack with a rope around his neck raced through her mind faster than she could even grasp them.

Without warning, she kicked her horse hard and took off as fast as she could towards the castle. She tried, with all her might, to outrun the images that chased close behind her.

CHAPTER 22

ANTICS

The Duke's castle, also known as Vasfale, was even more impressive up close than the stories had told. It was true that it was all built from rock, but Sarah didn't anticipate that it was made from one large piece of stone that seemed to come up from the ground. It sat on the edge of a cliff with only a drawbridge to get across to it. Off to the right a waterfall cascaded down and rolled over the side of the precipice.

When Sarah dared to glance over the stony edge, she saw nothing but plush greenery sprout from the side of the precipice as far down as her eyes would dare to look. It was as if a meadow crawled down the cliffside and tried to get to flat land. It was quite something to behold.

When she returned her focus to Vasfale, she found four guards stand statue-like above the raised drawbridge.

Sarah caught a glimpse of the Captain's humored smile as he yelled out, "Good Sirs!"

Not a single one of the guards acknowledged him.

"Would you be so kind as to drop the drawbridge so that we might get Lady Levine into the safety and comforts of the castle?"

Still, no one moved.

"Password?" shouted an unnatural high-pitched voice from above.

The Captain looked over to the General for some kind of guidance but the General's hard face did not crack.

"Is the password *Duke?*" yelled out the Captain.

"Nope. Guess again," came the quirky voice, this time it sounded far more absurd.

Sarah studied each of the guards, none of whom seemed to be the one talking.

"Castle?" guessed the Captain.

"Nope! Wrong again!"

"Festival? Ball? Ladies?"

"You are getting closer!"

"Long-horned Rooster," the General said, finally.

An uncomfortable moment of silence passed before hearty laughter burst out from above.

Sarah looked over to the General for some sort of explanation but he kept his focus on the guards.

When Sarah looked back, a man dressed in the finest fabrics, which hung slack on his body, stepped to the front rock wall and looked down at them. Even with the long shadows of dusk, it was hard not to be struck by his handsome face covered by dark stubble or the loose brown curls that landed just above his shoulders. He held up an enormous beer stein in the air as if to celebrate the arrival of the company.

"Dear General, I knew you would know the answer!"

The General bowed his head with gracious acknowledgement while the man took a huge swig from his glass. He wiped the froth from his lips when he finished, and turned his gaze to the rest of the company.

"My, my, my. This lovely creature would not happen to be Lady Levine, would it?" asked the man.

Sarah could feel the General's weighty eyes glance over to her. She couldn't help that her face contorted with confusion at the oddity of this man.

"It is," stated the General gruffly.

The strange man leaned on the wall and propped his head on hands, "Do tell me, Lady Levine, how was your travel with the good General?"

"Perilous," she replied shortly.

"Are you talking about the journey or the General?"

"Yes."

The man's eyes grew wide before he burst out into more laughter. In fact, he laughed so hard, he fell over on one of the guards who tried his best to remain at attention.

"Did you hear that, Captain? She has spunk, this one!"

"She does indeed!"

"Not to break up this amusing conversation, but would you kindly state the requirements for dropping this drawbridge? The last thing I feel like dealing with after such a long journey is the antics of a drunkard," said Sarah with frustration.

The humor was quickly wiped clean and replaced with seriousness from the young man.

"Well, well, well. Do excuse me, Lady Levine. I never meant to offend."

Sarah held her frustrated countenance as she bowed her head and acknowledged his apology. When she looked over to the Captain, he seemed to suppress a laugh while the General looked cruelly disappointed.

"You are quite a handful. I can tell already!" retorted the man.

"And you are ridiculous," blurted out Sarah.

The man smiled, bemused as Sarah took a couple steps closer with her horse and tried to hold the man's glare.

"Tell me General, is she always like this?"

"You will have to excuse Lady Levine, Sire. I have found in my travels with her that she is young and not used to our customs or manners," replied the General with annoyance laced in every word.

"Indeed!" replied the man.

Sarah snickered at the General and wished only that she wasn't in the company of a buffoon so that she might speak her mind to the General properly.

"I love it!" shouted the man with great zeal that recaptured Sarah's attention.

The man laughed even harder than before and took another swig.

"Lady Levine, I would like to introduce you to Duke Emrick of Baldwin," said the General.

A glaze coated over Sarah's eyes as her lips parted ever so slightly and she dropped her head into a bow.

"You are more beautiful than rumors have told," said the Duke.

Sarah could feel her cheeks get even hotter than they already were from her previous misstep.

"And now, all of a sudden, modest," noted the Duke.

Even though it was ever so slight, Sarah caught the General's head nod in mocking agreement.

"Well, it is quite rude of me to allow such a beauty to be left waiting. Lower the bridge," ordered the Duke.

As soon as the cogs on the drawbridge started to release, Sarah pushed her horse forward until she came to rest next to the General.

"I told you he would like your insolence," reminded the General, and then started his way over the bridge.

Crossing under the archway of the castle, Sarah found herself in the middle of a large courtyard. Being that the whole castle was made from the same stone, the walls appeared to be smooth and covered in some kind of moss. They stood just a little shorter than the outer wall of the castle.

On both the ground and the upper wall, several guards stood at attention just a few paces from each other on either side of the courtyard. At present, she wasn't sure if she was at a luxurious castle or a fort.

The Duke ran down a side staircase that followed the wall and led to the courtyard. He moved swiftly to Sarah's horse and held out his hands to her. Taking them, she slid off her horse and landed gently into his strong arms.

She found a comfort in his firm grip but it was drowned out by the overwhelming smell of ale.

"There now," said the Duke softly.

Sarah pulled back from him to give herself a moment to brush off the creases in her dress. When she looked back at the Duke, he grimaced. Before she knew what was going on, the Duke stepped forward and ran his thumb across her forehead. A sting burned across her cut. She had forgotten about it until that moment.

The Duke's hard look shot over to the General.

"Baer?"

The General, who stood a few feet away, nodded his head.

"I see," said the Duke, and then turned his focus back to Sarah. "I will deal with him in good time. As of right now, I will have my personal physician come see you once you are settled in your chambers."

"Thank you, Sire."

The Duke held his arm out to her. Sarah looked at it for a long moment, unsure if she should really take it, and then looked over to the General and the Captain.

"Come, come now, you cannot be so humble that you will not allow me to escort you to your room? Please, I feel like we got started on the wrong foot. Let me make amends," urged the Duke. "Besides, I would like to hear more about the Southlands and Ditrum. Seldom do I ever get down that way."

The Duke pulled Sarah forward towards the entrance way into the castle. Just before she stepped through the doors, she looked over her shoulder and caught one last glimpse of the General's hard expression.

In that moment she knew that their time together had come to an end. The journey to the castle was over and she was now safely with the Duke. Her name could be crossed off the General's proverbial list.

Sadness overcame her, but she did her best, with every step she took away from the General to leave her feelings behind with him.

CHAPTER 23

A GRAND ENTRANCE

*a*s they stepped into the entrance hall, Sarah was immediately swept away with the gaiety that danced through the air; it lightened even her dark spirits after such an arduous journey.

Down every hall were magnificent and large paintings of the Duke's family members. Most stood strong on top of a boulder or battlefield and displayed their crowning achievements.

Every side table Sarah passed was covered with vibrant bouquets of flowers that not only illuminated the corridors but also left a pleasing aroma to waft in the air.

As Sarah traveled alongside the Duke to her bedchamber, she noticed the clumps of young women strewn throughout the corridors as they talked in their exclusive groups. The ornamentation each girl had dangle around her neck and draped down her arms were far more than that to which Sarah was accustomed. Nothing in her possession could possibly match such decorations.

As the Duke and she passed each group, like clockwork, the girls would bow their heads to the Duke with a flirtatious giggle to follow. Then, that same gaiety would fade into a snicker when their eyes fell on Sarah.

She clinched more tightly to the Duke as she felt the disapproving looks assault her.

"You cannot worry yourself with them, Lady Levine. Most of these ladies have never been much farther than the gates at their own homes. They are not quite as worldly as yourself," uttered the Duke softly.

"I hardly consider myself worldly, Sire. I, too, have not been much farther then the fields just outside my house."

"Yes, but you are from Ditrum. That is a world away from here, as your travel here has shown you. Therefore, you are now worldly."

Sarah appreciated the comfort he tried to bring her, but it didn't make her feel any more welcome. Even the General's words reminded her that she didn't know the customs of Vasfale and that the Duke's logic was flawed.

"This place is quite fascinating," admitted Sarah as she tried to find a diversion.

"Really? How so?" replied the Duke.

"The whole castle seems to be carved from a single stone. How is that even possible?" she inquired.

"Leave it to you to notice the architecture before the fancies of the ball," said the Duke, amused.

Sarah tried to force a laugh at the Duke's comment but it faded quickly behind her fascination of the smoothness of the walls.

"It is one stone. The waterfall used to run over this rock for centuries, the water itself smoothed and molded it into its own masterpiece."

"Excuse me, Sire, but the waterfall could not have crafted this whole castle. That would be… impossible."

"Improbable perhaps, but not impossible."

Sarah's brow contorted with confusion. Those words were hers when she spoke to the old innkeeper in Lankenshire. The Duke clearly knew more than he was letting on.

The Duke came to a halt and looked at her.

"What my men tell me is true."

The Duke left his comment there while Sarah remained in an anxious silence.

"Here we are," said the Duke and gestured to the door off to the right of the hall.

Still holding onto Sarah, he moved closer to the door and opened it for her.

"If you need anything at all, you have your own personal hand-maid. Eshe?"

A woman with flawless, dark skin and a radiant smile stepped into the doorway from within the room.

"Yes, sir," answered Eshe as she moved closer to Sarah.

"Lady Levine has been on a long journey and needs tending to before the feast tonight."

"What kind of feast?" asked Sarah when she realized how famished she was.

"One fit for a King," said the Duke proudly.

Sarah tried to swallow the huge lump now in her throat. The only occasion she ever attended was a heavily attended dance in her own town, and every now and then her Aunt Bernice would throw a small party for fifty or so people. Certainly nothing that was the size of a ball at Vasfale.

Her train of thought ended when the Duke leaned over and kissed Sarah's hand. His lips were so gentle and soft against her skin that she almost forgot what a nuisance he had been when the company just twenty minutes earlier. His hands were tender and caring, unlike the General's callused ones. As for his smile, it was flawless and a comfort.

"This is where I will leave you. But I do hope to be promised at least one dance with you tonight?"

"Of course," Sarah said, resigned.

The Duke bowed his head to her, and then moved swiftly up the hall. Everyone's head followed him until he turned the corner. The mindless chatter resumed amongst the groups of girls scattered throughout the hall.

Sarah turned back to Eshe, who still looked at her with a contented smile, not only on her mouth but in her eyes as well.

"I have never been to anything like a ball before. I doubt I have an appropriate dress to wear."

"Do not worry. The Duke already has something picked out for you," confirmed the handmaiden.

"The Duke? Picked something out for me?" she asked and wondered how he could possibly even know her sizes.

Eshe grabbed a hold of Sarah's hand which gained Sarah's full attention.

"Things happen a little differently here than the rest of the world. If I may make a suggestion – just let it happen, I think you will find you will be happier."

Sarah found Eshe's outspokenness refreshing compared to others she had encountered over the course of this trip. There was no need to read facial reactions or her body posture, and her tone was pleasant.

"Please, come and see your room," Eshe said excitedly, and pulled Sarah through the door.

The room was just as delicately crafted to match the rest of the castle. The first thing that caught her eye was a huge painting that had a sheet draped over it.

"What is this?" Sarah asked with curiosity.

"Oh, the Tantum painting. Most people cannot handle looking at it for too long, so we put a sheet over it."

"That sounds mysterious. May I look?" asked Sarah.

"Be my guest."

Sarah's love of paintings and critical eye were prepared for a great many things, but wasn't sure what to expect from this one.

Eshe pulled the sheet away that left behind the picture of a white unicorn that nuzzled a little girl's shoulder by a river. The flow of the paint across the canvas made the river look convincingly real. She studied the picture closely before she slid her fingertips across the girl's pink cheek.

"You have much compassion, Lady Levine."

Sarah quickly lifted her hand and turned towards Eshe.

"How could you think all that from me touching a painting?"

"It was not your touch, but instead the look in your eyes when you did it. Words cannot describe the pain felt in that expression."

"The picture looks so real, do you not want to touch this unicorn?"

Eshe stepped closer and stood next to her in front of the painting.

"I cannot see what you see. This painting is very special in that way. It comes from Tantum."

"Tantum, I have never heard of this place."

"If you are from the Southlands then surely you have heard of Tanter trees," pointed out Eshe.

"I do know them. They turn the color of the seasons. Quite beautiful."

"I guess you could say this painting changes with the person instead of the season. As the story goes, mystics lived in the hills of Tantum. Though, this came to the Duke when he was moving his army though that piece of land and found the town had been abandoned. This painting was found in a monastery.

"From what little we can tell about it, everyone sees something different when they look at it. The Duke originally had it hung in the entrance hall but found it too distracting to many of the guests. It would capture their attention for long periods of time. So, the Duke decided to tuck it into this room."

"Any reason why Tantum was abandoned?"

"I would guess a raid."

"You speak very freely," Sarah noted.

"It might be considered one of my greatest faults," agreed the handmaiden.

"Well, the company I just traveled with did not share much of anything with me. Least of all his thoughts. It is refreshing to hear something other than my own frustrations."

"Ah. You were traveling with the General, yes?"

"I was."

"He is a noble but soft spoken man," agreed Eshe.

"That is one way to describe him," replied Sarah with a snicker.

"How would you describe him?"

"Expressionless and hard."

"Would you not become these things if you fought in many battles and watched many people die?" Eshe inquired.

Sarah found Eshe's words caused her a moment of pause. She had never really thought much about the fighting, killing, and loss of life the General must have suffered over his years. She remembered his story about his sister with clarity, but she had not thought much of the other losses he had gone through since that day.

"Are you a long way from home?" Sarah asked as she tried to redirect her train of thought.

"I come from a different part of the world. My parents and I were separated when I was just a little girl. My journey here was much like yours, I would guess. Perilous and, at the time, unwanted."

"Have you ever thought about going back to find them?" Sarah questioned with concern.

The look that filled Eshe's eye needed no words. It was clear the pain and suffering she must have lived through.

"Are you happy here?" Sarah continued.

"I am happy to be alive. And the Duke is a kind and generous person."

"Ah, but that did not answer my question," Sarah argued.

Eshe smiled, "Yes, I suppose you are right."

Eshe broke from the conversation, when two of the other handmaidens brought a stunning rose-colored dress from the closet and presented it. Sarah looked it over carefully and chuckled to herself.

"Does the dress displease you?" asked Eshe.

"Quite the contrary. It is a finer dress than I could ever wish for," Sarah let slip from her lips as she ran her fingers over the soft fabric. "Why did the Duke pick this for me?"

"Because he thought it would look nice on you. We have been hearing wonderful things about you, Lady Levine."

"Really? From whom?"

Eshe didn't respond except to walk over to a chest of drawers and grab a small, wooden jewelry box that had rested on top of it. When she held it out, Sarah ran her fingers over the bands of iron that were melded into the wood. They reminded her of the design of the iron torches that hung in the Hollow.

Sarah lifted the lid and saw several pink and white diamonds strung together harmoniously which led to one pink, oval shaped diamond that stood out from the rest.

"Do you like it?" asked Eshe.

Sarah didn't answer at first. Instead, she allowed her fingers to run freely along the stones until they reached the oval jewel in the middle.

"We can find you another one, if you would like."

Sarah's head shook slowly, still fully attracted to the decorative artwork at her fingertips as the weight of her body came to rest on the bed.

"It looks like something a princess from a fairy tale might wear."

"A feast in a castle with a handsome Duke, this happens in many fairy tales, yes?"

"It does. I just never imagined I could be part of one until now."

Eshe sat on the bed next to Sarah.

"From the sounds of your journey here, you are already part of a tale, fairy or any other. Now, Princess, you must get ready."

Sarah could feel the weight that she had carried for the last several days be lifted into an overwhelming happiness.

A light knock came at the door.

Eshe opened it and poked her head out into the hall. "Captain Lowe."

Sarah made her way over to him.

"I am sorry to bother you while you are settling in, but the Duke has asked me to bring his physician here to look at your injury."

Sarah half smiled and nodded while her eyes drifted out to the hall behind the Captain.

"He is not here."

"Who is not here?" she reitterated coyly.

"The General has other matters to attend to tonight."

"I was simply looking for the doctor."

The Captain gestured to the impatient man who stood a couple step behind him.

"Doctor?"

The jittery man regained his focus as he stepped up next to the Captain and bowed.

"How do you do? Oh, that looks like some cut. Let me get you all fixed up before the feast."

"I will be back in a short time to escort you down to the festivities," said the Captain.

Sarah's expression turned sour without her even knowing it.

"Would you prefer someone else to escort you?" The Captain shot back quickly. "The Duke thought you would be most comfortable with me since we had just traveled together."

Sarah corrected her posture so that she stood up straight and shook her head.

"I will see you shortly, Captain."

The Captain smiled and let the doctor into the room. "I will leave you in the doctor's good care. Now if you will excuse me?"

Sarah bowed her head before she readjusted her eyes to the doctor with a little jar of ointment in his hand.

"I suppose we should get to it," she said. "It will be hard enough to stand out in a room full of fawning admirers. I do not think a blemish is the best way to make an impression."

Eshe pulled Sarah's hair away from her face as the doctor drew closer with a damp cloth and the jar of ointment and placed both on the wound.

"I do not think this cut will even be noticed when you walk into the room," said Eshe.

Sarah lowered her head at Eshe's kind words but felt the storm of nerves and doubt building while she waited for the stinging of the cut on her forehead to subside.

CHAPTER 24

THE FIRE DANCE

*U*nlike Sarah's normal attire, the dress she wore was far more fitted and clung to her body so tightly that it made it difficult to breathe. While one of the handmaidens laced her up; another threw powder on her nose and color across her cheeks and lips. Finally, Sarah slid the necklace around her neck to complete her final look.

Eshe clasped her hands together in triumph while the other two handmaidens smiled contentedly with their final masterpiece.

"Well?" Sarah asked. "Do I look suitable?"

Eshe slowly guided Sarah over to a full-length mirror.

Sarah's breath caught in her chest when her eyes locked on the stranger who looked back at her. As she moved, the strange reflection followed, but Sarah found it hard to believe that the reflection could possibly be her.

The rose colored dress was not the only thing accented by jewelry, but also a series of knots and braids weaved through her hair. Across her forehead was a painted brown vine tiara that covered her cut.

Eshe was right – no one would notice her injury at all.

"Who is this person I see?" breathed Sarah as she watched her reflection follow her movements.

A light knock tapped on the door, but before Eshe could answer –

"Who is it?" Sarah shouted out.

"Your humble escort."

Sarah nodded to Eshe to let Captain Lowe enter.

The door creaked open slowly and the Captain stood tall in the doorway. His regal uniform was his attire for the night and his freshly shaved face made him almost unrecognizable. Sarah spun her heel to look at him in disbelief.

"I will have to let the Duke know that Lady Levine has fled from the castle leaving behind only this beautiful decoy," chuckled the Captain.

"Really?" muttered Sarah unsure of the unusual fashioned design of her whole attire.

"You are stunning," said Eshe as the handmaid nudged the Captain in the arm.

The Captain finally took a full step into the room. Sarah was taken in by his refinement that resided in his clean face and handsome clothes.

"You clean up nice, yourself Captain."

"Why thank you. I would like to think my wife would agree with you," he said.

Then, he fell into a bow while Sarah grabbed the folds of her dress and curtsied.

"Shall we?" asked the Captain and held out his arm to her.

"We shall," she replied.

Sarah smiled as her arm slid comfortably around his, and the two moved out the door.

The loud merriment echoed down the corridor as the two drew closer to the grand hall.

Sarah couldn't help but allow her eyes to wander to the interesting artifacts and statues that sat on white pillars throughout the hall. There were many porcelain vases with foreign characters painted across them so delicately, and each one told its own story.

"Are you alright?" questioned the Captain.

Sarah slowed her pace.

"What is it?" urged the Captain.

"I am not sure if I am ready to be on display. I mean, most of these people have lived the noble lifestyle their entire lives."

"Lady Levine, you are a noble woman as well," reminded the Captain.

"Yes, but a poor country one. I work the fields with my people. I have dirt under my fingernails and sweat on my brow."

"That does not remove you from your noble bloodline. If anything, it strengthens it between you and your people."

Sarah let a little sigh escape before she continued down the hall.

The two made their way to the open doors of the grand hall. Many girls dressed in exotic silks and danced in the middle area of the room. Huge banners with the Duke's family crest hung from all four stone pillars on both sides of the room. Three long tables were covered end to end with food and guests were placed in a U to allow the space in between to be used as a dance floor. Everyone laughed, drank, and cheered loudly for the dancers.

Much to Sarah's surprise, her eyes found the large figure that she wondered if he would even be there. The General sat at the head table right next to the Duke.

"I thought you said the General would not be here tonight," she whispered out of the side of her mouth to the Captain.

"I am just as surprised as you. Maybe he has been encouraged on our adventure to drink and be merry?" hinted the Captain happily.

Sarah rolled her eyes at the absurd notion.

"Ah!" yelled the Duke and rose from his seat with goblet in his hand. "My final guest has arrived! So, now we might begin the festive evening properly."

The Duke held his goblet out to Sarah. She stared blankly at him, not sure how she was to respond. Her breathing became labored but she tried to hide it.

"Curtsy," whispered the Captain.

Sarah complied and quickly took the Captain's arm to get out of the entranceway.

She then surveyed the room and found two empty table settings at the table off to the right. She and the Captain swiftly made their way to their seats.

"Now begins this week's festivities of gaiety and pleasure... *My* pleasure," said the Duke with his charming smile and a dashing wink. "By the end of this joyful occasion, one of you beautiful maidens will be my future, my all, my everything."

Some of the girls around the room broke into giddy laughter, while others started to fan themselves with small hand fans.

"Now if you will quickly take your seats, the entertainment is about to begin!" the Duke shouted as he clapped his hands together hard enough to created a little reverberation.

The torchlight was instantly extinguished and a gasp swept through the guests.

A single thunder drum pounded which echoed around the hall. A spark flew and a small ball of fire on a chain swung around in a circle above the head of a dancer. The speed of the drum beat in time with the swinging motion. Starting in a small circle close to the dancer's body, the chain loosened and the small ball of flame inched closer and closer to the tables.

The guests gasped at the magnificence. The dancer allowed the ball to drop to the stone floor which sparked high with an explosion of light. Many watched it burn for a long moment in silence, mesmerized.

Then multiple thunder drums around the room rang out as the dancer screamed and ran at the table on the far side of the room. The table shrieked loudly and didn't know if he would stop.

The dancer threw his chain in their direction just as he turned and ran at the table on the opposite side of the room. The ball of fire reached the first table just as the dancer reached the other. It was magical, how the chain flowed in perfect sequence with the dancer.

A second dancer could be seen as he moved through the darkness to the floor. Flames slid across what looked like dragon wings that, once extended, spread a quarter length of the table.

The dragon moved in an aggressive motion towards the first dancer.

The crowd gasped.

The warrior threw the ball of fire at the dragon but the dragon was too quick. He swooped out of the way and extinguished as he flew into the darkness towards the ceiling.

The low beats of the drums taunted the warrior. Sarah could see him look around the room. She hadn't noticed his blue eyes were glowing in the dark. It sent a shiver down her spine.

Again the dancer launched the ball of flames towards the middle of the room as he ran around to all the tables, screaming. The dancer tightened the reins of the chain and swung the ball over his head, and then slammed it on the ground. A burst of flames flared from the floor where the ball hit. He swung it again and again as if in an angry rant or as if he had lost his mind.

Then, in the upper corner of the hall, the dragon's flaming wings ignited again. This time the dragon leapt from his perch and flew around the room just above the guests' heads.

"Ooo," buzzed throughout the room in unison.

Sarah was so captured by the performance that she hadn't even realized the other dancers snuck behind everyone.

The warrior flung his ball of flames up at the dragon, but the dragon caught it. Slowly the chain caught on fire as the tense struggle continued between the dragon who tried to pull the warrior to one end of the room and the warrior who refused to yield.

Once the fire crawled the full length of the chain to reach the warrior, a big burst of flame exploded both near the warrior and up by the dragon. Sparks flew from the hands of all the dancers behind the tables that hit the floor in tiny bursts of blaze, and illuminated the whole room. Everything went dark.

The guests cheered uncontrollably. As the roar of the room grew, candlelight returned and allowed the guests to feel comfortable again.

A merry tune sprung from several fiddles and the dancers went to several guests and pulled them onto the dance floor. Sarah was a little surprised to see a hand extended out to her. At first, she looked at it with confusion, but then took it with excitement.

"I am not sure I will know this dance," she admitted to the gentleman.

"I shall lead you," he replied happily.

Sarah took his hand and allowed him to swing and twirl her about the dance floor. Her head spun and she couldn't stop laughing with her partner until finally the song came to an end.

Sarah clapped and cheered as loud as her voice would let her.

"Did you all enjoy that?" yelled out the Duke to his guests.

Applause instantly erupted.

"That dance was inspired by the infamous, hidden city of Branch. Now, friends, how would you all like to see another exotic dance from a land far, far away?"

Hoots and hollers rang out in agreement.

"There is one guest among us that I hear is quite the dancer. She displayed her talents along her travels with an exotic dance from the South."

Sarah began to feel flushed. A glare shot from her eyes to the Captain, who clapped along with the rest of the guests.

He leaned over to her with his crooked smile and said, "Well, you did."

"It would please me greatly if she would dance this infamous dance of The Conti Rose so that I might see with my own eyes if these stories are true. You know who you are, please come to the dance floor."

Sarah leaned into the Captain, "I thought you said you could keep a secret."

"Go on, get up there," the Captain urged back.

Sarah stepped front and center, and faced the Duke, who remained behind the table where he still stood.

"If I am to see this exciting dance properly, I alas cannot take part. So, who will take my place?" asked the Duke. "Who would like to dance The Conti Rose?"

Looking around the room, no one seemed brave enough to take the Duke's offer. Sarah turned slowly, with her hand extended out to all the tables. She secretly hoped that someone would want to accept it.

"Come now, friends, we should not be so timid," stated the Duke.

The only thing worse than being forced to the dance floor alone is to have no one to dance with. Sarah felt her body grow heavier with every passing moment.

"I will accept this dance with Lady Levine," said the low familiar voice. "After all, I believe I have danced it once with her before."

The General rose from his seat and walked around the table to meet face to face with Sarah.

"Well, well, well... this night just keeps getting better and better," rejoiced the Duke. "Can we get a round of applause for the coupl-"

The Duke was cut off by a sharp glower from both the General and Sarah.

"Dancers," the Duke finished by correcting his sentence.

The General held his terse expression Sarah had grown accustomed to over the past week. He wouldn't even look at her, and made her feel like this whole thing was her fault.

The General spun Sarah around so that her back was pressed tightly to his stomach and he leaned his head over her shoulder and leaned his cheek on hers. In that instant, she could feel his warm breath graze her neck as he looked towards the floor. His arm slid around her small frame and pulled it tightly to his own.

Sarah sensed the heavy fall of the General's head as he nodded to the musicians to begin. A slow, lustful tune began to play between two fiddles.

The General's giant hand slid from Sarah's waist all the way up her side until it took a hold of her hand and spun Sarah away from him. Then immediately, he pulled her back close, but this time she faced him.

When the General's dark brown eyes locked with Sarah's, everyone else in the room faded away into the background. Every step the General took, he guided Sarah into it with him. The dance was effortless, as her partner had clearly done this dance before. One last time, he spun her around him, and then dipped her back which allowed his face to come to rest near her chest. Both were breathless as the music stopped and the room seemed to suspend indefinitely in silence.

Nothing moved.

"You know the second starting position for this dance," realized Sarah aloud.

"And?" said the General, nonchalantly.

"I started in the first position when we were in Lankenshire. You have danced this before."

Then –

"Bravo!" screamed the Duke.

Following the Duke's lead, the room exploded into thunderous applause. The Duke continued to clap as he made his way around the table.

"Old friend! What other secrets have you been keeping from me?" inquired the Duke, aghast.

The General released Sarah so she could stand upright again. She kept her eyes low while she swept her hands over her dress nervously.

"Captain!" screamed the Duke.

"Yes, Sire?" replied the Captain and rose to his feet.

The Duke looked over at him while he pointed at the General.

"Did you know this man could dance like this?"

"Sire, I was as much in awe as you."

"And how long have you known him?"

"My whole life, your highness."

The Duke looked back at the General, who appeared still a little out of sorts.

"I as well..." hummed the Duke with curiosity in his tone.

"Dancing does not often present itself on the battlefield, Sire," stated the General.

He looked back at Sarah. "I tolerate it when I must, but it is not really for me."

Sarah couldn't stop the scoff that shot from her mouth.

The Duke glanced at Sarah, but then returned his focus to the

General. "Well, dear friend, I hope to see more of this sort of thing from you. Even if it is not for you, you do it so well."

The General bowed his head to the Duke's request.

Then, the Duke turned his full attention to Sarah as he held out his arm to her.

"I, unlike my General, prefer dancing. Would you be so kind as to allow me the next one? After all, you did promise me a dance tonight."

Sarah bowed her head and forced a brilliant smile. "I would be delighted."

"Wonderful! Everyone, please, come join us!"

Sarah took the Duke's arm as the dance floor flooded once more with people. As she moved farther away, Sarah's lips pursed as she looked over her shoulder to see the General's reaction. When she turned, his large figure was nowhere to be found.

Anger and annoyance filled her to the brim at his constant display of indifference towards her. But when the music started and the Duke lead her into the first move, she let it all fade away into an enjoyable dance with someone else. Someone who was actually gave her a little attention, attention that she couldn't deny was marvelous.

CHAPTER 25

AN HONEST CONVERSATION

*T*he night grew old as the last song came and went. Sarah's feet were blistered and sore from dancing so much, but the evening had been filled with more pleasure than she could have ever expected.

During all her days of travel, she dreaded this festival and now, she wondered what all the fuss was about. Everyone had been right; the Duke was a charming man that she could get on with.

Just as she collected her things, the Captain approached her.

"My Lady, are you ready to retire for the evening?"

"Yes," she sigh9ed with exhaustion.

Sarah took a couple steps towards him, then stopped and stared at him quizzically.

"I thought you and the Duke left earlier."

"You cannot possibly think you would last longer at this party than me? Well that would just be... preposterous," explained the Captain.

Sarah threw her hands up in the air with a laugh.

"Well, maybe the Duke had something important he needed you to do for him? Or did he get everything about our journey out of you already?" said Sarah, venomously.

The Captain rolled his eyes and sighed.

"I cannot help that the Duke has his ways of finding out information," implied the Captain.

"Clearly."

"Think of me as you will. I did nothing wrong," grunted the Captain. "Now, I will see you to your room."

The Captain held out his arm which Sarah instantly took. The two started on their way down the hall.

They traveled down two side halls before the silence began to grate on Sarah's nerves.

"I cannot believe I am admitting this out loud, but I quite enjoyed my time tonight," Sarah confessed.

The Captain nodded his head in agreement.

"If there is anything the Duke knows how to do, it is to throw a party."

"You were right about him... he is quite charming."

"Am I hearing you correctly? Did you just say..."

"You were right!" said Sarah more emphatically and bumped the Captain's shoulder with hers, embarrassed. "That is after you get through his larks, if I may say in all honesty."

The halls were empty of guests and only a maid here or there could be seen before they disappeared down another hall or into a room. Seldom, if ever, was Sarah the last remaining guest at the few parties she did attend, but tonight was the exception.

As the gaiety of the night faded completely away, Sarah felt a sudden change in her mood. The image of the Duke drifted from her mind and was replaced with the General as he saved her on the dance floor. She looked around nervously, not sure exactly what she expected to find until her eyes landed on the Captain's face.

Even though he looked forward, she could already tell by his devious expression that he knew where her mind had wandered.

"Captain?"

"Yes?"

Sarah chewed on her lower lip as she ran over her thoughts once more before she spoke.

"Where did the General go?"

"Lady Levine, if I may," said the Captain in an attempt to cut her off. "It will do you no good, these thoughts you are having."

"What thoughts?" she asked, a little self-conscious.

The Captain scanned the hallway with his eyes before he turned towards her. Turmoil and fret was buried deep within his light eyes like she had never seen before from him.

"Come with me," said the Captain as he pulled Sarah down the next hall and into a small study.

He lit a couple candles that sat on the desk and gestured for Sarah to sit in one of the chairs in front of it.

Sarah took her time as she moved through the room, careful not to touch anything in her path. The Captain returned to the doorway and poked his head out into the hall to make sure they were alone before he closed the study door.

After Sarah was comfortably seated, she folded her hands neatly in her lap and nervously awaited the conversation.

The Captain came to sit in the chair next to Sarah. She noticed that he seemed slightly flustered which was quite unusual for him and continued to confuse her.

"What is it? You are making me nervous," she confessed.

"This is only my belief, and mine alone…"

"Alright?"

"The General would kill me for saying this to you, but I must do what I think is right."

"Captain? What is it?"

"He loves you."

The words rang loudly in Sarah's ears. The very sound of them made her stomach turn and her heart race. A warm feeling washed over her whole body. Unlike when she felt angry or embarrassed, there was a sense of happiness.

"He does?" she stammered.

"I had my suspicions along our travels but it was confirmed for me tonight."

Sarah nodded her head at the weightiness of his statement.

"What should I do?" she inquired.

"That is up to you, but if I were you…"

Sarah nodded her head, anxiously and hung onto every word.

"Then let him go."

As quickly as the joy arose in her every fiber, it was ripped away again.

"Why do you say this?" she asked, unsure of why his message seemed to have changed since the tavern in Lankenshire.

"The General is a warrior who has lived a hard life of fighting and killing. No doubt you caught a glimpse of it in the Banting Woods."

The image of Jack's red face while the General almost choked the air out of him entered her mind.

"He has never been known for affection, at least not the kind you seek from him. I know you are frustrated with his constantly letting you down, but you have created a conflict within him. A conflict that he does not know how to combat."

"Maybe that is a good thing."

"Confusion in the head General of the Duke's army is a very bad thing. Dangerous even. He cannot be distracted, especially with Lord Baer becoming stronger every passing day," argued the Captain.

"You seemed so encouraging back in Lankenshire. Has he said something to you?"

The Captain sat stoically and looked conflicted on how to respond. Finally, he shook his head 'no.'

"Then, why have you changed your mind about the General and me?" asked Sarah, distressed.

"At first, this whole venture for the General was amusing. The men and I got a good laugh out of it. But we are not in some small town anymore, Lady Levine. We are in Vasfale. You must see the danger you are putting the General in."

Sarah's head dropped in shame at his words. Her fingers slid across the soft fabric of her rose colored dress as she tried to calm herself. Her eyes began to well up and her throat tightened.

The Captain slid forward in his seat and forced her to look up at him. The look of determination and seriousness was like none she had seen in the Captain.

"I know you care for him very much. I could see it that night by the campfire, just like I saw it when you were in his arms tonight. But it is time to say your goodbyes."

"How could I possibly?" she replied and felt like she could choke on her words.

"Harshly. The more firm you are about it, the more he will not turn back."

Tears spilled over and down Sarah's cheeks.

"How could *I* possibly? I cannot help the way I feel. I never meant for any of this to happen. So many times I wish I would have just run away with Jack and never come back," she stated emphatically. Especially punching out the last couple of words.

The Captain's face softened while he pulled a handkerchief from his pocket and offered it to her. Sarah slid it out of his hand.

"What I suggest to you is not an easy task, but you must do it for him."

The Captain stood up and motioned for Sarah to follow him. The two made their way over to the window behind the desk. The Captain pulled open the curtain that had been drawn so Sarah could see out to a small pool of water at the bottom of the waterfall just behind the castle.

She wasn't sure what she was looking for at first, but then she noticed a large figure move that could easily be noticed.

"You must make him believe that you do not love him," reiterated the Captain.

Sarah kept her focus on the General's form outside. Her stomach continued to turn as if she drank soured milk. Her mind raced furiously with everything she should say or wanted to say, or *had* to say to him. Never in her life could she have predicted when she met this brusque creature in her sitting room only a week earlier would she feel like this now. That she would be in love with him now.

The ache and want to be closer to the General overwhelmed her.

To be with him. To love him. Now that she acknowledged all of these feelings she had for him, what was she to do?

Sarah heard the study door open and then close. When she turned, she realized she was alone with nothing but her thoughts to keep her company.

When she looked back out at the General, she already knew what she had to do, however much she hated it.

CHAPTER 26

DECISIONS

*E*verything Sarah could see blurred behind a curtain of tears. Cupping her hands over her face, she allowed all her frustrations to go into the thin fabric of her sleeve.

"Now, now, deary. Do not cry. You tell Old Madge what is ailing you."

Sarah's head shot up at the sound of the rugged voice. Old Madge sat at her small, wooden table just a couple of feet away while she sipped her usual cup of tea. The longer Sarah stared at her, the bedchamber that was once around Sarah melted away and was replaced with the shabby interior of Old Madge's single room cottage.

Sarah rose to her feet and looked around anxiously until her eyes landed on the crooked smile of the old woman.

"Is this a dream?"

"Yes," affirmed Old Madge.

"Then no matter what I say or do, it will not matter," grumbled Sarah as she placed her hands over her face with dismay.

"Nonsense!"

Sarah's instantly dropped to see the jovial woman. Old Madge patted the seat next to her and invited Sarah to come sit. Sarah moved to the empty seat and tucked her hands into her lap.

"Do you think the beans do not matter? How do you think you got those?"

"You gave them to me," said Sarah.

"And how did I give them to you?" hummed the old woman in a suggestive tone.

"You handed them to me in this cottage when I was in the woods. You were there. I was there."

"Ahhhh," resonated in the old woman's throat. "I handed them to you in a dream and you brought them with you to when you were awake. State of mind and state of being are two very different things. Do remember that."

Sarah could not figure out this absurd woman.

All of a sudden, a howl rang out just on the other side of Old Madge's front door.

"He will never learn," teased the Old Madge with a lighthearted chuckle.

A loud bang hit the front door hard enough that caused Sarah to spin around in her seat.

"What is that?" she asked breathlessly.

"He will always be following you, Sarah. He loves you that much."

Another loud bang slammed into the door. Sarah watched the door shift in its frame as the massive figure, just on the other side, slammed into it again.

"He has made his choice as wrong as it was."

"Who has made what choice? I do not understand!"

"He has chosen a bleak road to travel and I caution you to not travel it with him. You have the ability to know everything before even he does."

Another loud howl cried out, so loud this time that Sarah had to cover her ears.

The old woman sipped her tea calmly despite the fact her door was about to give way to the heavy force that continuously ran into it.

"Old Madge, please! I need your help," whimpered Sarah.

Another bang hit the door. Old Madge took one last sip from her teacup and slammed it down on the table.

"Alright, alright!" she hollered. "Don't knock my door off of its hinges, you big bad wolf!"

The old woman rose unsteadily to her feet and crossed over to the door. Sarah's eyes followed her slow pace.

"Sarah, you do not need my help, you just need to make up your mind."

"About what?"

"You are about to find out."

Just then, Old Madge threw open the front door and a large wolf leaped into the cottage. He was darkly shaded and his eye glowed against the flicking firelight. A low growl sat in the back of his throat as he crouched low just a few steps away from Sarah.

She jumped to her feet which knocked her chair over on the floor.

Like a slow dance, every step the wolf took towards Sarah; she took a step back.

"What am I supposed to do? Old Madge? Old Madge?"

Sarah's eyes glanced quickly around the room to find that the old woman had disappeared. That left the wolf there alone to maul her.

"Great!" she grumbled.

The wolf took another step forward, which caused Sarah to raise her hands for protection. She tried to use a soothing tone to calm the growling beast.

"This is just a dream. It is just a dream," Sarah said over and over again and tried to convince herself that she would not be harmed.

The wolf crouched low to the ground, and then he lunged with his full weight, knocking her over. The wolf's head was trapped between Sarah's tiny hands as he tried to snap at her face.

Sarah slammed her eyes shut. She knew in that moment that she physically was no match for this animal. She felt a sharp pain strike her arm as the wolf scratched at her.

"Stop! Stop it!" she screamed as loud as she could.

Silence fell.

When Sarah's eyes opened again, she sat up in her bed in the castle. She looked around frantically, still disoriented by her dream. When she realized she was safe, she allowed her body to relax back against the headboard of the bed.

A sliver of light made its way through the curtain.

"Morning," she whispered in relief.

A gentle tap came at the door.

"Yes?"

Eshe entered in with her brilliant smile that she always held.

"The guests are gathering for breakfast in the hall," Eshe said while she moved over to the curtains and drew them back from the window.

Sarah held up her hands to shield her eyes from the light that now poured into the room.

"Oh my goodness, what has happened to your arm?" Eshe asked with concern.

"What are you talking about?"

When Sarah looked down, she saw claw marks freshly dug into her skin.

"We must call for the doctor," Eshe stated and hastily went out the door.

"It was just a dream," said Sarah as she tried to convince herself that nothing should have happened in her dream that would effect her while she was awake.

Running her fingers across the marks, a stinging sensation suddenly burned furiously. Her brow crinkled tightly as she hissed in pain.

"It was just a dream," repeated Sarah. "It was just..."

Sarah looked down at the scratches on her arm once more, but this time it was with wonderment.

"That is how I know! My dreams!" shouted Sarah.

Eshe boomed through the door with the doctor at her side.

"What happened?" asked the doctor, confounded by the scratches on Sarah's arm.

"Bad dream."

"I would say. Well, let me get you cleaned up and downstairs in time for the unicorn chase."

"The what? I thought the unicorn chase was just a story my father told me."

The doctor looked over the rim of his spectacles, "You father told you the truth. Consider it more of a game than finding a magical creature."

Ointment and bandages were smothered around Sarah's arm, and Eshe helped her dress quickly.

The images of Old Madge and the large wolf kept Sarah company while she made her way down to the grand hall.

Old Madge always spoke in riddles. Sarah felt triumphant in finally understanding one piece of the old woman's crazy puzzle. Though, the question that still lingered was what the significance was of all the graphic dreams she has had since the night before her excursion.

Sarah stopped just shy of the door into the grand hall.

"What decision do I have to make?" She repeated Old Madge's question.

"Having a morning discussion with yourself?" said a familiar jovial voice.

When Sarah turned, the Captain walked towards her through the foyer. He removed his gloves before he bowed to her.

The curtsy Sarah dipped into was abrupt and short.

"Are you alright?" asked the Captain as his brow grew quizzical. "You seem out of sorts."

Sarah felt annoyed by his presence after his betrayal of her confidence to the Duke. Then to change his tune about her and the General's growing affection for one another. Though she understood what he meant by the dangers she was putting the General in, still the Captain was her closest confidant and was suppose to support her decisions. All she wished to do was make her way into breakfast without much being said between them.

"I am just a little hungry is all," she lied.

The Captain stepped into the doorway of the grand hall and gestured with his hand for Sarah to enter.

"You have come to the right place."

As Sarah passed him, she leaned over just for a second, and said, "As much as you pretend to be my friend, you betrayed me. I will not forget that."

Sarah looked up to make sure the Captain understood her meaning and was greeted with his amused smirk.

"Well then, please excuse me," replied the Captain.

Sarah took a step back, partly in disbelief and partly in anger. But before she could retort, the Captain turned and walked away.

CHAPTER 27

THE UNICORN CHASE

*T*he grand hall was filled with people who were half awake as they nibbled off their plates of food in front of them. Sarah wondered if she was the only noble person who knew how to celebrate properly? The thought festered even further when she realized she was the last person to arrive at the castle and was least prepared for the previous nights dinner.

Once she had a plate of breaks for herself, Sarah allowed her eyes the freedom to search the room for the General. He sat at the head table next to that Duke as he had done before. The General, too, looked awake and alert.

Sarah's nerves started to return as the warning from the Captain with his unexpected conversation played out in her mind. What was she to do?

A man dressed in the Duke's house colors marched to the middle of the room, pulled a horn from under his arm, and blasted a call to arms. All the guests jumped in their seats at the rude interruption.

"Friends!" shouted the Duke as he jumped over the head table and walked out to the middle of the floor to stand next to the trumpeter.

"It is time for the unicorn chase to begin!" he said, happily.

A farmer walked through the main doors with a cage. He held it out to the Duke as he bowed low to the ground.

"Thank you, my good sir," said the Duke graciously and took the cage from him.

"This, dear friends, is our unicorn."

He held the cage up so the entire room could see what laid inside. The largest rooster Sarah could ever recall laying eyes on sat in his confinement and occasionally cooed. It must have been the size of three chickens combined. From what little she could see, an ivory colored stump grew from its forehead that loosely resembled a horn.

"This is a long-horned rooster that my top General brought from his homeland of Gaente."

The Duke bowed to the General with graciousness, who, with his stern expression, bowed his head back in acknowledgement.

"But I wish to warn you now my nimble guests. Let me assure you that this is no ordinary rooster. He is quicker than lightning, and tougher than the biggest beast you have ever come across," said the Duke, before he ran his fingers along the bars of the cage.

The rooster pecked the Duke's hand which instantly drew blood. The crowd gasped. The Duke dropped the cage and clutched the gash on his hand, but an odd smirk was still present on his face.

"And, might I add, a feisty creature."

The entire room broke into laughter and applause at the Duke's heroism.

The Duke pulled a rare stone that was plated in gold and hung from a green ribbon out of his pocket and held it up to the room. The room reverberated with 'oohs' and 'ahhs'.

"This, ladies and gentlemen, is the prize to be won. This stone is from my very own Vasfale Falls. That is, *if* you can outwit this noble creature…"

The room went silent. The beautiful stone that dangled from the Duke's hand captured every eye.

"But it is more than just a stone. If a maiden can capture this, she shall not only have the first dance with me at the last evening's ball, but also sit at my side for dinner. Should one of you noble gentlemen be the victor, he shall receive a bag of one hundred gold pieces and the choice of one of my finest mares in my stables. How does that sound to everyone?"

The crowd erupted into thunderous applause.

"Shall we have the games begin?" asked the Duke.

"Yes!" the room shouted back in unison.

The Duke was the first to walk out of the balcony doors, while all the guests followed after him.

* * *

BY THE TIME Sarah got outside, the huge group of enthusiastic guests had gathered in a circle around the Duke and the illustrious rooster. The Vasfale stone had already been placed around the poor long-horned rooster's neck while in the clutches of the Duke.

Sarah thought that the chase would not take long because the grounds outside consisted of the garden that was lined with a stone wall covered in ivy and the waterfall. Though the land was large enough, surely, the beast wouldn't stray outside of that area.

"Let the games begin!" shouted the Duke and threw the long-horned rooster into the air.

The bird flapped back down and once he hit the ground, he took off at a fast pace. Chaos ensued as the guests ran this way and that. Lords and Ladies alike fell flat on their faces as they jumped and lunged for the feathery unicorn.

Slowly, the group of people moved away from the entrance out to the garden as they took chase. Sheer amusement filled Sarah to the brim as she watched such buffoonery. Once she realized she stood alone, Sarah took time to survey the grounds.

As her eyes glided across the landscape, they came to an abrupt halt when they landed on the General, who stood a couple steps in front of her at the railing of the balcony. Knots tied tightly in her stomach as she observed him stand stoic-like, and watched the chase in the garden below.

Step by step, Sarah's feet carried her closer to him. Upon her approach, the General's head turned to look at her. A sheepish grin pressed into her lips as if she were caught doing a bad deed.

"Are you not going to chase the unicorn?" she asked.

The General looked back down at the group in the distance without an answer. Sarah moved next to him to join in the splendor.

"Friends!" shouted the Duke and staggered up the staircase towards the two of them.

"Why are you not taking chase? Does the unicorn's dowry not please you?"

"I know the complexities of chasing a scared animal, Sire. Nothing could make me willingly run after a bird that is as fast as lightning without starvation being present," admitted Sarah.

"Fascinating," hummed the Duke with his charming smile, and then he took a swig of ale. "You come from the Southlands."

"Ditrum, Sire," reminded Sarah, not sure he could retain the information.

"Good farmland, if I recall correctly," stated the Duke, proud of himself.

"Indeed. Some of the best in the land, if I may say so," agreed Sarah.

"I must admit," started the Duke as he swooped his arm around Sarah's waist and pulled her close to him. "There is something very attractive about a noble country girl that knows how to work the land."

Sarah's eyes narrowed as she realized he was trying to swoon her. Looking over the Duke's shoulder, she could see the General just stand there. She wanted him so very much to come and protect her, but knew that this was why she was at the castle in the first place. She was meant for the Duke.

The Duke tried to pull Sarah into a kiss despite her unwillingness to accept it.

"I do not know how you can claim that Ditrum has the best farm country when you personally saw the great farmland of Somar," grumbled the General.

The Duke stopped in his pursuit of Sarah and looked over at the General, mildly disappointed.

"Pride in one's crops is nothing to mock, General. To Lady Levine, her crops are the best in all the land."

The General sneered. Sarah couldn't follow where his cruelness came from.

"Her opinions are commonly ill-informed."

At this, the Duke released Sarah's frame and turned his full attention to the General.

"Why are you being so hard on Lady Levine, Gregor?" asked the Duke before he finished off his drink.

"Truth is not always kind, your majesty."

The Duke paused for a moment while he appeared to mull over the General's words. Then, two young ladies filled with giggles, stumbled into the garden just below the balcony.

"My Lord! We were hoping you might come join us in the garden for our own little chase?" they wooed the Duke.

The Duke's ears perked up and he was filled with eagerness.

"Well, duty calls," he replied.

Then, he glanced over at the General, who still stood resigned and looked down unimpressed at the girls below. The Duke put his hand on the General's shoulder.

"General, take it easy on Lady Levine. She may turn out to be my Duchess someday soon."

The General dropped his head just enough to show he understood before the Duke ran down the stairs. He joined the girls; quickly sliding his arms around each one's waist, and the three moved into the maze of bushes.

Sarah found herself alone with the General once more. She stepped next to him and enjoyed the quiet between them. Unfortunately, his cruel words he had just spoke to the Duke pushed through the silence and remained fresh in Sarah's mind.

"Why must you mock me so in front of the Duke, of all people? Did I, in some way, offend you?"

"Yes," replied the General shortly.

"By what exactly?"

"By the way you are. By who you are. The way you carry yourself into a room as if there is no one else good enough to stand next to you. Not even the Duke."

"That is *absurd!*"

"Is it? When all eyes were on you last night for 'your' dance, did you not think it strange that no one would dance with you?"

"No one knows that dance. They were probably not wanting to make fools of themselves."

"No one knows it?" repeated the General in a knowing tone.

"You clearly did! Is that why you came out to dance with me?"

"I pitied you. You looked like a poor child begging for food. A moment longer and you probably would have started crying."

The sting of the General's harsh words cut Sarah deeper than she could have expected. How could this man who saved her life on many occasions say all these hurtful things?

"Maddi was right – you are a miserable man. You cannot get past your own 'duty' and see what is standing right in front of you. I am only sorry I have wasted time thinking about you."

The General turned and took a strong step towards Sarah. As he towered over her, she felt sure that he meant to intimidate her, but she was so full of rage from his cross words; she didn't care what he did.

"Careful," growled the General.

"Or what? What will you do?" Sarah snapped back.

The General's eyes probed every inch of Sarah's face. She could tell that he thought very strongly about what would come next. There was an unexplainable longing that flew into his eyes as they drifted to to look at her.

Sarah could feel her whole body tremble as she took a deep breath in and exhaled it. Not sure what possessed her, she slid her hand up to his cheek. She could feel the General start to lean a little closer to her as if she drew him in. Her eyes slid closed as she desperately wanted to feel his lips caress hers again.

The warmth of his breath brushed over her nose and cheek.

Suddenly, she felt the General shake her hand free from his face and pull away. When her eyes opened again, the General had already turned and moved down the steps to the garden. Every step he took was heavy and they weighed heavily on her.

"Am I no longer your worthy opponent?" shouted Sarah after him.

The General slowed his pace, and then held out his arm to her.

"We must join the chase or the Duke will ask questions."

Sarah knew what the General meant by that. As if a loyal soldier in the General's army, she practically marched down the stairs and took his arm as she was ordered to do.

As they moved through the garden in search of the long-horned rooster, Sarah tried her best to keep up with the giant strides of the General. It was unnatural to move next to his large frame but as uncomfortable as she was, she still preferred being with the General than anyone else she knew.

CHAPTER 28

SURPRISE SURPRISE

The sheer size of the General's steps made it difficult for Sarah to hang onto his arm. Feeling as though she were being dragged down the path, Sarah finally let go of him.

The General took a couple steps more before he came to a halt. Sarah noticed his head drop but couldn't see his face well enough to read his expression.

Certain that he became more pained the longer she was with him, she said, "I believe I can find my own way to the chase."

"I am fully aware of your capabilities."

"Then you know I am capable of making up a story that will free you from any kind of obligation you might feel you have to escort me," Sarah pointed out.

The General's chin slid to his shoulder just far enough so that Sarah could catch his condemnation of her suggestion. When the General didn't move, Sarah knew he felt it was his 'duty' to escort her. In which case, he would wait there for her all day.

"You have more important things to do than be here," said Sarah.

The General stared at her blankly.

"Have a good day, General," she said curtly, and then stepped past him as she moved farther into the garden.

But the instant she brushed past the enormous figure, his firm grip clutched her forearm.

"You presume too much, Lady Levine," said the General.

"It is difficult to tell what you want from me, General. It is easier to assume that you would prefer to be with your men than with me," said Sarah in defeat. "And when you do speak to me, it is with such harshness that I am left without words."

"Perhaps I spoke with such severity just now, not to hurt you but to help you."

"Help me?"

"You looked uncomfortable when the Duke pulled you close to him. Many girls would have been overjoyed, but not you."

"So you insulted me? What help did that bring?"

"He let you go, did he not?" pointed out the General.

Sarah took a moment of pause to reflect on his insults since she arrived at the castle.

"Maybe if I had walked away from you back in Lankenshire, it would have been easier for you," admitted Sarah.

The General looked at her with such longing that even she couldn't mistake his feelings.

"Would you have allowed Jack to take me with him that last night we camped in the woods?" asked Sarah sincerely.

"No more than I would be alright if the Duke chooses you for his bride."

A perfect storm of relief and nervousness shot through Sarah's body. She didn't fully comprehend that the General just said the words she had longed to hear the whole journey. But those words did cause her lower lip to quiver.

"Are you saying..." Sarah stammered.

"I am saying that I have seen happiness ripped away from people who deserve it and given to those who do not."

"You believe I deserve happiness? That might be the kindest thing you have ever said to me."

Sarah moved close to the General once more, and tried with every ounce of strength she had to pull him in to her.

"I know what you wish, but I cannot give it to you, Lady Levine," argued the General.

"Do you care for me? There are times when you look at me and I believe you do. You wish me to be happy."

"I do wish that for you," he agreed.

"Then why will you not give me the one thing that I wish for more than anything else?"

The General placed his large, callused hand over her tiny one.

"Because it is not mine to give."

"Always duty bound," muttered Sarah.

A speedy flutter broke between the two of them as the long-horned rooster, who still carried the stone, sprinted by.

Sarah's eyes fixed on the unsuspecting bird as she hunched down in a cat-like stance, ready to pounce.

"Careful. He is faster than you, and is smarter than the average rooster," advised the General.

Sarah didn't flinch at the comment, but instead crept closer to the colorful bird. Just like a flash of lightning, the rooster took off in a hurry through the back wall of the garden. Sarah was quick to chase after it.

"I thought you were not interested in the unicorn chase," yelled the General.

Sarah veered away from the rooster and shot into the woods that lay just beyond the garden walls. She made her way a few rows of trees deep, and kept the bird in sight. As quietly as possible, she snuck along parallel with it until finally the bird slowed his pace.

Crouching low to the ground, just behind a tree, Sarah could hear the rooster move closer to where she hid. Every muscle in her body tensed as she tried to control her breathing.

The rustle of leaves kicked up as the rooster took a few steps farther into the woods.

More leaves crunched but this time the steps were heavier. A perplexed look crossed Sarah's face. She tried to refocus on the lighter steps that worked their way towards her, but a sound rung out that completely threw off her intended attack.

A gentle, low note hummed a soothing tune.

More leaves rustled that caused Sarah to lunge around the tree before she was prepared.

"Umf," she grunted as she landed hard onto the empty ground where the long-horned rooster had just stood.

When she looked up, Sarah shook her head in disbelief, for the long-horned rooster rested comfortably in the arms of the General. While the General stroked the bird's chest, he hummed the notes of a calm tune.

"You sing?" asked Sarah as she pulled herself up to her feet and brushed her dress clean of the forest floor debris.

The General rubbed his nose humbly into the rooster, and nuzzled it for a moment, and then said, "I am not supposed to tell anyone that there is only one way to catch a long-horned rooster and that is to sing to it."

Sarah was impressed with him on many levels. Moving next to the General, she stretched out her hands to stroke the bird's chest, but not before her finger was nicked by the bird's beak. A stream of blood trickled down her finger.

"Ouch," hissed Sarah and tried to shake out the pain.

"Not exactly friendly with people," said the General before he released the bird back onto the ground. The rooster promptly took off again.

"Makes him far more difficult to catch," finished the General.

Sarah placed her finger between her lips, and tried to calm the pain when the General pulled her hand from her lips and brought her finger close to his. A warm breath of air blew across the tip of her stinging finger.

In a matter of seconds the pain subsided.

"How did you do that?"

"I brought the long-horned rooster here from my homeland, remember?" said the General. "Do you think that this is the first time I have dealt with a pinched finger?"

"After meeting the Duke, I suppose he has been pecked a couple of times."

The rooster could be heard as it took off through the woods. By the time Sarah turned, the rooster was gone.

"Sad to think that bird lives such a lonely life," said Sarah.

"You might be surprised to learn that he has a mate. A goose that is as spectacular as he... and just as difficult, I might add."

Sarah giggled light-heartedly at the thought, when she felt a flash bolt throughout her body. When she brushed her hand across her forehead, it was drenched in sweat. The world around her began to spin and blur into unrecognizable shapes. Lightheaded, she staggered a couple steps backwards when the General caught her.

"Sarah," said the General with concern.

"What is happening to me?"

All of a sudden, her head felt heavy and her body no longer cooperated. Tingling rushed down her arms and into her fingertips. It even went all the way down into her toes.

"Sarah!" the General said louder, but it was drowned out by a high-pitched squeal that rang in her ears.

The world in front of her washed away into a haze. She started to wheeze. She could feel him pick her up and start move with her in his arms.

"Sarah, stay with me," said the General as he tried to remain calm.

The blur in her vision spun around and around until finally everything went to dark.

CHAPTER 29

NIGHTMARES

The dizziness continued on into the darkness. Sarah felt the ability to move her arms drain away. Her knees began to wobble until she completely lost her balance. She collapsed into the darkness and fell hard do on the cold earth.

"What is happening to me?" Sarah muttered as her voice dissipated into the emptiness.

"Sarah?" whispered softly behind her.

Sarah couldn't move to see who said her name, but she could hear a rustle through what she thought were leaves.

"Sarah?" whispered again.

Who could possibly be here? she thought to herself.

A pair of gray eyes appeared right in front of her. They stood out as clearly as the moon in a cloudless night sky. Slowly, the eyes were accompanied by a nose and lips until the recognizable face of Jack was composed in its entirety.

He scooped Sarah into his arms and rocked her motionless body back and forth as he tried to comfort her.

"Are you hurt?" he asked as he looked her over, but then began to rock her again.

Sarah tried to open her mouth to speak, but she couldn't move. She was at his mercy.

Jack looked around in the darkness suspiciously. His head shot in every direction as if he waited for something, or perhaps someone.

"I am sorry about all this, Sari... this is all my fault."

Before she knew what was going on, Jack slid something small into her hand. Though she could not see it, she could feel that at least one side of it was smooth.

"I know you are not well, but you cannot stay in the castle longer. It is not safe."

Looking past Jack's panicked face, small pieces of the forest took shape in her view. The red leaves of the Tanter trees from just outside her house started to etch their way into Sarah's sight.

"You must go. As soon as you wake!" said Jack emphatically.

A familiar howl cried out behind them. The noise was so intense that adrenaline coursed through her body and allowed her to move a little. With great effort, Sarah tried to muffle the wolf's cries as she placed her hands over her ears, but it was now permanently clasped around the object Jack had just placed in it.

"Ahh!" Sarah screamed at the top of her lungs as she crumpled into a ball of aggravated pain. She could feel Jack wrap his arms around her. He held her so tightly with his uncommonly strong grip.

"I am sorry, Sari. I tried. I tried," Jack whispered into her ear.

Just then, a large muscular hand reached around Jack's neck and ripped him backwards into the darkness.

"Sarah!" he choked out.

The howl grew louder and louder. All Sarah could do to release her fears was to scream at the top of her lungs.

"Jaaaaaack!"

The reds and yellows from the Tanter trees blended together and spun like a pinwheel, around and around. Tears poured uncontrollably from Sarah's eyes. She cared nothing for respect or dignity at that moment. She just wanted to be in control of her body and have some understanding of what was happening.

She felt hot and her whole body was covered in sweat. Her eyes felt too heavy to keep open and her body too weak to stand on its own.

"Jaaaaaaack!" she attempted to scream but it faded away into nothing.

Just then a burst of cold air smacked her across the face from seemingly nowhere. She used all the energy that remained to force her eyes open one more time.

Her view was fuzzy at first. A large figure sat next to her bed in a chair and dabbed a cold washcloth to her cheeks. Unable to make out the General's face clearly, but she still knew it was him because of his large frame.

Right behind him was the doctor and Eshe.

Sarah knew she would not be conscious for long. Heaviness and exhaustion held too firm to her body to allow her to remain awake.

"Jack," she whispered the warning. "Jack."

The General's face shift at the sound of her friend's name. As much as she wished her lips would form other words, Jack was the only thing she could say.

The General rose from his chair to allow the doctor to move closer to his patient. From what little Sarah could make out, the portly doctor examined her while the General handed the damp cloth to Eshe.

"I must go," he mummbled, and then promptly made his way out to the hall.

The door closed behind him and shifted the air through the room. Sarah felt it would be better to go back to the dream world than to stay in this harsh reality much longer.

No struggle came when she gave way to the heaviness that now overtook her.

As she fell back into the darkness again, this time it was a smaller hand that reached from the shadows. An old, weathered hand pulled Sarah gently forward.

At the very touch, she felt the pain and tension leave her body. All of a sudden, she felt light and airy. Her hand was still clasped shut around the object Jack gave her, but it no longer created panic within her.

Only one explanation could be given in that moment.

"Old Madge," said Sarah.

The head of gray hair formed in front of her that eventually attached to the arm that walked her forward.

"Where are we going?"

The set of gray eyes turned to look at her.

"A cup of tea."

"Tea?"

The old woman grinned and nodded her head excitedly.

"A lot can be explained over a good cup of tea."

Sarah felt it best not to argue with a woman that didn't seem altogether there.

Just as it had been before, Old Madge came to a halt next to a fallen tree. The vines came from every which direction to create the cottage. As they entered, Sarah noticed the same parts of the front wall were still missing and she no longer felt it was a mistake.

It looked very much like it had the first time Sarah saw it. Though, there was a bit more clarity to the room. She noticed the bookshelf in the corner that was covered with bottles filled with a few more heres and theres, along with several books.

"Why am I here, Old Madge?" asked Sarah as she sat down at the little kitchen table.

The old woman slid a cup of tea across the table to Sarah, and then poured herself one too.

"I know this journey has turned into more than you bargained for," stated the old woman.

Sarah found her head bobbed up and down in agreement.

"You have a case of love and a decision before you, my dear."

"What do you mean?" asked Sarah, genuinely confused.

"You started with a fox but fell in love with an ox," said the old woman as she cackled.

"What?" muttered Sarah.

"Though he is strong indeed, will his love be enough to succeed?

Past the war and the flame, the duty and the shame? Can he drop down his wall? Will he heed your call?"

"What lunacy is this?"

"I believe he would travel the world below and above, just to hear one word of your love," finished Old Madge, and then took a sip of her tea with humor and deviousness in her eyes.

"It cannot be true."

"Why not?"

"The General is too duty bound to care for things like love. Affection, maybe, but not love. Someone quite close to him confirmed it for me on my trip to Vasfale."

"Maddi was wrong."

Sarah leaned away from Old Madge, mouth open in shock.

"How do you know her name?"

Again a light-hearted giggle shook the old woman's body as she slowly rose from the table and moved towards the bookshelf.

"I know you think me crazy, Sarah Levine."

The two gray eyes looked over her shoulder to catch Sarah's astonished reaction. Sarah's mouth still hung slightly ajar while her eyes followed the old woman's fingers as they reached out for a small book.

"But I assure you, I know more about your travels than you do."

Old Madge struggled to pull a small, dark book from the shelf. It looked as though the book was resistant to come.

"Come here, dagnabit!"

The book released itself from the shelf and smacked Old Madge in the face. She cleared her throat and collected herself.

She hugged it tight to her chest and uttered a few words under her breath. A deep sigh exhaled from her mouth before she turned with a sincere smile and came back to her seat.

Putting the book down on the table, she looked it over one last time before she pushed it over to Sarah.

"What is this?" asked Sarah, confused.

"This is a story that will help you understand your own better, but it will only be opened to you at the right time."

Sarah's face twisted with more confusion.

"Gregor loves you, Sarah. There are no two ways about it."

This was not the first time this notion had been suggested, but for some reason it hit harder when it came from Old Madge.

"He hardly ever shows emotion. I do not know how you could possibly tell," said Sarah.

"Because he is coming right now to ask for my help. When you know our history better, it will help you understand how much you mean to him," replied the old woman.

Sarah's head dropped. Was this just a dream of everything she longed to hear? Or was this more? There was no way to tell at this time.

Sarah could feel Old Madge's hands land gently on top of hers. When she looked up, she was taken with the fact that Old Madge looked like a proud parent as she watched her child grow up before her very eyes. A moment passed between the two.

"I know this is a lot to take in right now, but you have a much more pressing issue."

"What is it?"

The old woman's lips skewed to one side of her face while she looked for the right words.

"Jack," Old Madge finally said.

"What about him?"

"He is bringing trouble to the gates of Vasfale. He will be alluring and strong. You must not give into him, however much you want to. Be careful that you do not reveal too much to him. I will try to protect you as best I can, but at the end of it all, it is up to you to make that choice," said Old Madge.

"What could I possibly…"

The old woman looked down at Sarah's waist.

"The beans?" Sarah whispered.

Old Madge nodded her head.

"I never said anything to him about them."

"I know you didn't, but that doesn't mean he doesn't know about them," responded Old Madge.

"But-"

"He knows" the old woman cut her off.

This was the first thing that the Old Madge said that Sarah could see apprehension.

"Do not worry, they are with me always," confirmed Sarah and patted the hidden pocket on her dress. When her hand hit the fabric, it didn't collide with the small bottle as she anticipated. Instead, it hit her skin.

Sarah looked down at her dress in panic.

"Where are they?" she shrieked.

"Take this book. Drink your tea, and when you wake, find them. They are very dangerous in another person's possession. Especially because they were meant for you."

"What is their intent? You never explained what they do," said Sarah.

"You will find out when you truly wish to know."

"Why can you not just tell me?"

Old Madge's eyes darted back and forth between Sarah's.

"I..." the old woman started. "I cannot. Even if I wished to! That's not how this game is played. Just find them."

Sarah nodded her head confidently and she knew what she had to do after she wakes. She swiped the book up in her hands and chugged down the tea as quick as she could.

At first she felt nothing. Then a warm happy feeling started in her lips and worked across her cheeks, through her chest, and eventually throughout her entire body.

Laughter burst from her lips as she felt light as a cloud. She laughed harder and harder until her eyes watered from laughing so hard. She tried to wipe them away, but then she laughed even harder.

The hazy image of Old Madge washed away behind the laughter. The light in the room grew brighter and brighter until it melted into the early evening sunlight that came through her window at the castle.

CHAPTER 30

THE GENERAL'S ABSENCE

Sarah sat up straight in her bed and gasped hard for air. She placed her hands on her aching ribs because her body had been tricked into laughing too hard. They certainly felt bruised.

"Calm yourself," said Eshe in her soothing voice.

Sarah looked frantically around for Old Madge, or even Jack.

"Jack!" she whispered to herself, and then looked at Eshe. "What happened?"

"You fell ill during the unicorn chase. The General carried you here, screaming for the doctor," explained Eshe.

Identifying the bedchamber started to bring some comfort to Sarah after her series of nightmares.

Eshe took a wet cloth from a bowl that sat on the bedside table and wrung it out before she placed it onto Sarah's forehead.

"I would like to send for the doctor. The Duke, too, wished to know when you woke."

The pounding in Sarah's head made her wonder if she should see anyone, but she was happy to be away from the nightmares that haunted her the last several nights.

Sarah gave Eshe consent to summon whomever wished to see her.

The handmaiden rose and moved towards the door. Just before

she opened it, Sarah said, "Eshe, the General too. I would like to see him as soon as possible."

A distressed look crossed Eshe's face and her lips curled under her teeth.

"Wha... What is it?" Sarah stammered and sat up anxiously. "Is he alright?"

Eshe put her hands up to calm Sarah.

"He is fine, it is just the General is not here, My Lady."

"Where is he?" inquired Sarah.

"I cannot be sure. After you fell ill, the General sat next to you all day and long into the night. Then..."

"And then?"

"You woke up in hysterics. Screaming for 'Jack'? Well, the General rose without saying a word and left in great haste."

Adrenaline coursed through every fiber of Sarah's being. In the blurry visions that she could remember, she tried to send a warning of Jack's presence. Instead, she feared that the General misinterpreted the warning and only heard her friend's name.

"Eshe, I need to know... where has he gone?" Sarah asked as she took the cloth from her forehead.

"He left the castle. I am not sure to where," said Eshe before she dismissed herself to the hall.

"Jack," growled Sarah. She hadn't realized that at the very mention of his name she had twisted the cloth in her hands into a ball. "How could my dearest friend do this to me?"

She threw the cloth into the bowl on her night table which splashed water everywhere.

Jack had always been a good friend who always looked after her in her darkest of moments. His heart, she felt, was in the right place. Still, he never knew where to draw the line. He always erred on the side of recklessness.

Sarah scooped up one of the dry towels and sopped up the puddle of water that had spilled. As she wiped across the table, her cloth landed on something quite unexpected.

Slowly, she picked up the green ribbon and allowed the small jewel that had been draped around the long-horned rooster's neck to dangle from her fingers.

"Oh, no."

Just then a light knock tapped on the door.

"Who is it?" asked Sarah as she clenched the jewel tightly in her hand.

"Anton Lowe."

"Captain!"

She curled the trinket into her hand under the covers. Leaning backwards, she rested comfortably against the headboard while the Captain entered the room. He removed his hat and slowly moved to the empty seat next to the bed.

"You are a sight for sore eyes," confessed Sarah.

"Am I? I was worried after the last time we spoke; I thought for sure you may never speak with me again. I was only here to make sure that you were feeling better," he said.

"I am feeling better, thank you. I wish the Duke had not known about the dance in Lankenshire, but that should all be water under the bridge now."

The Captain folded his hands neatly in his lap and leaned back in the seat.

"May I be frank with you?" said the Captain.

"Please."

"I will not deny that you have been a breath of fresh air for the General. Even the men think so. I only expressed my concerns the other night because I can see now how difficult this is for him."

Sarah raised her brow at his remark.

"He is stepping out of his element and that puts attention on him. Attention he does not want. Dangerous, even."

"Because he danced with me?"

"Because he *chose* to dance with you."

"No one else in the room knew the dance and the Duke wanted to see it," argued Sarah.

"The Duke noticed the General was the one to take the offer. This time it was humorous to him, but that may not always be the case."

Sarah threw her hands up in the air to stop him from speaking.

"Maybe none of that would have happened had the Duke not known about the Conti Rose in the first place. Ever think of that?"

"I know I said this the other night, but if you truly care about him, it would be best just to turn your attention to the Duke. At least until he picks his Duchess."

"What if he chooses me?" asked Sarah, deflated.

The Captain looked down and seemed unsure how to answer.

The moments of when the Captain appeared to tell her to stay away from the General flickered through her mind. She squeezed the jewel tightly in her hand.

"I take your counsel to heart, and I will do my best. That is all I can offer."

"Fair enough," settled the Captain.

"Can I at least ask where the General went?"

"I cannot say."

Sarah licked her dry lips and exhaled a deep sigh.

"Captain, I am afraid he will be in danger. Jack has been-"

"Jack! Yes, you said his name many times while you slept," said the Captain, cutting her off.

"I know. He has been in many of my dreams."

The Captain looked deviously at her as though there were some romantic attachments there.

"Honestly, after all the time we spent together on our journey, you think I have feelings for Jack? First the General, and now Jack."

"Well, Lady Levine, I do not like to point things out when you are in an ill state."

"But you are going to anyway," snapped Sarah.

"He is your friend."

"I know."

"You did try to run away with him."

"Only on the first night!"

"He tried to sneak into our camp and take you again," pointed out the Captain.

"And yet, I told him I was going to stay."

The Captain's eyes thinned and he studied Sarah closely. Sarah leaned forward and placed a reassuring hand on the Captain's shoulder.

"I cannot be with Jack. My heart will never belong to him."

"Then why did you keep saying his name while you slept?" he asked as if he caught her in a lie.

"He was in my dream, but he was up to something... something dangerous," said Sarah as she became lost in her thoughts.

"It was just a bad dream," said the Captain as he tried to comfort her.

"That is where you are mistaken, Captain. I cannot explain it all to you now, but I must warn the General."

"He is gone."

"Then the Duke! Am I allowed to speak with him?"

"He is quite busy with this week's festivities."

Sarah rose quickly from her bed and threw a robe around her.

"The beans," whispered an old voice.

Panic struck Sarah as she quickly ran to her bags in the closet. She threw all the contents on the floor and rummaged through them until she found her petticoat. She wiped her hand over the material, she found the pocket was empty.

"What are you looking for?" asked the Captain.

Sarah didn't even hear his question. She was too lost in the idea that her beans were gone and mostlikmly in the possession of Jack. Were they magic? If so, then what did him having them really mean for her?

Her eyes fell on the book Old Madge had given her in her last dream. She picked it up and tried in vain to open it.

"What are you looking for?" repeated the Captain.

Sarah gave up her attempt as she stepped out of the closet and looked out her window at the night sky. "What time is it?"

"Well after eight in the evening. Many of the guests have retired for the evening. That is why I thought I could slip away unnoticed to check on you before I turn in."

"Then the Duke should still be awake. And if I am feeling better, which I am, then I would think the Duke would be most anxious to hear about it," suggested Sarah.

"I am glad to see you have retained your stubbornness," the Captain joked.

"Please, Captain," pleaded Sarah. "I must let him know that something is about to happen."

The Captain looked unsure of Sarah's plan, but then opened the door.

"Well, I suppose you know your friend better than any of us. You would know what he is capable of."

"I am sorry to say I do," said Sarah, just before she hurried out of the door and pulled the Captain along with her.

CHAPTER 31

BAG OF GOLD

*D*espite the fact that Sarah needed the Captain to tell her where to go, she still dragged him from hallway to hallway. Every time she got to the end of one hall or a stairway, the Captain would point a direction and Sarah would quickly follow.

She noticed a moment where the Captain looked a little faint, but his enthusiasm eventually returned.

"Where are we going again?" he asked.

"The Duke," replied Sarah.

"Ah, yes," said the Captain as he snapped his fingers and marched down another hall.

"Where might the Duke be at this hour?" asked Sarah and looked cautiously down the empty corridor before she followed after him.

"I would think his study, which is just down the next hall," replied the Captain.

Sarah quickened her step so much that she moved a couple paces past the entrance way to the Duke's study.

The Captain grabbed a hold of Sarah's arm to encourage her to stop.

"I know you are quite interested to get to the Duke in a timely fashion but you are going too fast for your own good." whispered the Captain.

Sarah looked around, slightly annoyed with the Captain for being a hindrance. The Captain leaned his back against the wall and looked a little weary.

"Well then, point out the door and I will continue by myself."

The Captain gestured over his shoulder to the doorway behind him. Sarah's whole body slouched as she rolled her eyes, disappointed in herself for missing it.

As she passed the Captain, she patted him on the shoulder as a thank you, and then stepped into the entrance that led to the Duke's study. Even the little hallway was impressive. The ceiling looked like a marble stone archway found in a church. Intricate patterns of loops and swirls were carved into the stone that created the appearance of gusting clouds. On the edges were one or two trees carved into the wall with branches that crawled across the marble.

The image of the vines at Old Madge's cottage popped into her mind. A beast of sorts was carved into one side and on the other was a beautiful girl.

Sarah was so captured by the artistry that she almost forgot why she was even there. She shook her head when she woke from the momentary trance and turned to look into the study.

What her eyes landed on first caught her off guard and she jumped back out into the main hall.

"What is it?" asked the Captain. "Is the Duke not there?"

Sarah didn't respond. Instead, she peeked around the corner again, and then turned back around to face the Captain.

"I thought the General had left Vasfale?"

"He did. He left last night."

"Well it appears that he is in with the Duke," Sarah blurted out.

"Are you sure?" asked the Captain, not fully believing her.

He didn't wait for the answer before he brushed past Sarah and glanced into the room to see for himself. He turned as quickly as Sarah had.

"That is strange indeed. He mentioned he had a two-day journey before him."

"Where was he going?" pleaded Sarah.

"I cannot say."

Sarah crossed her arms and tapped her toe to demand an answer.

"Captain?" she growled as she lost her patience. "What does it matter if he is here?"

"I cannot," said the Captain more firmly.

"I wish I could hear what they are talking about. It looks as though they are in a deep conversation," said Sarah.

The Captain's eyes grew enthusiastically and his scheming smile made its way to his lips.

"That, I can help you with."

The Captain grabbed Sarah's arm and tugged her down the hallway, and turned the corner. At the end of the next hall was a staircase that the Captain flew up with Sarah close behind.

Once they were on the next floor, they moved quickly down the hall until they stood before the doorway which lead into the room that mirrored where the study was a floor below.

"What is this?" asked Sarah.

"It is our guests, Sir Anthony and Lady Valerie's, bedchambers for the week."

"Will they not be in there?"

"Luckily, they like to go swimming in the falls every night. It created quite a stir the night before last. Still, they do it every night, like some ritual."

Sarah's humored expression said it all. The Captain looked both ways down the hall before he pushed the door open. He grabbed a candle from one of the holders on the wall and the two snuck into the room.

"How does being here help us?"

The Captain walked to the far side of the room and stepped on many of the floorboards until one of them squeaked. He hastily fell to the floor and pulled back the rug.

"Some time ago, I will not say when, the General and I were up here surveying some things."

"Surveying some things?"

"Yes, we will call it that. Anyway, we got a little unruly and well, I burned a little hole in the floor. We decided since it is hidden to the Duke's view and muffled by the rug, we felt it best that nothing be said."

"Hm. That does not sound like the General," remarked Sarah.

"You know, he is duty bound to his men and all of that."

Sarah wanted to roll her eyes, but she knew the Captain was right.

"Very well. So, how does this help us?" she asked.

"You can see into the Duke's study from that hole we created. You might not be able to see the people in there, but you can see a little corner of the desk. You can also put your ear to the floor to listen."

Sarah was so overjoyed with the notion, she clasped the Captain's face and kissed him on the cheek.

"Oh Lady Levine. I appreciate the gesture, but I am spoken for," said the Captain, flattered. Sarah just continued to glow.

The Captain pointed to the small spot on the floor. Sarah moved over and knelt down. She had to run her hand along the wooden floorboard before she located a small knot in the wood.

At first, she looked through, but when she couldn't see anything, she placed her ear on the floor instead.

"You have been on quite a journey from the sounds of it," said the Duke.

"Indeed," retorted the General.

"You realize some of these 'fair maidens' would have never made it here safely if it were not for your protection. Many would have gotten lost, and for others it was just too treacherous."

"I agree," stated the General.

"Lady Levine, for instance, seemed quite worn out from your trip. She could not even bear a moment of humor when she got to the gate," pointed out the Duke.

Sarah covered her mouth and tried to hold back the scoff that pressed against her lips.

"Honestly, Sire, I do not even think you should have brought her here. There are far more worthy ladies that are far more suitable."

"Really?" replied the Duke.

"Really?" repeated Sarah under her breath, annoyed.

"Really. The journey was long and you have seen her. She comes from a different culture. Hard to believe she is from the same land as you with the way she speaks at times."

Sarah felt her heart skip a couple beats. Every word that came out of the General's mouth hit her hard, over and over again. It was as though the moments they shared together never happened and she alone held onto hope that a relationship with this heartless giant was possible.Though, she also now knew that he had a tendency to say harsh words about her to protect her.

"I think you are being unfair, Gregor. Lady Levine seems very grounded in her character. I never have to wonder if she is telling me the truth or not," stated the Duke.

"Of course," agreed Gregor.

"Most people I meet are too afraid to talk to me. And when they do, they tell me only what they think I wish to hear."

"You are the Duke."

"Lady Levine is mysterious and intriguing. I would like to know more about her," admitted the Duke with a swoon in his tone.

A moment of silence fell between the two men before the Duke continued.

"What do you think?" nudged the Duke.

"I am not sure why you are asking me. You sound like you have already made up your mind about her."

"What do you think?" demanded the Duke.

"I think you should be happy," stated the General.

"That is your answer?"

"I fight wars for you, Sire. Once you turn to matters of matchmaking, I would defer to others for advice, such as Captain Lowe."

"Maybe I will ask him then."

A long pause ensued, then came a sound of a drawer as it pulled out from the desk and something was shuffled around.

A second later, Sarah heard a loud clank. When she pulled away and looked through the peep hole, all she could see was a small velvet bag, filled to the brim with gold coins, that sat on the corner of the desk.

"What is this?" asked the General.

"For your troubles. For bringing Lady Levine to me."

"It was an honor and my duty," stated the General.

"And you succeeded admirably. Please, allow me to show you my appreciation."

All Sarah could see was the back of the General's head as he stepped closer to the desk and looked down at the bag.

"This appears to be more than the agreed to amount," said the General.

"Double," replied the Duke.

After a couple seconds, the General swiped the bag up into his huge hand.

Sarah could take no more. Enraged by the feeling like she was nothing more than bought property with no soul or emotions, she flipped the rug back into place.

"Are they finished?" inquired the Captain. "You did not listen very long."

"I heard enough," she barked.

Sarah gritted her teeth and clenched her fists. She knew that she didn't fit in here. That this land was far from her home and yes, the culture was different. Maybe she was a little headstrong, but this country girl had to keep her wits about her.

She brushed past the Captain and out the door.

"That good, huh?" she heard the Captain call after her.

She couldn't even stop to thank him for his time. Too angry. Too blinded by emotions she stomped down the hall.

Her stride quickened until she ran. Tears fell uncontrollably as she moved down the maze of hallways.

Finally, she turned into the grand hall. As she made her way to the far side of the room, she was able to find the door the Duke used to lead the guests out to the gardens of for the unicorn chase.

Sarah made her way out of the door, down to the stair by the balcony where she stood with the General, and just ran until she had no energy left.

CHAPTER 32

MAGICAL MEMORIES

*T*he night air felt chilled against Sarah's skin, but she ran anyway. She ran through the garden, down the wide corridor of trees which were being decorated for the ball. She continued past the main water fountain as it bubbled, and darted out of the western archway that led to the falls.

The moon captured the water as it cascaded down in such a way that it could be seen when it bounced off of every rock and landed in the pool below.

As she slowed on her approach, Sarah gulped for air while she felt her heart race quickly within her chest.

The terrain down to the bank was covered in mismatched boulders and cobblestones. Removing her shoes, she slid her feet across the cold stones. More gracefully than she could imagine, Sarah moved from boulder to pebbles until she reached the bank of the water at the base of the falls.

Sarah dipped her hand into the water covered with the shimmering moon light, but the water was too frigid to keep her hand there for too long. Instead, she leaned against a boulder that was twice her size.

There was no energy left to cry or to even be angry. So, she sat and looked out at the water as it flowed over the cliff like a paintbrush across a canvas and came to rest in the masterpiece below.

The sound of laughter trickled through the air. At first, Sarah thought it was Lord Anthony and his wife who had made such a stir over the last week. But as the laughter continued, she could tell that the voices were far more youthful and free of life's worries.

Looking down the rocky bank, Sarah clapped eyes on a boy at the age of around twelve with blond unkempt hair and pale blue-green eyes. He giggled continuously while he poked the water with a long stick. Right next to him was a little girl with darker hair that blended in with the shadows of the night.

"What are you doing?" huffed the girl.

"I am practicing slaying the dragon who lives here," said the little boy, proudly.

"You are?" replied the little girl, impressed.

When the boy nodded, his golden hair flew uncaringly in every direction. He then picked up a rock and tossed it into the pond. It skipped once before it clumped down into the water.

He tried to skip another stone, but it only bounced once on the water before it fell to the depths below.

"Are you trying to make the dragon angry?" asked the little girl, curiously.

"No, I am trying to summon him to fight me."

"You will never get his attention like that. Try this," suggested the girl, and skimmed a rock across the water that skipped five times before it glided under the water seamlessly.

The boy crossed his arms and appeared to be angry at being bested by the young girl. When the girl turned to see his sour expression, she moved closer to him and grabbed a hold of his arm.

"Come on, Jack. Do not be a grumble-sprout."

"Mmm," moaned the boy.

The girl let him go and gave him a hard look over.

"You may want to be a grumble-sprout, but I know a cure."

Stepping closer to the water, the girl dipped her hand in, much like

Sarah had done only moments earlier, and pulled a vine of suckle flowers out and held them up to her friend.

At first, the boy turned his nose up to her offer. The girl placed the first stem of honey onto her own tongue and hummed with pleasure.

"Mmmm. You have no idea what you are missing," she giggled with glee.

The boy dropped his hands by his sides while he leaned closer to the girl and looked eager for a taste.

The girl pulled the stem through the heart of the suckle flower and held it out to him. The boy stuck his tongue out and she placed the stem right on the tip.

Both of them laughed heartily as the boy's face melted into contentment. The girl wrapped her arm underneath him, and then allowed her fingers to lace intricately with his.

"You are my best friend, Jack."

The boy rested his head down on the top of the little girl's.

"You are mine too, Sari."

"You think we will be friends forever?" she asked, not sure of the answer.

"I hope so."

"What if the monsters comes and try to take me away like last time?" she asked. "You sure took a couple knocks from them."

"They can hit and punch all they want, but I will still be standing long after they are gone."

The girl sat up a little and looked at the boy with seriousness.

"You will?"

"I will," he said emphatically.

"Promise?" the girl followed.

"Promise."

"What if the monsters grow stronger than you? You would not allow them to hurt you, would you?"

The boy squeezed her tightly and tried to comfort her from her worries.

"Do not worry yourself about any of this for I have a secret weapon in my possession that will protect us forever."

"What is it?" asked the girl with her voice filled with wonder.

A sneaky smile that had more deceitfulness than a boy his age should have, crept onto his face as he said, "Magic."

"Magic?" repeated the little girl.

"Magic," said Sarah simultaneously as she recalled this memory with more clarity.

"Sari, I will do whatever it takes. I care about you that much," replied the little boy with great assurance.

The girl sat quietly while she pulled on the stems of the suckle flowers in her hand, and then she smiled. Allowing her head to fall, she curled up into the boy's arms.

Sarah's lips moved in sink with the little girl's voice.

"I have never felt safer than I do right now, Jack."

"Me too," agreed the boy, and looked out to the pond in front of him.

Sarah could see the cunning that she couldn't see when she was a little girl.

The memory slowly faded until the two children disappeared. Sarah was left alone with just the sound of water as it smashed against the rocks at the bottom of the falls.

"Magic," reiterated Sarah, as if it were the key word that she had waited for to be deciphered in her dreams.

"Magic," she repeated once more.

A flash of the wolf popped into her mind, then the long-horned rooster when it pecked Sarah's finger.

"Magic?"

An image of Jack as he was dragged through the forest floor by a rope around his throat came next in the flow of images. Then an image of Jack at the campfire with no trace of a rope burn.

Something Jack gave her locked in her hand. The diamond that sat comfortably on her side table, perhaps? The Duke. The General. Lord Baer. The Captain. Jack.

The remnants of the wolf's howl shook her out of her dazed state.

"Jack is using magic. 'He made his choice to walk down that dark road.' That is what Old Madge has been trying to warn me about," stated Sarah.

A horse's whinny shot through the night sky and captured Sarah's attention.

She rose quickly and ran back towards the castle.

Sarah's mind raced in every direction as she tried to figure it all out. The elaborate puzzle that sat before her had more pieces which played bigger roles in her life than she originally thought.

Jack's determination to save her from the General and the Duke had already put her life in danger several times.

Another whinny sounded as if the horse was distressed.

She ran back up to the castle, along the stair by the balcony, cut through the grand hall out to the entrance hall, and quickly made her way to the front doorway of the castle.

Pushing the front door open, Sarah looked out to the courtyard. A large figure stood next to his large horse as he held out a piece of paper to the Duke.

The Duke took it and studied it closely before he handed it back to the General.

"This is not good," said the Duke.

"No," replied the General solemnly as his eyes caught Sarah in the doorway. He gestured to her with his head which caused the Duke to turn as see her.

Sarah felt her heart leap into her throat. Whatever was on that paper was not good, and she knew instantly that it had something to do with her.

CHAPTER 33

THE NOTE

"What is going on?" asked Sarah gravely.

The General looked riddled with concern. Gone was his hard expression of indifference.

"I am just back from my travels to Deyle, do you know it?"

"Yes. It is a town on the east corner of the Allogot Forest."

"I met an old acquaintance there…" He paused.

"Old Madge?" inquired Sarah.

The General's face hardened at the name.

"She had troubling news that I needed to hear in person. When I got there, she handed me this," finished the General.

He held out the little piece of rolled up parchment to Sarah. She looked at it, a little confused, before the Duke said, "It will be alright. Take it."

Sarah pulled it from the large gloved hand and unrolled it.

With all these powers in my possession I can now love my love with no hindrance. I owe my undying devotion to you for helping me find the strength that lived within me all along.

J.S.

. . .

"Jack," whispered Sarah.

"Do you know what he is speaking of with these powers?" inquired the Duke.

The cryptic note had Sarah just as puzzled as the two men. Then a single word rose to her conscience and exhaled between her lips.

"Magic," she breathed.

"Excuse me?" asked the Duke.

Sarah shook her head back and forth, trying fervently to wake herself from the nightmare situation building itself around her. Then, she looked up to catch both the Duke and the General's confused faces.

"I do not think you would believe me even if I told you."

"Try me," said the Duke sternly.

"Magic. I think Jack has some kind of magic in his possession. A dark magic."

The lack of surprise on the men's faces told her everything she needed to know. They looked at each other as if they knew something Sarah did not.

"What is it?" pleaded Sarah.

"You have affirmed a suspicion that I have carried since that day in the woods with the fallen tree," stated the General.

"What is that exactly?"

"Your friend is in love with you and he will stop at nothing until he gets you back," replied the General.

Sarah's face soured.

"He believes he is protecting me," said Sarah a little shaky.

"He might be, but with it comes trouble," said the Duke.

"You may have not even realized you were encouraging him," followed the General.

"You were with me at the campfire when Jack tried to take me with him. I said 'no.' I chose differently. I chose you," said Sarah before she realized what words came out of her mouth.

"What does she mean by this?" snapped the Duke.

Sarah covered her lips in disbelief.

"General?"

"Lady Levine's friend, Jack, snuck into our camp and tried to take her with him. She chose to come with me… to Vasfale," replied the General calmly.

"And how does anyone sneak up on my best General?"

"I knew he was there. I just wanted to see what he would do. He had been following us for quite some time, then he brought Baer into it."

"I knew you had run into problems with Baer, but this is the first I am hearing about this Jack fellow. Why is that?" growled the Duke.

"I thought he was gone."

"Clearly he is not, and now we must figure out what we are up against," stated the Duke.

"I already know the answer to that," said the General.

"How?"

"I asked the one person I know that dabbles in the world of magic. She is quite aware of what is going on with Jack."

Sarah could feel the color drain from her face as the horror struck her.

"Did she help him as is suggested in this letter?" Sarah struggled to get out and hoped against all odds that Old Madge hadn't set a trap for her.

"Not consciously, no," said the General reluctantly.

Sarah felt a slight sigh of relief before her breathing become labored and shorter. She took a couple steps forward, horrified as all the deceit and lies mounted in her mind.

"General," she said, then collapsed into his arms.

The sheer strength of his body comforted her.

"Lady Levine!" screamed the Duke with concern.

The General rolled her to her side so that he could see her properly. Her eyes were half closed but she was still conscious.

"She will be alright. She just needs to lie down," said the General to the Duke.

"We should get her to her room," agreed the Duke with a nod.

"I will take her. Then I will meet in the Stratagem to discuss tactics for tomorrow night."

The General pulled Sarah up into his arms before he started to move. She could feel the heaviness of his steps, the slow pace and care he took to make her comfortable.

The amount of contentment she felt while she remained in his arms made her wish that her time with him would never end.

"You know Old Madge," whispered Sarah.

"I do," confirmed the General. "She told me a little of your encounters. She did not reveal much, though."

"How do you know her?" asked Sarah.

A sadness flashed in his eyes that made Sarah regret that she had even asked him the question.

"Nevermind, it is not important," Sarah followed quickly.

The General pushed open Sarah's bedchamber door, and placed her back into her bed. Gently, he pulled the covers up around her.

When he turned to go, Sarah reached out and caught his hand.

"I have spent a lot of time believing that you had no feeling for me," said Sarah. "You have treated me so poorly on so many occasions."

"I know," said the General and took a moment to see her. He slid his hand so he now held hers properly.

"And yet, I hear you would not leave my side when I was ill," she said.

The General sat down in the chair next to her bed.

"I cannot say all that I wish to, but know there is much left unsaid between us."

"We are alone. Please tell me," she begged.

"Perhaps I am waiting for another dance."

Without warning a laugh burst from Sarah's lips. Even a small smile crept up on the General's face.

"A joke, how unlike you."

"It is known to happen on the rare occasion," he admitted.

"Is that right?"

"It is. But now you must rest. The ball is tomorrow and you must..."

"Yes?"

"You must rest," finished the General.

He gave her a half smile, and then rose to his feet.

"I must confess, I am scared to fall asleep. Jack or even Old Madge might be there, waiting for me. What if this time I do not wake again?"

The General took a long moment and then said, "If anyone is there, just tell them 'Fee, fi, fo, fum'."

"Fee, fi, fo, fum? What does that mean?" asked Sarah, a little taken aback.

"It is a chant my mother taught me. She said it is to curse those who are unwanted."

Sarah was unsure if the chant would protect her from dark magic but she would try anything to keep the old woman and Jack away from her.

The General knelt down beside her again.

"Say it with me – Fee, fi, fo, fum."

Together they said it again. "Fee, fi, fo, fum."

Sarah was so lost in repetition of the chant over and over in her head, she hadn't even realized that the General stroked her hair. When it came to her attention, she placed her hand on his and stopped the motion.

Then, the General leaned in and kissed Sarah on the forehead. His lips lingered there longer than expected, but Sarah had no complaints.

"I must go, the Duke is waiting for me."

Sarah nodded with consent and watched the General as he made his way out of her room.

Too many confused thoughts clouded her mind. Was she just a prize that the General turned over for a bag of gold or did he actually have feelings for her?

In that moment, butterflies clipped the corners of her stomach and she thought the latter to be true.

With the words of protection fresh on her lips and the thought of the General's true feelings in the foreground of her mind, she allowed the exhaustion to take hold.

Just before her eyes drifted closed, she caught a glimpse of the Tantum painting on the wall. Two blue-green eyes glowered at her.

Fear was present, but she could not keep her eyes open any longer to examine the painting further.

Instead, she continued her chant in the hopes that her nightmares would not return.

"Fee, fi, fo, fum. Fee, fi, fo, fum."

CHAPTER 34

THE PAINTING SPEAKS

 hen Sarah's eyes opened, she was pleased to see the late morning sun peek through her curtains and the nightmares that had taunted her were nowhere to be found.

"Yes," she said as she thrust her hands triumphantly into the air.

The "Fee, fi, fo, fum" chant worked, for it was the first good night's sleep she'd had since the day she left her house.

She leaned over and pulled the little string that would summon her breakfast.

Only a matter of minutes passed before Eshe knocked on the door.

"Come in!" said Sarah, eagerly.

Eshe seemed pleasant as ever when she placed the tray of food down across Sarah's lap.

"I hope this will suffice, My Lady."

When the cover was pulled off the silver platter, she saw an array of cheeses, meats, and fruit placed is a beautiful pattern across the plate.

"This looks delicious!" said Sarah before she dug into her meal.

While she ate, Eshe walked to each of the three windows and drew the curtains back that allowed the proper morning light into the room.

"Eshe, will you sit with me? I fear I have not made any friends since I have arrived."

"Of course, My Lady."

Eshe moved awkwardly closer to the bed and waited. Her eyes shifted around the room as if she looked for a subject matter to speak on.

"Is everyone enjoying the general splendor of the occasion?" asked Sarah as she munched on her bite of food.

"Yes, everyone seems pleased. Though, many of the girls are trying to figure out whom the Duke will pick for his bride. All of them are hopeful."

Sarah cut a slice of cheese and popped it in her mouth.

"Only broken hearts will come of that kind of thinking. After all, he can only choose one."

Eshe looked coyly at Sarah.

"Many say he favors you, My Lady."

Sarah almost choked on the piece of cheese in her mouth.

"There is no way he would possibly pick me."

Eshe was unmoved in her position.

"You are serious?" said Sarah.

"People say he has shown more attention to you than anyone else."

"I have also traveled the farthest, and I was ill."

Eshe bowed her head to acknowledge that she agreed with both points.

"I will leave you to your breakfast. In no time at all, I will be back and we will get you ready for the ball."

"I cannot believe it is tonight."

"Yes. And we shall transform you into a princess."

"I do not know about that, but I will certainly try."

Eshe bowed her head and excused herself from the room.

Sarah munched on a few more bits of food before she sat the tray off to her side.

Stretching her hands in front of her, a big yawn billowed out. It took a moment for Sarah's eyes to focus properly. As they did, she noticed the painting on her wall had changed again.

Rising from the bed to get a closer look, Sarah could see the blue-green eyes that tried to taunt her the previous night were gone. Now, the little girl from the original painting was curled up near the ceiling and looked down at the room.

Below was the Duke and he sat grandly at his desk with a small bag of gold near his fingers. Standing before him was Jack. He wore a suit of fancy armor and carried a war hammer on one side with a sword on the other.

"This is not like Jack. He is not a warrior. And why would the Duke be paying him?" Sarah whispered to herself.

When she ran her finger over the velvet bag that held gold, she was certain she could feel the soft plushness of the fabric against her skin. When she scrutinized Jack's face, she could swear the paint shifted on the canvas so that his eyes now looked up at the girl on the ceiling.

"Sarah," whispered a voice.

Sarah took a big step backwards.

"Who is there?"

Not wanting to let fear get the best of her, Sarah approached the picture again. This time far more cautiously.

"I know this bag," she observed. "I saw it last night. The Duke was giving it to the General."

Her thoughts overtook her mouth as her eyes shifted across the canvas. Back and forth they shot between the bag of gold and Jack.

"The General could not have been there at that time last night. The Captain thought even if he were on his way back from Deyle, he would not be here until late. The General actually arrived when I found him in the courtyard with the Duke. How could he be in two places at once?" Sarah's mind raced. "How?"

Sarah placed her finger on the dried paint that outlined her friend's figure.

"Jack, what are you doing?"

No sooner had the words come out of her mouth than the dried eyes shifted and looked at her. A deceitful smile forced its way through the cracks of the painting.

"I will never let anything ever hurt you, Sari," said the painted Jack. "Ever."

Just then, the painting on the wall swirled around the desk until it and the Duke were replaced by the General.

As large as the General was, he was distracted by the girl up on the ceiling.

Jack's painted body ripped the sword from its sheath and stabbed it firmly into the General's back all the way through his stomach. The General collapsed to the ground but still he reached out for the girl.

"No!" Sarah cried out in horror.

Jack walked over to him and kicked the General in the ribs.

"Jack, no!" Sarah screamed as she watched the monstrosity unfold in front of her.

The General's body went limp and his deep brown eyes glossed over. It was then that Jack pulled the girl from the ceiling and coddled her in his arms as he walked out of the door in the painting.

"There, there. All is made right again. You are safe now."

Sarah watched in agony as Jack took the little girl and left the confines of the painting.

"The Captain was right, I have distracted the General."

Sarah wanted to run in every direction through the castle and look for the General, but she knew that she could not save him by being in his presence. In fact, she must try to give him the most distance she could in the short time before the ball.

She could not allow her wants and desires to overtake his safety.

Not being able to bear the image the painting had provided, she took the sheet that had once covered the Tantum painting, and draped it back over it.

Nothing about what she saw felt right. In fact, a hint of dread loomed about her in knowing the ball was only a few hours away. And if she knew nothing else about Jack, he loved to make a spectacle to distract people while he tried to take control of the situation.

The last consistent thing Sarah always knew to be true was; there had never been a situation that Jack was able to control and all of them would inevitably end in disaster.

CHAPTER 35

CHANGE OF MOOD

*T*hankfully, the rest of the day was relatively uneventful. Sarah thought for sure that this was the calm before the storm. After seeing the possibility of what the night might hold, it left discomfort in the air.

There was some relief when the handmaidens arrived to help Sarah ready herself for the ball. Led by Eshe, they puffed and pulled Sarah into her stunning princess form.

Eshe placed the last golden clip into Sarah's hair that made her outfit complete.

The finishing touch was a gold-plated mask with diamond studs that trimmed the frame. In the middle of the headpiece was the jewel she won from the unicorn chase. Pulling the string, she slid the mask perfectly over her nose and eyes that completely concealed her identity.

"How do I look?"

"Like a princess," admired Eshe.

Sarah stared at her masked figure in the mirror. Much like the first night at the castle, she barely recognized herself. Never had she been so decorated with jewelry and the fine delicacies.

"I could not have been made a princess without your help, Eshe," said Sarah with a smile, and hugged her.

"You will certainly be the talk of the ball," confessed Eshe with much delight.

Once ready, Sarah wasted no time as she scurried down the path that led her to the grand hall.

Upon entering, she noticed the room had golden silks strung from wall to wall highlighted by extravagant candleholders on every column. Two long tables rested in the middle of the room with many eclectic platters of food from all over the country. A few people milled around it and tried to decide what they should try next.

At the far end of the room were the three sets of double doors that had been pulled open so people could move easily out to the gardens.

When Sarah stepped out into the night air, she longed for its coolness to calm her nerves. Her breath was instantly swept away with the grandeur of the festivities.

Sarah stepped to the balcony rail and looked out at many of the guests as they danced in their beautiful gowns and suits. Every single identity hidden by the decorative masks across everyones' faces.

As for the dance floor, the Duke had turned his garden into an outdoor ballroom. The large rectangular lawn that could easily hold the two hundred guests was lined by a ten foot tall hedge. On those hedges were golden shaded flowers with five petals that came to points much like a star. Strands of white globe candles were strung on several strings which made their way up to a single pinnacle at the center of the lawn and created the illusion of a canopy.

"It is hard not to be impressed with the opulence," said a raspy voice.

When Sarah turned, the familiar thin figure stood next to her and puffed on his pipe. Though he had a mask on that just barely covered his eyes, there was no mistaking the carelessness of Raff's unkempt hair.

"Raff?" Sarah exhaled, exhilarated.

Before she knew it, Sarah had thrown her arms around the old man, thankful for the reinforcement of his company. The old man patted her on the arm and looked a little uncomfortable with the affection.

"What are you doing here?" she asked as she pulled away from him.

"I was sent for."

"Sent for?" echoed Sarah, a little confused.

"Yes. Gregor asked me to be here."

"Why?"

Raff's crooked smile was endearing but left his forthrightness at the wayside.

"You know, I didn't ask."

"Still you came?"

"Of course. The General hasn't asked me for too many favors in his life. Figured I could comply for this one."

"I suppose that makes sense," agreed Sarah.

The two leaned on the balcony and watched the joy and dancing down below. All the women wore puffy, colorful ball gowns ornamented with diamond rings and vibrant stone necklaces, while the men were in their finest suits only distinguished if they had military attire on.

Sarah didn't grasp until her gaze made it half way through the crowd, what it was she searched for.

"He is not here," said the old man.

Sarah dropped her head as she poorly tried to cover up that she looked for the General.

"Mm," hummed from Raff's lips as he surveyed all the grounds. His eyes traveled over the wave of people until they landed on Sarah. As much as she tried to ignore it, she could feel the loftiness of his eyes.

"Is there something on your mind?" Sarah finally asked.

"I could ask you the same question," he replied.

Sarah turned to him, but could not bring herself to look up. Instead, she diverted her attention down to her hands which were clasped together in front of her waist.

"I do not know what you mean by that?"

"Yes you do."

Sarah's eyes flickered up but the heaviness of Raff's gaze was too much for her to bear, so they went right back down.

"I am scared to say," muttered Sarah, barely audible.

"Because?"

"Because I am afraid you will think I am ridiculous."

This time, it was Raff's turn to look away with a light chuckle.

"Not possible," said Raff sincerely. "You are one of the most grounded people I have had the privilege to meet."

With these encouraging words, Sarah finally found the confidence to look at him. He half smiled in return for her bravery and chewed on his pipe.

"Come now, tell me what is on your mind," he asked again.

"I have a friend."

"Jack?"

Sarah froze at the sound of his name. Not sure if it was the fear that the Tantum painting showed her the truth or the fact that even Raff knew Jack's name, whatever it was, it struck her to the core.

"How did you know his name?"

"It doesn't matter. What has he done?"

"It is not what he has done but what I think he is going to do," confessed Sarah. "I think he is going to hurt the General and maybe even the Duke."

"Do you know how?"

"Jack is going to kill him when he is least expecting it. Because… because…" Sarah stammered.

Raff placed a calming hand on Sarah's shoulder.

"It's alright. I won't judge your thoughts," said Raff in a fatherly tone.

"Because I am distracting the General," Sarah pushed out.

Raff's hand slid back to his pipe as smoke spilled over his lips.

"I think you give yourself too much praise, Lady Levine."

Sarah wasn't sure if the old man was trying to restore her faith in the General's abilities or just trying to calm her nerves. Either way, both things occurred, simultaneously.

"How did you come by this information?" asked Raff, a bit more sternly.

Sarah's hands twisted around one another until finally she turned away.

"You would not believe me."

"Out of all the people you know, I am more likely to believe you than almost anyone else… Please, I must know."

"A painting revealed it to me."

"The painting from Tantum," he said, knowingly.

"You know of it?"

Sarah was relieved by the soft expression on the old man's face. It was obvious he didn't think she was crazy, but instead seemed he understood even more.

"That painting is a riddle to most," said Raff. "It seems as if you have it figured out, though."

"Is it telling a truth?" asked Sarah apprehensively.

"A version of it, I suppose."

"Jack stabbed him. Stabbed the General when he was reaching out to a little girl who I can only presume is me. I cannot be responsible for the death of the General!"

"Are you sure the girl was you?"

Sarah nodded. "I believe so."

"You never know, it could be your daughter years from now," suggested the old man.

The image of the dried painted sword going through the General's body overwhelmed Sarah.

"Sarah, if the General dies, it will not be your fault. He is a brave man who has been in many battles. This is no different."

"But Jack has magic!"

"Magic, you say?" Raff looked as though he didn't expect that answer. "Even magic has its limitations."

"I have also been warned by this old woman in my dreams."

"What woman?" said Raff sharply.

"Her name is Old Madge."

Raff's eyes quickly shot to all four corners of the garden and then up to the hedges that surrounded it. Suspicion covered his entire face.

"Let me give you a piece of advice. Leave her be! Do *not* talk to her, she will just misguide you," barked Raff before he slid the pipe back into his mouth.

Sarah looked around, taken aback by the sudden change of mood from Raff. The General and Raff knew Old Madge, and neither seemed to think very highly of her. There was no telling how much she has guided, or perhaps misguided, Sarah over the last couple of weeks.

"Thank you for trusting me with this information, Lady Levine. Now I know why I am here. But now you must go and dance with the Duke."

"What?" said Sarah, jarred by the quick change of subject.

Raff gestured down to the dance floor where the Duke stood in the middle of a circle of guests.

Being wrapped up in the intense conversation, Sarah hadn't even realized that the music had stopped playing.

When she looked over to him, the Duke knelt down in the middle of the garden and held a hand out in Sarah's direction.

"Lady Levine, will you honor me with this next dance?"

The coolness of Sarah's mask kept the heat from rising in her cheeks. She bowed her head and started down the staircase to the garden.

Just before Raff was out of her sight, she looked back at him for assurance, which he simply bowed his head to her.

The guest parted as the Duke came to greet Sarah at the bottom of the stairs.

"Which dance would you prefer?" asked the Duke as he escorted her out to the empty dance floor.

"Whatever you wish," replied Sarah as she looked around at the guests suspiciously and wondered if Jack was amongst them somewhere.

When she finished measuring up the audience, she looked back at the Duke. She could tell, even through his mask, he appeared to be disappointed.

"Well, if I cannot inspire you to this dance perhaps I can find someone else who will."

The Duke held out his hand to the crowd.

"Who thinks they can inspire this fair maiden from our South-lands to dance with him?"

The crowd remained still. All the guests looked around at one another to see if anyone could possibly be bold enough to take the Duke's place.

Sarah was embarrassed it had come to this for a second time since she had been at Vasfale.

"If I may dare to take the place of the Duke," said a somewhat recognizable voice.

A man with a slightly muscular build and sandy blond hair stepped forward. He wore a suit made of the finest fabrics, his outfit finished with a gold and green mask that covered over half his face. He took another step forward and bowed to the Duke.

The Duke smiled and bowed his head back with approval.

Then the man stepped up to Sarah and took her hand into his.

She was transfixed by him and found she glided easily with him without complaint.

He turned to face her and his blue-green eyes confirmed who this mysterious man truly was. However; there appeared to be distinct flecks of gray that cut across the familiar colors of his eyes.

"Jack," Sarah exhaled.

CHAPTER 36

THE MYSTERY MAN

"Would you care for the Alomon, or are you up for the Stotson?" asked the man.

"The Alomon will do," replied Sarah with a little quiver in her voice.

The music began to play and the two moved effortlessly through the sea of couples that started to surround them. Before Sarah knew it, they blended perfectly into the scene. Just the way Jack always liked it, but could never succeed at doing so.

"What happened to you? How did you get in here?" Sarah inquired.

"I have been here for quite some time, Lady Levine. Though, I believe you already knew that," said Jack in a tone more terse than Sarah was used to hearing from him.

As the two floated across the dance floor, Sarah could feel the strength of Jack's arms pull her into the next step.

Something had changed.

Jack's eyes still captured her attention, but there was a restlessness to them that she hadn't noticed before. Turmoil backed by self-assurance.

Sarah found her body unconsciously press more closely to his with every passing second. Be it for comfort or a newfound attraction for him, she didn't know. Everything just felt right. It felt familiar. It felt comfortable in a way she hadn't felt before.

Caught in a trance, the world outside of the two of them faded away. It was just Jack and Sarah dancing together. No one else mattered. Sarah didn't even find it odd that she couldn't tear her eyes away from his.

Jack pulled Sarah's hand up to his lips and kissed them while the two continued to move as one fluid body through the motions of the slow dance.

"You have been in my dreams lately," admitted Sarah, whether she wanted to or not.

"Is that so?" replied Jack in a knowing tone.

"Yes."

"Were they good dreams?"

Everything was hazy and euphoric. Sarah couldn't help but smile brilliantly as she longed to kiss Jack's lips.

"Yes," she replied, not fully in control of her response.

"Well if you were there and I was there, I do not know how it could not be wonderful," said Jack, charmingly.

Sarah bit her lower lip while she rested her head against Jack's shoulder.

"I know that I was afraid."

"I promised, since the day that I met you, Lady Levine, that I would protect you from anything that scared you."

"You did," she said and pulled herself far enough away that she could look at him again.

Jack slid his hand onto Sarah's cheek.

"And I always will. Even if I have to protect you from yourself."

Sarah wasn't sure what his words meant, nor did she care. She felt so impassioned that she thrust her lips forward until they pressed against his.

Jack's lips were soft and warm like a spring afternoon. The energy that swam around her made Sarah's legs tremble. The thought that she could kiss him all night made her giddy inside.

An unusual gust of wind swept through the garden.

"Sarah," whispered Old Madge's voice.

It was enough to catch Sarah's attention, but not enough for her to pull away from her elation.

Instead, Sarah's nose nuzzled into Jack's neck. She felt his lips caress her forehead, lovingly.

"I have wanted to be with you for a long time, Sari."

"I know you have. I could not tell you what was holding me back."

"Whatever it was, it is gone now," said Jack pleased, and pulled his arms more tightly around her waist.

"Sarah," whispered again, but this time it was the sound of the General's voice.

It rattled her. Enough to break her away from the passionate moment she shared with her friend.

Shaking her head, Sarah looked around at the other guests as they continued the dance around them. None of them even seemed to notice that Sarah and Jack were there.

She backed away from Jack and looked at him in his new handsome form. Her head began to pound.

"What has happened to you? Something has changed," she said as the haze around her dissipated and the sharpness of reality set in.

Jack tried to pull Sarah back into his arms, but Sarah shied away. A high-pitched trill began to ring in her ears.

"What did you do to me?" she asked and glared at Jack with disgust.

"Much has changed that I cannot explain to you now," he implied.

"Magic," she hissed.

"Yes," he said, unapologetically. "Magic."

"You swore to protect me," she whimpered.

"And I am doing it the best way I know how," Jack growled back.

"By magic!" she barked.

"By loving you."

"I will never love you, Jack," said Sarah as she choked back her disappointed tears. "If for no other reason than you never asked me to love you. You always told me that I should!"

Hurt was present on Jack's face.

"You will always be his duty, never his wife," he insinuated.

It felt like a bucket of cold water was dumped on her head. The reaction shot through her arm as Sarah reared back and slapped Jack as hard as she could across the face. Jack slowly turned back to Sarah's scowl.

"I love him, Jack," she said sincerely.

"Then you know how I feel. To love without getting it in return."

The song hit its final note, and all the guests applauded the musicians.

Jack straightened up his posture, and then swooped into a graceful bow.

"What are you doing?" said Sarah, confused.

"I am saying goodbye. It has been made clear that you do not want me here and I have other matters that need my attention."

"I never meant for things to turn like this between us, Jack. I care about you very much."

"That is not good enough for me."

"It is just, I thought I knew you," expressed Sarah.

"And now?"

"And now I believe you have taken something that belongs to me," she finished as held out her open palm and waited for him to return her bottle of beans.

"What is it you think I have?" replied Jack.

"You know what it is," barked Sarah.

Jack's eyes danced back and forth between Sarah's before he pulled a velvet bag of gold out from seemingly nowhere and dropped it into her hand.

The perfect storm of emotions collided within Sarah. At first she was heartbroken, then angry, followed by frustration. The last several minutes had been a whirlwind that she couldn't understand.

"What is this?" she asked.

"The price that the man you love was paid for your delivery to Vasfale."

Rage filled Sarah. Tears streaked down her checks while her whole body shook with fury.

"Forgive me," said Jack. "I tried to warn you."

Just then, Sarah felt a firm hand on her shoulder. When she turned, she saw the masked face of the Captain.

"Lady Levine, may I have the pleasure of the next dance?"

"Of course," she agreed.

"Are you alright?" asked the Captain with great concern.

When Sarah turned back to Jack, he had disappeared. She looked all around but didn't see him anywhere.

"Sarah, you look pale. Are you ill?" asked the Captain.

Sarah shook her head while she took the Captain's hand.

"I will be fine."

The Captain looked down at the bag of gold in her hand.

"Lady Levine, please consider this dance on me," chuckled the Captain.

Sarah blushed a little, and dropped the small bag of coins on a table she passed on the way to the dance floor.

"I supposed I can come back for this later."

As she spoke, the Captain held out his hand to her.

"Are you ready?" he asked.

Sarah smiled and curtsied to him. The Captain bowed and then took her by the hand and guided her farther out onto the grassy floor.

"You must be ready when we start this dance."

"Is that right?" chuckled Sarah.

"Before I can answer that, we must pick a dance. I would suggest the Conti Rose, but I feel that might be reserved for someone else," said the Captain, jokingly. "How about the Whicksen? Do you know that one?"

"I do," professed Sarah.

The Captain took a hold of Sarah and pulled her in close to him.

He used his hand to guide her head to his shoulder so that they were in a tight embrace.

He leaned down so his lips were near her ear and whispered, "Baer is here."

CHAPTER 37

THE FATAL DANCE

The Captain instructed with one hand for the musicians to start.

"About twenty seconds into this dance, Baer's men are going to jump from behind the shrubs and attack," said the Captain.

"How do you know this?" asked Sarah, alarmed by the news.

"The same way I know everything - the General."

"Should we not bring the guard here to protect us?" advised Sarah, as she looked around panicked.

The strings started to sing the lovely tune and the Captain shifted Sarah into the sequence of steps. Like an involuntary counter going off in her head, she counted - one, two, three, four.

"The most important thing is to remain calm and trust that the General knows what he is doing," counseled the Captain.

Sarah couldn't help but clench more tightly to him in anticipation.

Eleven, twelve, thirteen...

The Captain had locked eyes with someone in the audience and nodded his head. He then grabbed a hold of Sarah before he spun them both around. Again, he locked eyes with someone else and nodded.

Eighteen, nineteen, twenty...

The Captain spun Sarah back into the crowd and drew his sword as the horde of men jumped through the hedge with swords pulled. The Captain's archers drew back their bows and aimed them at the evil men on the outskirts of the lawn.

The guests squealed and gasped at the invaders that now surrounded them.

"Shut up!" screamed one callous voice.

Lord Baer broke through his men, and moved briskly to the middle of the floor where Captain Lowe stood, ready to fight.

Baer drew his sword and pointed it at the Captain. "There is only one man I wish to kill tonight."

"I suppose I am not worthy of such an honor," chuckled the Captain.

The Duke stepped forward.

"Bernard, I wondered when you would grace me with your presence. Shame you always have a need to start a fight on festive occasions. Could you possibly put down your swords and just have a drink with us instead?"

The Duke walked nonchalantly behind Captain Lowe.

Baer lunged forward, but the Captain clanked his sword away.

"Where is he?" demanded Baer.

The Captain glanced over at the Duke.

"Do you know who he is talking about?" mocked the Captain.

"Not a clue," said the Duke in a humored tone and took a sip from the glass in his hand.

"Rah!" raged Baer and threw his sword forward.

The Captain countered again.

"Really, I do believe you need to learn to control your temper," said the Captain.

Swords clashed again and again. Baer's eyes narrowed as the Captain lunged at him, but was deflected away. A counter strike swung around at the Captain, but he pulled his sword up just in time to protect his chest. The two pushed against each other through their swords.

Their full weight pushed back and forth until Baer flung the Captain backwards. The Captain found his balance before he clashed swords with Baer once more.

This time the Captain got the upper hand and shifted his weight so that Baer was going lower to the ground.

"Do you yield?" grunted the Captain.

"Grr," groaned Baer as the Captain had pushed him down to his knees. Sarah was unnerved with how similar Baer sounded to his brother with his battle cry.

"Do you yield?" shouted the Captain again.

Baer released his sword and allowed it to fall to the ground. He was hunched over in defeat. The Captain leaned over and asked again, "I will accept your defeat as an honorable one."

Baer's head shot up. Pulling a knife from his sleeve, he lunged forward and stabbed Captain Lowe in the stomach. A gasp escaped the Captain's lips, as Baer threw his weight into it. The Captain collapsed in a heap on the ground.

"You do that," grumbled Baer, and spat on Captain Lowe's motionless body.

Baer staggered to his feet, picked up his sword and pointed it at the Duke.

"Where is he? Where is your prized General?"

A whinny sounded, and the General's horse trotted into view on the far end of the lawn. The General sat tall and made the beast look even bigger than it already was.

Baer snickered as he turned his gaze to his target.

Sarah's stomach turned into knots, not sure if she was happy to see the General or if she would have felt better had he never come at all. Looking at the Captain's lifeless body laying face down only made the possibility of the same outcome for the General more real.

"Well, brother. Glad you could finally join us. Though you did miss your Captain's noble exit."

The General kept his cold and calculated glare on Baer while his horse danced side to side in a taunting fashion.

"Let us finish this. Just you and me," ordered the General.

Baer looked around at all the frightened guests, and then to his men.

"Gladly," agreed Baer.

Nodding his head to the terms, swords were sheathed and tension in the bows were relaxed amongst the two warring armies.

The General dismounted his horse and took two steps forward, throwing his sword down.

"Just you and me," the General repeated.

Baer, too, threw his sword on the ground.

"That means all your hidden knives as well," shouted Raff.

Sarah wasn't sure when the old man had made his way down to the lawn, but it must have been during all the excitement of the sword fight between Baer and the Captain.

Baer pulled another knife out that was sheathed in his other sleeve and two that were tucked in his belt.

"You never understood the word *all,*" Raff said as he shook his head with disapproval.

Baer pulled another knife from the back of his boot while he sneered at the old man that stood in front of him.

Raff looked over to the General and nodded his head to proceed.

"This is simple," explained Raff. "A fight until someone concedes or is dead. Whichever comes first. You may begin."

The two larger than life men stepped towards each other while the rest of the crowd scattered back towards the hedge walls to watch the fight that was about to unfold.

"GRAH!" shouted the General and ran towards Baer.

"RAH!" Baer screamed back.

The two ran full speed until they crashed into each other in what looked like a bear hug. They tried to squeeze the air out of each other until Baer threw the General sideways. Then he pounced onto the General and wrapped his hands around his neck. The General got his feet under Baer's stomach and pushed him as hard as he could, flinging Baer head over foot to the ground.

Both rolled over before they put their fists up and were ready to resume their attack.

Baer took a swing at the General, but he missed. The General punched him several times in the side before he struck Baer hard across the face. Baer shook it off and countered with two strong blows to the General's face which split open his eye.

Sarah stepped out from the crowd with her hands to her lips. She stood alone, separate from the rest.

"Uh-oh," huffed Baer as the fighting paused and each man caught his breath. "Your lady love knows what is about to happen. Making her a widow before you ever made her your bride."

The General looked down at the ground where the Captain's body lay, but he did not turn to look at Sarah.

The General held up his fists again. Baer nodded and the two resumed.

This time the General swung at Baer's chest but Baer jumped out of the way. The General overextended and exposed his back. Baer took the opportunity of the General's venerable position and tackled him to the ground. He slid his full arm around the General's throat and squeezed.

"I have longed for this moment the whole of my life," said Baer as he slowly and deliberately choked the air out of the General's body.

Even from that short distance, Sarah could see the General's eyes turn red.

Baer whispered something into the General's ear before he pulled the General's head back far enough that the General was forced to make eye contact with Sarah. The General reached out to her, just like in the painting.

The color drained from his face, and his hollow eyes narrowed into thin slits.

Aware that Baer had slid his hand around one of his daggers lying on the ground, Sarah was consumed with rage. It coursed through every inch of her fiber. She lost her senses when she felt her body run with full force forward at the large figure of Baer.

"Graw!" she screamed, as if she, too, was a warrior in this fight.

When her tiny frame barreled into Baer's hard one, she glanced off of him, as if she had done nothing at all. A hard hit smacked the side of her face and the weight of the world felt like it landed on top of her when she hit the ground.

"GRAH!" growled the General and threw his weight around so he now faced Baer. He punched his brother in the nose with all his might.

Baer doubled over in pain while the General rolled on top of him. Punch after bloody punch, the General struck him until Baer stopped moving.

Sarah shook her head and struggled to lift herself off the ground.

Even though it was unmistakable that Baer was unconscious, if not dead, the General kept punching before he screamed all the rage he had.

"Gregor," Sarah said softly and put a calm hand on his shoulder. "It is over."

"I am sorry it ever had to end this way," muttered the General.

Sarah stood and watched him with a sympathetic hand on his shoulder.

Before she knew what had happened, a tight grip wrapped around her neck and yanked her backwards. As the grip tightened and the man's other arm locked the back of her head, he was ready to snap her neck.

"Just when you thought everything was going to be alright," said one of Baer's men who held Sarah captive.

Glancing around, Baer's horde had resumed their fighting positions, while Captain Lowe's men were ready to protect the Duke and his guests.

The Duke held his hands up to the man in an effort to calm him down.

"Now, Sir. What would you possibly want with one of my guests?"

"She is not just any guest – she is his!" the man hissed and gestured to the General.

"Lord Baer was very clear with what we were supposed to do with her should he…"

The man looked down at Baer's corpse.

"You know you will not make it out of here alive if you hurt her in any way," stated the General.

"You think we care!"

"Good answer," said the Duke. "Captain?"

A knife flung past Sarah's eyes and into the captor's head. He crumpled behind her, dead.

Sarah staggered forward while she felt the air flooded back into her lungs.

When Sarah finally had the strength to look up again, her mouth fell open. She shook her head, not sure she could trust her eyes. Captain Lowe stood at the edge of the lawn where she thought he had died... fallen over... dead...

Maybe she had died at this man's hands?

The Captain held out the other two knives he had slowly retrieved from Baer that had left on the ground next to the Captain. The General rose and patted the Captain on the back.

"Well done, Captain."

"I thought you were killed," cried Sarah.

The Captain shook his head with his usual smirk and pulled open his shirt to reveal a thick cover of Highland leather.

"Another gift from Gaente. Highland leather is very rare to come by, but it is impervious to blades," said the General.

"Did you hear that? I am impervious," joked the Captain. "Now, my men and I need to escort all these traitors down to their cells until the Duke decides what to do with them."

The Captain and his men took Baer's body away, along with Baer's men and left the guests in silence.

The Duke approached the General and Sarah while Raff followed a couple steps behind him.

"I knew you would eventually deal with this unfinished business between you and your brother," confessed the Duke.

The General looked down where Baer's body had just been, and nodded his head with sadness.

"Now my friend, you have inspired my long-awaited decision."

"Which is?"

The Duke took Sarah's hand and smiled.

He then turned to the crowd and said, "Guests. Maidens from near and far, who have come with hopes of winning my hand in marriage. After much thought, and a long and trying week. I have made my decision..."

CHAPTER 38

AN EXPLANATION

*S*arah sat by herself on a bench near the balcony rail that overlooked the garden. A few guests meandered around aimlessly as they looked at the array of flowers and got one last breath of grandeur in before everyone returned to their homes.

Two young ladies snickered at Sarah as they passed by her before they continued down to the garden. Sarah just watched on with indifference.

"They will get over their disappointment in time," said the Duke.

When Sarah turned, he had already moved towards her with two goblets in his hand.

She was about to stand and greet him properly, but he shook his head.

"Sit, sit, sit."

Sarah remained where she was while the Duke came to sit next to her. As he did, he handed one of the glasses to her.

"Cheers!' he said in his playful voice.

They clinked glasses and Sarah took a sip. Her face instantly contorted.

"Is this water?" she said, surprised.

The Duke nodded his head.

"This is most unexpected," admitted Sarah.

"It was bound to happen sooner or later, right?" said the Duke.

Both chuckled, and then fell into an awkward silence.

The two took a moment to look out at the lush greenery before them. The intricate colors from several of the girls' dresses moved in soothing patterns as the background while the flowers popped against the fabrics. There was some delight to all the beauty that sat in front of them.

"Are you sure you are making the right decision?" Sarah finally asked.

"I believe so," said the Duke. "What about you? Are you happy with my decision?"

"Sire, if you are choosing a life of bachelorhood, then who am I to judge?"

A group of three more girls passed by them. The girls winked and giggled at the Duke before they inevitably snickered at Sarah.

"I just do not know how I could possibly be blamed for your choice."

"You have held my attention for the whole of the week. Girls come easily into jealousy over such folly. What they do not understand is why you had my attention," explained the Duke.

Sarah's brow furrowed with confusion.

"Come. Walk with me."

The Duke rose and offered his arm to her. He led her down to the garden that still looked a little worn from the previous night's events.

"I want you to know, I am sorry your journey here was so tiresome. It seemed to get only more tumultuous after you arrived."

"That was no doing of yours, Duke," said Sarah, reassuringly.

As they moved slowly through the yard, they made their way out amongst the flowers that were in full bloom.

"Be that as it may, I do apologize all the same."

Sarah bowed her head graciously.

"Now, what is next for you, Lady Levine?"

Sarah found herself bite on her lower lip in thought.

"I suppose I will return to my home."

"It is funny that you should say such a thing."

"Why? Where do you think I should go?"

"You know, before you ever arrived at the castle, I had caught wind of just how special you were," admitted the Duke.

"I do not know what you mean. There is nothing special about me. I am just a country girl from Ditrum."

"Ahh... Lady Levine, why are you lying to me?"

"Sire?" replied Sarah, a little nervous on where this conversation was going.

"I believe you to be a witch. Come now, admit it," demanded the Duke with some humor still present in his voice.

"I assure you, I have no special powers," said Sarah with more concern.

"And yet, you bewitched the heart of my greatest General."

Sarah's eyes widened in disbelief. Had she been that transparent to everyone?

"But..." Sarah started but the Duke placed a hand over her mouth to silence her.

"Word got to me before you ever arrived here that you got the great General Gregor Furst to the dance floor."

"I was making a point to him."

"And you clearly made it, if I do say so," he agreed.

Sarah looked around, not sure if she could believe her ears on what was being said. Nor could she be confident her tongue would not say something that would damn the General.

The Duke stepped forward and took Sarah's hands into his.

"Please do not misunderstand me," he said gently. "The first night, when I asked you to show your dance to the room, I wanted to see if Gregor would get up and dance with you. Before either of you arrived, I had ordered the rest of the room to remain in their seats. The Captain, too."

"The Captain."

"Speaking of Anton. I want to squash any rumors that he was the one who told me about you and the good General. He is loyal to Gregor and would never divulge such information to me."

"I suppose one of the other soldiers then," guessed Sarah.

"They, too, are loyal to the General. They would rather be hung from their toenails before spreading such gossip."

"Then who? Please, tell me," pleaded Sarah as her curiosity got the the better of her.

"Normally I would not say, but I have a feeling Raff would not care either way."

"Raff? He was not in Lankenshire for that dance."

"He did not have to be. Neither did I, to be honest. You see, the General is not known for being a sentimental man."

"I gathered," blurted out Sarah.

"But you are different for him. You had his attention from the moment he met you, I think. I could have suspected something when he took my place in the Conti Rose. Did I get the name right?"

"He said he pitied me."

"He may have said that, but then he protected you from me in the garden," pointed out the Duke.

"What are you talking about?"

"He confirmed it for me once more when I tried to woo you at the beginning of the unicorn chase. The General had no other way of shielding you from me than to insult you. He knew it would bother me that one of my guests had been disrespected. And the amount of insults he threw at you, it was completely out of character for him. I also noticed how freely he disagrees with you. We have had our disagreements over the years but he usually keeps it to himself."

"You are the Duke."

"Maybe. Or maybe it is something else that loosens his tongue entirely?"

Sarah could feel the heat rise into her cheeks again. She quickly turned every insult by the General into a moment of him saying he cared for her and became overwhelmed by the beautiful possibilities.

"He would never say he cared about me. He has always kept me at arm's length."

"Really?" asked the Duke.

"Well…"

"Sarah, he is an honorable man. He knew that you were here as a possible suitor for me. He is loyal and puts duty above all."

"Stubborn as a mule."

"That he is. My decision last night was not about me. It was instead to open up the possibilities for him, if he is willing to take it."

Sarah closed her eyes and exhaled a deep sigh.

"He will never say the words I have longed to hear from him. He simply will not."

"I do not know about that, Lady Levine. I believe you have one or two more tricks up your sleeve."

With that, the Duke leaned forward and kissed her. Sarah was caught completely off her guard by his abrupt change in behavior. She quickly pulled away.

"Maybe I have one or two more tricks up my sleeve too. Now, I must go," said the Duke, not missing a beat. "Several of the guests will be leaving shortly, and I must give them my thanks."

The Duke turned and waved oddly to someone off in the distance.

When Sarah turned, her eyes landed firmly on the General as he stood and stared at them. His face was hard with a hint of disappointment present. In no time at all, he stormed off around the side of the castle.

All the color drained from Sarah's face as her head dropped into her hands. How could the Duke have done that? What kind of person is cruel enough to lead his friend into believing something was going on when it was, in fact, not?

CHAPTER 39

THE LONG RIDE HOME

Sarah took one last look around her room to make sure she hadn't forgotten anything. A light knock tapped the bedchamber door.

"Yes?"

Eshe stepped into the room with her contented smile.

"My Lady, your carriage is ready for you in the courtyard," she said.

"I will be right out. Please, just give me a moment," Sarah requested.

Eshe bowed her head and stepped out into the hall.

Sarah looked out the window, enjoying the magnificence of the waterfall one last time. What stories she will have to tell her father when she arrived at home.

As she turned, she couldn't help but notice the Tantum painting that still hid under the sheet. Did she have the strength, in light of all that had happened, to look at the fortune the picture wanted to tell her today?

A part of her didn't want to see it, but curiosity got the better of her.

Sarah yanked the sheet clear from the painting and just stared at it.

In the cracked paint across the canvas was a hand with only the palm lit. In the palm was four beans and the trinket that was won at the unicorn chase.

Sarah's head tilted towards her shoulder as she studied the painting. Four beans. When Old Madge gave her the bottle, there were six. Where did the two other beans go?

She thought back to the previous night and how strangely she had reacted to Jack. Being attracted to Jack after all their years of friendship. Something didn't feel right and she was terribly embarrassed with how much she had swooned over him.

"Magic," she whispered to herself. "Maybe they are magic beans?"

But looking more closely at the weathered beans, Sarah shook her head at the preposterous notion.

Then her eyes shifted over to the stone. How did she get that? Jack would have never wanted her to be with the Duke, so why was it there?

'Maybe I have some tricks up my sleeves too,' echoed in her ears.

"The stone! He wants to see if I would get up and dance with him!"

Her cryptic answer lingered in the air for a moment before Sarah went into the closet and found her golden mask that she wore the night before. Still placed firmly in the center of the headpiece was the stone from the unicorn chase. It took no effort at all for her to pull it off the head dress and slide it into her pocket.

She took off for the door but when she tried to exit, she nearly collided, head first, into the Captain.

"Oh, Captain," she gasped.

"Lady Levine. I am here to see you safely down to your carriage."

"You are?"

The Captain bowed his head with a grin. Sarah smirked back.

"You know, I do believe I will miss that devious smile of yours," she confessed.

"Me? Devious smile? I know not of what you speak," denied the Captain, humorously.

"Uh huh," said Sarah, taking his arm as the two started down the hall.

Only a few steps were taken when Sarah stopped.

"What is it?" asked the Captain.

"Captain, I feel like I owe you an apology."

"For what, exactly?"

"The Duke explained that you had nothing to do with his knowledge of what happened in Lankenshire, or Branch... or when we took camp in the woods. And for that, I am truly grateful and sorry for my mistrust in you and your men."

"Well, I was not expecting such a kind apology nor do I think it is warranted. You have been through a lot during your time away from your home. I would not trust any of this lot either. Self included."

"That is kind of you to say," said Sarah, pleased.

They continued on their way towards the entrance hall.

"So what is next for you, Captain Lowe? Now that you are done protecting maidens on the roads to Vasfale."

"I think I will return home to see my wife and children. I have been away just long enough that she might be happy to see me again."

The two broke out into hearty laughter. It was a nice change of pace to feel the threat and dangers of her trip to the castle were gone. All that remained now was what to do with the affection that remained for the General.

When she stepped out into to courtyard, she saw all the Captain's men already mounted on their horses in front and behind her carriage. Raff, too, was on horseback ready to go.

She turned to the Captain and smiled.

"You did not think we would leave you to the wolves on your return home, now did you?" said the Captain.

With that, the Captain released Sarah's arm and headed over to his horse.

The Duke stood a couple steps away with his back to her. The one person she could not find was the General.

A hint of annoyance rushed through her veins as she approached the Duke.

"Smile as pleasantly as you can and say 'good morning'. Then make your way to the carriage," She repeated Raff's words of wisdom.

"Ah, Lady Levine, you seem all packed up and ready to start your journey home. I assure you that it will be smoother on your return."

"I truly hope so," she said with a brilliant smile as she slipped her hand into her pocket.

"Duke, I believe this belongs to you," said Sarah and handed the jewel back to him.

"Ah, the unicorn chase. That prize belongs to you. After all, you did catch the long-horned rooster."

"I do not believe so. I think instead, you placed this in my room for the General to see when he would not leave my bedside."

"Lady Levine..."

"Sire, you have been working hard to see if the General and I really care for each other. This is just one more of your trials. And though, I am not sure after all that has happened at Vasfale if the General would ever look at me again. But at least I know where I stand," proclaimed Sarah, and held the jewel out to him.

For the first time since she had been at the castle, Sarah saw the Duke look uncomfortable. He slid the jewel into his hand and placed it into his pocket.

"You are a very clever girl," stated the Duke.

"I hope all is not lost to your..."

The words 'ridiculous antics' wanted to come out of her mouth, but in light of the fact that she spoke to the Duke, she thought better of it.

"...sense of humor," she finished as kindly as she could.

"I am quite sure they are not," replied the Duke with both of his eyebrows raised. "Now, I wish you safe on your travels home."

Sarah curtsied to him, and then turned towards the carriage.

Her eyes skimmed the entire courtyard as she looked for the General, once more, but she knew he was too ill tempered to forgive her so quickly. She hoped that he would come running through the front doors of the castle and beg her not to leave. Her ears remained perked and hopeful every step she took towards her carriage.

When she took the last step that placed her in front of the carriage door, she turned one last time, but there was still no General.

The footman opened the door for her. Pulling the steps down, he offered her a helpful hand into the carriage.

"I have her."

Sarah's head shot up to see a gloved hand come out from the darkness of the back seat.

When she didn't respond right away, the General stepped out into the daylight.

"General," Sarah breathed.

The General's ever-heavy gaze landed on her. It felt heavier and filled with more judgment, as if that were even possible.

"Earlier, when the Duke was speaking with me in the garden, he was telling me about all the trials he was putting you through. Well, actually putting us through," she said and tried to explain the misunderstanding.

No more words were spoken.

The General thrusted his lips onto Sarah's and silenced her for good. She could feel his strong frame pull her closer to his body as the embrace continued for a long moment.

"Let us hear it for the General and Lady Levine!" yelled the Captain.

"Atou! Atou!" shouted back the company.

The General's lips broke from Sarah's. He leaned over and placed his forehead onto hers.

"I have wanted this for some time now," he whispered.

"As have I," agreed Sarah with a contented smile.

"Before we return you home, I have one question I never thought I would ask any woman."

Butterflies took off through Sarah's stomach.

"Duke, would you be so kind?"

The Duke walked over to the General and handed him the stone from his pocket. The General took it and slid it into a silver frame with clasps that held the stone perfectly in place.

"I have never met my match until you, Sarah. You shall always be my one and only worthy opponent."

"Always?"

"Always," he confirmed.

Sarah's eyes filled with joy at the happy turn of events.

"One that I hope to keep forever," finished the General and held out the ring to her.

Tears streaked down Sarah's cheeks as she took the ring from the General.

"Is that a yes?" shouted the Captain as he forced her to respond out loud.

Sarah slid the ring onto her finger and pulled the General into a kiss once more.

"That is a yes!" yelled the Duke triumphantly.

"Alright, love birds! That will be enough. There is a long journey ahead of us and we want to make it to the first town before nightfall," grumbled Raff.

The General smirked at Sarah as he took her hand and they both climbed into the back of the carriage.

"My dear General," said the Duke. "There are words that Lady Levine has been longing to hear. Please do not make her wait the entire trip to hear them."

Sarah turned away, a little embarrassed at the Duke's candor. The General waved the Duke off, and then tapped the ceiling of the carriage to go.

"Drive on," ordered the General.

He wrapped a comforting arm around Sarah. She gladly curled into him and rested her head on his chest.

"I love you, Sarah," he whispered into her ear. "Always."

She clenched his hand tighter into hers and hoped with all hope that she would never have to let him go.

"I love you too, Gregor. Always."

Happiness overtook her more than she could ever imagine as the company began to move down the path that would lead Sarah home.

CHAPTER 40

A GOOD OL' FASHIONED FAIRY TALE

"Good morning," said a curious little man as he hopped down off the tree branch and landed on the dirt path right in front of the young boy.

The boy's eyes glanced across the nearby meadows as he tried to decipher where this strange little man could have come from.

"Good morning to you, Sir," replied the boy with a quizzical brow. "Can I help you with something?"

"Let me see…" said the little man as he scooted around the boy and looked at the cow that tagged along behind. "I could not help but notice that you are walking your cow towards town. Are you planning on selling it?"

The young man's head bobbed up and down in acknowledgement.

"That is fantastic news. You know why?"

"I can only venture a guess, Sir," the boy replied sharply as he played along with this little man's antics.

"Because I am in need of such a cow."

"Really?" The boy let slip out with more enthusiasm than he meant.

"Really!"

"I must warn you though, she is dry of milk at the moment."

"Cows have more uses than just milking and meat. She could help me carry heavy loads of wood and to a hermit such as myself, she would be welcomed company."

"Hmm," The boy's lips hummed. "What will you give me for her?"

The little man tilted his head this way and that in thought until he snapped his fingers.

"I have it! Just the thing for you!" he shouted energetically and then thrust his hand into his pants pocket. When it reappeared, in his palm, sat three white beans.

The boy turned up his nose at the sight of them. "You must be joking. I am not selling my cow for three lousy, old beans."

The little man's eyes popped. "Three lousy beans! Three lousy beans! What is your name boy?"

"Jackson, sir."

"Well, Jackson, you clearly do not have a clue what kind of beans these are! These are *Giant* beans!"

"I dare say, they are nothing of the sort."

"I do not mean they are giant, I mean they belong to a Giant, well his wife actually. And once planted in the earth, a beanstalk will grow to such heights and lead you to a place where there is more gold than you will ever want for."

The boy rubbed his chin while he studied the Giant beans. "Please tell me, if they would make a man rich, then why have you not used them?"

The little man looked all around, curiously. Then, he gestured for the boy to lean in closer.

"I am not courageous enough," whispered the little man.

"What do you mean?" asked the boy and pulled back with a look of intrigue, but then leaned in closer to hear the answer.

"A ferocious Giant lives at the end of this beanstalk. You must be aware of him if you go up there. He has already tried to kill me twice."

"You seem like you survived."

The little man rubbed the front of his neck. "Just barely."

The boy turned away and said, "This does not sound like a good enough deal."

"BUT!" screamed the little man as he interrupted the boy's refusal. "The Giant's wife, who is the most beautiful woman who you will ever lay eyes on in your life, will keep you safe from her husband."

An elongated moment of silence settled between the two. Then the boy scooped the beans out of the little man's hands and replaced them with the reins to his cow.

"Enjoy the old girl," the boy muttered while he patted the cow's neck. "She is good company indeed."

"Thank you," said the little man and bowed to the boy.

The boy quickly pocketed the beans and turned to head back towards his home.

The little man watched the young boy travel the road until he turned the bend and was out of sight.

Devious laughter rumbled in the little man's belly that shook him about the harder he laughed.

"Fee, fi, fo, fum, now you *will* smell the blood of Jack Stiltskin!"

And with that, he snapped his fingers and disappeared.

* * *

SARAH SAT STRAIGHT UP in her bed and gasped for air. She clenched her husband's hand who laid next to her while beads of sweat ran down her face.

"What is it?" asked Gregor, not fully awake.

"Jack! He has returned!"

ABOUT ~THE FAIRY TALER~

Cay Templeton (~The Fairy Taler~) grew up in a small, country town in Maryland. The quiet gave her time to think, to listen, and to wander. Between the differences of the town and the country that laid just beyond, Cay developed a sense for things under the surface.

As she grew up, Cay learned to recognize those differences: rich versus poor, liberal versus conservative, and city versus country. Through investigation, Cay began to understand that there's never one side that has the full story. As people take sides, they miss out on other perspectives and even lose track of things that could help them.

Chasing her love for storytelling, Cay earned BA's in Film and Theatre from Towson University. She then went on to Wilkes University, where she earned an MA in Creative Writing.

A month after she graduated, she found herself working in the D.C. Production Office on the film *National Treasure 2: Book of Secrets*. Once the film completed there, she found the courage to pack up and begin her biggest journey yet – across the country to Hollywood.

To this day, Cay works on writing more installments to the Second Side Series. The theme of missing perspectives runs through her signature twisted fairy tale series: *Reversal of Beauty, Gossip: The Evil Stepmother's Tale, Stalked: The Conti Rose,* and *Stalked: The Eastern Passage.*

~The Fairy Taler~ is always on the lookout for the next fairy tale that has a 'Second Side' to it which people should hear.

THE SECOND SIDE SERIES

The Second Side Series

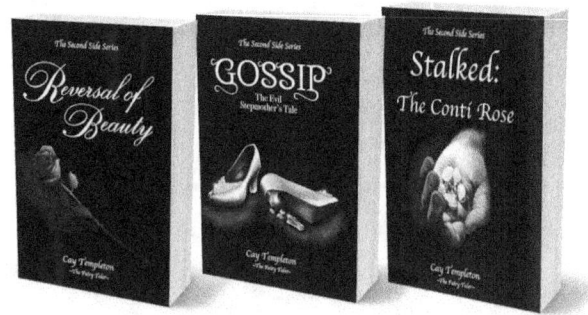

Written By:
~The Fairy Taler~

Check out The Second Side Series Website!
TheSecondSide.com

www.ingramcontent.com/pod-product-compliance
Lightning Source LLC
Chambersburg PA
CBHW070726280626
47159CB00023B/2772